FAERIE WRATH

THE CHANGELING CHRONICLES: BOOK FOUR

EMMA L. ADAMS

On light feet, I stalked across the living room floor towards my target. The sword sheathed at my waist was sharper than any instrument that existed in the mortal realm, forged in wood that came from the heart of the faerie realm. I had several daggers in my pockets, too, along with an array of handmade witch charms, and I was no slouch in hand-to-hand combat either.

None of those things were any use whatsoever when the enemy was dead.

I'd had more experience with ghosts than most people in the room, but being buddies with a necromancer Guardian was no help whatsoever against the living.

"It destroyed my house!" screeched the middle-aged woman cowering behind the sofa. "I want compensation!"

Honestly, I didn't blame the ghost for staying out of sight, given that she'd spent the past half-hour screaming loudly enough to fracture my eardrums, but not being able to see my target was a major downside. If I hadn't been carrying a saltshaker instead of a sword, I might have looked a little more impressive, but no luck there either. Just call me Ivy Lane, mercenary-turned-exorcist.

"Ivy," Isabel called across the room. "The trap's ready."

"Good." We'd put a circle of salt around the perimeter and blocked off the hall, but the kitchen and living room were joined by a single door and were crammed with so many antiques that the house might as well have had a sign on its roof advertising the bill we'd have to pick up if our elusive spirit caused any more mayhem.

I continued on my path across the room, testing every step carefully. Poltergeists were notorious pranksters, and this one had already tripped up the necromancer apprentice, Colby, causing him to face-plant into his own trapping spell. Spirit banishment was usually the sort of job given to necromancers alone, but their guild was swamped with requests to put down wandering undead, so the woman who owned this house had called Isabel and me instead. After a fierce debate with the necromancer guild's leader, we'd managed to secure an apprentice to accompany us, but Colby occupied such a low spot in the guild's hierarchy that he was practically squatting in the basement.

"What are you doing?" Mrs Bennet watched from behind the sofa with reproachful eyes. "Where's the ghost?"

"Same place it always was." I kept my eyes on the corner where the necromancer apprentice claimed the spirit was hiding. Since he was the one with the spirit sight, I'd have to take his word for it. Unlike the faeries, no bait would work on the dead, so my only option was to use force.

I sprinkled the salt onto the floor near the ghost's hiding spot. Isabel watched, looking far more the part of an exorcist than I did with the array of witch charms and protective symbols chalked on her brown arms. At her side was the decidedly less impressive necromancer apprentice looked decidedly less impressive. Skinny and pale, Colby was eighteen at most and kept tripping over the end of a coat made for someone half a foot taller than him. If I'd been Lord Evander, I wouldn't have sent him on his first real mission alongside a former mercenary who had to keep biting her tongue to avoid telling Mrs Bennet exactly where to shove her antique china. I'd also have told him to stop glancing over at the doorway into the hall, where Isabel had employed an illusion spell to hide the trap he'd set up for the ghost, before he gave the game away.

Not that the ghost had anywhere to run. I threw more salt in a diagonal pattern, covering the area near the room's corner. Salt couldn't actively harm ghosts, but if a spirit managed to solidify, being doused in salt would supposedly cause it to dissolve into ectoplasm. Not that this spirit was that strong, but instinct would drive the ghost avoid the areas of the room we'd covered in salt. Sure enough, the faint hint of a breeze on the back of my neck indicated my target was on the move.

"You," said Mrs Bennet, "are ruining my carpets. What are you doing?"

The macarena, I thought at her, sidestepping the pile of stuffing that had once been three cushions. The poltergeist had torn up half the furniture before we'd got here, and I might have felt sorry for her if she hadn't spent the past half-hour berating us for not performing an exorcism to her satisfaction.

A breeze lifted my hair again, and I turned, my gaze following the flutter of curtains and the faint rattle of cabinet doors. Isabel and I locked eyes and nodded, envisioning our invisible menace nearing the trap.

"Gotcha." I stepped forward, and a loud creak halted me in my tracks.

One of the cabinets gave an alarming wobble, and then an expensive-looking plate clattered to the ground.

"What?" I stared. "The trap's supposed to negate kinetic energy, isn't it?"

"The ghost isn't in the trap!" The necromancer apprentice threw his arms over his head as a plate soared at him and shattered against the back wall.

Mrs Bennet screeched like a fire engine. Tearing her straggling grey hair from its roots, she advanced on Isabel and me. "You *vandals*."

"Wait, don't step in the trap—" Isabel started to protest, too late. When Mrs Bennet reached the doorway, the illusion concealing the trap fell away and vibrant red bars enclosed the old woman.

Another plate flew across the room and hit the back wall in a shower of broken china. Mrs Bennet screamed again. My eardrums burned.

"What—?" I spun on my heel as three plates flew to the ceiling and smashed, trying to pinpoint where they'd been thrown from, but the one person in the room with spirit sight had ducked behind the sofa to avoid being struck by a flying plate.

"Colby!" I yelled at him. "Tell us where the spirit is!"

Isabel, as a witch, couldn't see the runaway poltergeist, either. She moved towards the screaming old woman instead, while I ducked more projectiles and waved the saltshaker in all directions in the hopes of hitting my target.

"Stop wrecking my furniture and get me out of here!" screamed Mrs Bennet.

I very nearly said it was an improvement to have her behind bars where she wouldn't get under our feet, but I somehow managed to hold my tongue. As I marched over to the necromancer apprentice, an armchair swung around and knocked me off my feet. I landed in a roll, coming upright with the taste of salt on my tongue.

Isabel knelt down and began trying to free Mrs Bennet

from the trap, while I grabbed Colby by the scruff of his neck and dragged him away from the sofa. "Set up another trap. Or let me do it. How'd you misjudge where it was hiding?"

Another crash. Bits of china showered over our heads and forced Isabel to go into retreat. Mrs Bennet stomped her feet and yelled, but her hands passed straight through the transparent lines forming the cage and she was unable to free herself.

"I swear the spirit was right there." Colby rubbed his arm where a larger piece of china had struck him. "I don't know how it tricked me."

"You're supposed to be the expert." Wait a moment. "There isn't more than one, is there?" Two ghosts tag-teaming would explain how they'd got the jump on us so easily.

"I don't know," he mumbled. "I saw *something* in that corner, though, I swear."

"Great."

Out of the corner of my eye, I watched Isabel crouch again. When the trap switched off, Mrs Bennett sprinted across the room and tripped headlong over an armchair. At the side, three mugs left the cabinet and started juggling themselves in midair.

"Colby, give me the spare salt." I took the saltshaker from him and tossed it to Isabel, who took careful aim at the cabinet. Between us, we might have a chance of salvaging this situation... if Mrs Bennet didn't thwart us again.

Isabel threw half the container of salt towards the cabinet. There wasn't much space in the room that was salt-free at this point. Including Mrs Bennet, who remained hunched on the armchair and didn't seem inclined to get out of our way.

Colby and I edged along the back wall, ducking around the framed pictures of mountain scenery that had somehow remained in place throughout all the chaos. A sudden cold laugh echoed around the room, sharp as a shock of icy water. Mrs Bennet screamed again, this time in pure terror, while the necromancer apprentice lost his head altogether. He broke away from the wall and legged it across the room.

"Don't!" I yelled, too late.

A frying pan sailed out of the kitchen and struck him in the back of his head. Colby dropped to the floor like a stone.

"Oh, shit." From this distance, he looked dazed, not unconscious, but the laughter had sent Mrs Bennet into mild hysterics. She flailed and screamed and tore at the armchair, as though she hoped it'd portal her into another dimension far away from here.

Enough of this. I took my own salt canister and caught Isabel's eye. In unison, we took aim, scanning the room. A rustle of wind stirred my hair, telling me that the spirit was on the move again, but we'd lost our one team member with the spirit sight and might as well be fighting in the dark.

Another laugh sounded. A mug shattered overhead, followed by a second, and then a warning creak drew my attention back to the picture frames. *Uh-oh.* One of the frames began shaking violently, sending bits of plaster dust raining down onto the carpet.

"Watch out!" Isabel ran, and so did I, as the giant wooden-framed landscape on the back wall crashed to the floor in a shower of glass.

"Vandals!" Mrs Bennet howled. "Stop!"

Apparently, the ghost wanted her to shut up, too, because the huge wooden frame lifted upwards and tilted towards the woman cowering on the sofa.

I didn't stop to think. I pulled the sword from its sheath at my side, pointed it at the painting, and shot a stream of vibrant blue energy across the room. Instead of landing on its owner, the heavy wooden frame was sent flying back into the kitchen doorway in a flare of light that shattered what remained of the glass.

Mrs Bennet whimpered, gawping at me. "What—magic—?"

"Witch magic," I said to her in explanation. She wouldn't know any better. I was the only person in the room who could see and use faerie magic, let alone wield a sword forged by the Sidhe themselves. The pleased hum in my hands reminded me it'd been a while since I'd used it on a job, let alone on a more challenging adversary than a pesky ghost.

I re-sheathed the sword and walked past a shell-shocked Mrs Bennet to Isabel. She crouched in the doorway, checking Colby's pulse.

"He's all right, I think. A healing spell will sort him out."

"Except he can't see our ghost." Even my unusual ability to cross the veil at will didn't give me any capacity to see spirits in the waking world, and I doubted old Frank would be pleased if I broke my resolution. I'd promised to keep the number of impromptu trips to the other side to a minimum, but in situations like this, it was difficult to resist.

The blue glow from my sheathed sword grew brighter. *Okay... that's odd.* The sword was supposed to react to faeries, not ghosts.

I crouched beside Colby, whose eyelids flickered. "Hey. Where's that spirit sensor of yours?"

He gave an incoherent groan. I sighed inwardly and dug into the pocket of his ridiculously overlong coat. A remote control-shaped device covered in dials bleeped and flashed blue. Spirit sensors were around ten percent accurate, but somehow the necromancers had never come up with something better, so we were stuck with it. The sensor continued to beep, the sound growing louder as another breeze lifted the hairs on my scalp. There weren't many hiding places left.

The armchair slid across the floor with Mrs Bennet still lying on it. She uttered a squawk of fear, hanging on for dear life.

Isabel lifted her container of salt. I did likewise, giving up on the spirit sensor for now, and we took aim at the armchair from both sides. The chair screeched to a halt as the twin streams of salt sent the spirit fleeing towards the only remaining route of escape.

I didn't need to have a spirit sensor in hand to see the moment the trapping spell activated again. Reddish bars appeared once more, and a flickering shape materialised within. Greyish and indistinct, it formed a vaguely humanoid outline, surprisingly small for something that had caused so much destruction.

"Finally." I high-fived Isabel with the hand that still clutched the saltshaker. Job done, and with minimal damage. Well, aside from Mrs Bennet's house, but she'd caused half the chaos herself by being so bloody obstinate.

The spirit sensor gave another shrill beep. I lifted my gaze. "Colby, is this thing defective?"

"Maybe it's reacting to the trap." Isabel jumped, too, when a distinct thud sounded from upstairs. "Is there anyone up there?"

Mrs Bennet sobbed, clinging to the armchair with both hands. "No! What is happening in my house?"

"Very good question." There was undeniably a ghost caught in the trap, but the distinct noise from upstairs reawakened my theory that there was more than one spirit present. "Colby?"

He half-lay against the wall, drooling, totally out of it.

Isabel lifted her gaze. "Is there another ghost up there? If there is…"

"We need a second trap." More crashing sounded overhead, and I shot Isabel an alarmed look as I sprinted into the hall.

In its sheath, my sword's glow grew brighter, illuminating the path through the shadows encasing the stairs. *No fucking way.* Actual ghosts were supposed to be a rarity anyway, because the necromancer Guardians quickly sent any wayward spirits over the veil. A good job, considering how incompetent the *living* necromancers were, but to have two spirits in one house was less likely than stumbling upon a cache of gold while raiding a troll's nest. Let alone a ghost that triggered my fae-sensitive sword.

I took the stairs three at a time and ran out into the landing, hearing more crashes from behind a closed door. I waved the saltshaker, wishing I hadn't used most of the contents up on the downstairs rooms. "Show yourself."

The door flew open, and a powerful gust of wind practically shoved me into the bedroom. Drawers flew left and right, spilling their contents on the carpet. A chair flew at me, and when I ducked, it struck the inside of the door frame, its wooden legs breaking off. Another laugh followed, sending chills down my back. The dead were hardly the biggest danger out there in the night, but disembodied laughter would be enough to send even the most fearless mercenary fleeing in the opposite direction.

"Very scary." I began sprinkling a line of salt along the doorway to stop the spectre from escaping into the landing. Unfortunately, Mrs Bennet had left the window open, so I could only hope that the spirit was getting too much of a kick out of causing chaos in the house to fly off into the night.

"Someone bring more salt up here!" I called downstairs, ducking another airborne desk chair that left a fist-sized dent in the wall where it struck. I didn't have enough salt to cover the whole room, but I'd start with the window and go from there.

As I ran that way, the bed slid towards me along the thickly carpeted floor. I jumped, using the bed as a spring, and landed in a forward roll, aiming my saltshaker at the area in front of the window. *Right. Now I've got it enclosed in one room.*

The door slammed behind me.

"Ah." I tensed. "Er… Isabel?"

More laughter sounded, and invisible hands tore at my hair, yanking me backwards.

"Hey!" I swatted at the air, half-falling against the bed. This spirit had some nerve. Most couldn't muster enough energy to grab onto a living person. All they could do was throw shit around. This one was far stronger than it should be.

I tugged my hair free and flung the saltshaker into the air, but barely a sprinkle escaped. Crap. I was all out. My hands went to my sword instead, though it'd have zero effect against a ghost. *Why* was it glowing? Mrs Bennet didn't have a piskie infestation as well as a ghost one, did she?

"Ivy Lane," hissed a whispering voice.

I froze, my hand on the hilt. "What? You can speak?"

More to the point, it knew my *name.* Spirits usually weren't able to communicate with anyone but a necromancer. Hence why people who didn't know better opted for Ouija Boards and other questionable tactics. Mrs Bennet had only noticed her unwelcome visitor when it started destroying her upholstery.

"Ivy Lane," repeated the spirit.

"What?" I dropped my gaze to the blade sheathed at my side, its bluish glow as bright as when I stood nose to nose with a faerie. This was no common spirit.

A flickering shape appeared on the ceiling, upside-down

and grinning. Four feet tall, its most dominant feature was its wide mouth full of sharpened teeth. A hobgoblin.

I was right. This was no ordinary ghost. It was a half-faerie.

Unlike regular faeries, half-bloods passed over the veil when they died. Pure faeries *could* die, in very rare circumstances, but as far as I was aware, they didn't leave a ghost behind in the same way. My sword's pulsing glow had never reacted to a spirit before, but I didn't go out of my way to put myself in situations where half-fae ghosts crossed my path.

"What do you want with me?"

"Entertainment." The hobgoblin offered me an upside-down grin. "I've heard all about you, Ivy Lane."

"You shouldn't even be able to speak."

"Or do this?"

The bed rose into the air, sending me sliding onto the floor. One of the daggers I carried in my pocket came loose and rose upward, forcing me to roll over to avoid being stabbed by my own weapon.

That's what I get for bringing a knife to a ghost fight. The knife whizzed around in midair, and I ducked again, unable to believe the spirit had that level of control. What the hell kind of power trip was this ghost on?

My blade hummed as I drew on its power to enhance my speed far beyond my normal human instincts, leaping onto the dresser. "Am I entertaining you?" I yelled over my shoulder, as the chest of drawers creaked and tipped, spilling half its contents onto the floor.

Outside, someone thumped on the door.

"Don't come in!" I warned. "This one won't be contained in a trap."

Not strictly true, but I was officially over being made a fool of. I withdrew my sword from its sheath in a shower of blue light. The spirit, being half-blood, would be able to see exactly how fearsome the blade looked when I held the sword high, letting the bright-blue light envelop the room.

"This is your last warning."

I'd used my magic to knock ghosts around when the veil had been low and death energy had been flying around everywhere. I didn't have a clue whether it'd work now, but the ghost's transparent face showed a flicker of fear. "That magic you wield is not meant for humans."

"Tough shit. Get down from there, or I'll make you wish you'd never learned my name."

The door flew open, and Isabel ran into the room. She held up the spirit sensor, which I must have dropped on the way in. "Where is it?"

"On the ceiling, but—"

She hit the sensor. A jet of pure white shot out, and the hobgoblin let go of the ceiling light. The ghost screamed, writhed, and then exploded in a shower of green slime.

"Oops," said Isabel. "I didn't know that'd happen."

Pushing slime-soaked hair from my eyes, I turned to her. "What *was* that?"

"Necromancer emergency backup weapon. I think it has concentrated salt in it. So that's what happens when you use it on a ghost. I did wonder." She gave me a shaky smile. "Now that's an idea for a new tripwire spell."

"Ghostbusters, eat your heart out." I shook more ectoplasm off my sleeve. "How the hell are we meant to explain this to the mage council?"

2

"This is a fine mess, isn't it?" said Drake. The copper-haired fire mage wore a wide grin as he approached, followed by the more stern-faced Lady Granville. This case must rank pretty high in the Mage Lords' list of major screw-ups if two members of the mage council were here, but at least Drake was less of a notorious stickler for the rules than his companion. He was also one of the few mages whom I'd befriended since I'd started working with them. "Vance is busy with clients, by the way. That's why he sent me instead."

I didn't doubt that. Unlike Isabel and me, the mages hadn't struggled with work drying up over the Christmas period. It didn't help that we'd lost half our clientele thanks to Larsen, my former employer, lowering his rates the same day Isabel and I had set up our new business, but frankly, I rarely bothered to think about my ex-boss these days.

"What exactly is *that*?" Lady Granville indicated the ecto-plasm on my sleeves with a distasteful expression that she reserved solely for me and the occasional spider that got into the mages' headquarters. I was pretty sure that she'd implode if she set eyes upon some of the shit I saw on a regular basis.

"Ectoplasm," I said. "From when the ghost exploded."

"Exploded?" said Lady Granville. "I was under the impression the three of you knew what you were doing."

"We did," I said ineffectually. "We were told to prepare for one spirit. We didn't expect to be attacked by two. It shouldn't have had that much kinetic power. Most spirits can't so much as lift a teaspoon."

I looked at Colby, who'd recovered from his blow to the head thanks to a quick-acting healing spell provided by Isabel and had set about banishing the second spirit with minimal fuss. Not that anyone ever noticed when we *did* follow the plan.

"Vandals and madmen!" screeched Mrs Bennet from the corner of the wrecked living room. She'd been shrieking incoherently for the last twenty minutes while we waited for help, ignoring Isabel's attempts to offer reassurances. My own efforts to clear up the mess had also been in vain. The bedroom was covered in ectoplasm, the furniture and carpets were ruined, and broken china lay everywhere downstairs. Luckily the mages would be paying for compensation and not us... assuming we gave the council a satisfying explanation.

"You clearly stated in your initial report was that the job was to deal with a spiritual incursion into a human home in as professional a manner as possible." Lady Granville zeroed in on me. "This is in no way reflective of our procedures at the mage guild."

"We were professional right up until the ghost multiplied itself and started smashing plates over our heads." Her complete unwillingness to lift a finger to help put me in mind of a better dressed and even more annoying version of Larsen. Maybe she and my ex-boss ought to get together.

"I want compensation!" screamed Mrs Bennet.

You'll get it, you old toad.

Just not from me. Hence why I had to bite my tongue around the senior Mage Lord. Why had Vance not shown up instead?

Drake snickered.

I gave him the evil eye and turned to our necromancer assistant, who was fiddling with the dial on the side of the spirit sensor. "Anything?"

"The veil tests as normal," said Colby. "No amol—anomo—"

"Anomalies?" suggested Isabel.

"Yeah. That." He rubbed the back of his head. Isabel had given him the healing spell before concussion set in, but he wasn't exactly on the ball even when he hadn't been hit in the head with a frying pan. "I don't get how the ghost evaded my spirit sensor."

"Probably because it's ten percent accurate." You'd think that someone in the necromancer guild's hundreds-year-old history would have invented a better method. "And the presence of one masked the other."

"You saw it, though."

Thanks for that, Colby. "I heard it. You were out cold."

"You did see it." Mrs Bennet pinned me with a wild-eyed stare. "You *talked* to it. I heard."

Why had she chosen that moment to pay attention?

"Faeries can choose to reveal themselves to whoever they want to," I said, mostly for Lady Granville's benefit. "Seems the same rule applies to ghosts. Hobgoblins aren't too smart whether they're alive or dead, and evidently, taunting someone with the Sight was hard to resist."

The council knew I was Sighted—it'd been hard to keep *that* off my application—but there also wasn't a category in the mages' listings for humans who held the magic of one of the Sidhe. Much to the annoyance of people like Lady Granville, who wanted nothing more than to put me into a neat box. And then throw away the key.

Isabel gave me a look that suggested she didn't see through my bravado, but I didn't need to freak out Mrs Bennet any further by speculating aloud on how a half-faerie ghost had packed such a magical punch this far from the Ley Line.

It was looking for you, too. It knew who you were.

I shoved the thoughts aside to confront later. "Did either of you question the other spirit?"

Colby shook his head. "It was too far gone to talk, so I banished it."

That figured. I didn't blame him for wanting rid of the ghost who'd destroyed the downstairs room, but that left us with nobody left who might explain why the spirit upstairs had been so abnormally strong.

"So we don't know what caused enough of an energy surge to draw two spirits here?" Not my magic, surely. I hadn't used any until the second spirit appeared.

"Spectral energy is drawn to certain areas," said Colby hesitantly. "Usually places where violent deaths have occurred."

"Are you accusing me of murder, *boy*?" screamed Mrs Bennet.

"No." Colby blanched. "No, of course not."

Lady Granville gave a disapproving sniff. "The Mage Lords will gladly provide compensation for the damages. I shall be in touch after we process the reports."

That's it? "Don't you want to find out the second spirit's identity? That one wasn't fae."

Whether Lord Evander would deign to drag himself out here was debateable, but it bugged the crap out of me that two violent spirits had come to the same house without catching the attention of the necromancers.

"No," said Lady Granville. "Our part in this mission is over."

That figured. Sticking to the rules by the letter was ranked at the top of her priority list, whether there was a troll beating down the door or ghosts running amok around the house. I was pretty sure she'd survived the faerie invasion by sticking her fingers in her ears and reciting a textbook at the invading Sidhe until they left her alone out of sheer annoyance.

"I think we should wait for the necromancers to show up." Drake nodded to Colby. "Wanna call your boss?"

"Absolutely not," said Lady Granville. "We need to file our reports within an hour of the incident. We shouldn't disturb this lady any longer."

"I… shouldn't call the boss," Colby said, the hint of an apology in his voice. "There's nothing left to find here."

Sure about that? The kid was terrified of his boss, though he was also scared of me, too. The first time we'd met, I'd strong-armed Colby into stealing from Lord Evander's office by paying him a visit via the spirit world, and I was pretty sure he'd live in fear of his boss learning of his deception for the rest of his life. And, with them both being necromancers, probably the afterlife as well.

I knew a losing battle when I saw one, though. Drake caught my eye, shrugged, and we traipsed out of the room after Lady Granville. Isabel and Colby followed, the latter carrying his surviving necromantic equipment.

"You're really going to come to the meeting covered in ectoplasm?" asked Drake.

"Yes." The first time I'd shown up to meet with the mage council wearing clothes stained with blood and monster guts, they'd looked so scandalised that it'd been entirely worth the tedium of sitting through a four-hour meeting, and I'd since learned that I could dress like an exact clone of one of them and certain individuals would still claim I fell short of their standards.

The cold January air slapped us in the face as we crossed Mrs Bennet's immaculate garden to the two sleek black cars parked outside. I huddled in my thick coat, my gaze travelling back to the sheen of blue-tinged faerie magic hovering over the upstairs window. Death energy fuelled spirits. As I'd seen more than once, death energy and my own faerie magic weren't all that different.

A chill that had nothing to do with the cold took hold of me as I recalled the last ghost I'd encountered, months before, and his vow that he'd return and take my life in recompense for his.

Calder's voice whispered in my ear. *"I'll kill your mage first."*

———

"Faerie ghosts," said Isabel around a mouthful of toast, seated at the desk in our office. "Seriously. Why does everything weird come after you?"

"Very good question." I blew on my coffee to cool it down, wrapping my hands around the mug for warmth. When our former neighbours moved out of the upstairs flat, they'd enacted a last act of defiance by leaving the heating broken and a leaking hole in the ceiling. Now we'd converted the main room into our office, we spent a lot of time sitting in the cold. "Because I'm faerie bait."

"Even for dead ones." Isabel shook her head over the stack of papers in front of her. "Do you want to know how much the damages were?"

"Nope. The mages have already offered to pay." I leaned

over the desk to read the topmost paper in yet another stack. "What's that?"

"Risk assessment forms from the mage guild. For the landlord, you know."

"Yay." In order to prove to our landlord that we planned to use the upstairs flat as an office and not to hold house parties, we'd been forced to develop a more organised system for paperwork. Usually I handled phone calls while Isabel dealt with the admin, but now the mages had got involved and I was technically *their* employee, we'd been saddled with filing a detailed report on last night's clusterfuck of a job. "Lucky we don't have too much of a backlog yet."

"Because we haven't *had* any new clients for two weeks," said Isabel.

"It was Christmas," I reminded her. "We can do a January special or something. Hire us to find a missing heirloom and we'll throw in an exorcism for free."

Isabel snorted. "I'm swearing off exorcisms for a while. Are the necromancers really overrun?"

"Sounds like it, from what Vance said. Maybe the Ghosts of Christmas Past and Present got lost in transit."

It was a week after New Year's Day, so new cases would start trickling in soon, but we didn't need to kickstart the year by landing ourselves in debt over a pair of spectres any more than we needed to make terrorising old ladies a recurring habit.

I was hardly complaining that we hadn't had many unpleasant cases to ruin our holiday. I'd spent Christmas and New Years at the manor, which had been a welcome change from sitting at home pulling a lonely cracker with Erwin the piskie while Isabel went to the coven's endless stream of holiday events. Since I didn't have any surviving family, I typically found the holidays bloody depressing.

Not that spending ample time around the mages was all

sunshine and piskie dust. There'd been no shortage of snooty upper-class sorts at the manor who looked at me like I was an ogre in human clothing or outright ignored me, but the upsides were more than enough to make up for the inconvenience of spending any length of time around Lady Granville.

Isabel set aside one of the papers. "Most of the costs are for removing ectoplasm from the carpets. The cleansing spell didn't work."

"Figures," I muttered. "Vance is coming over in a bit. I'll get him to double-check these to make sure I didn't get anything wrong."

It'd be just like the council to throw in a trick question that would reverse the blame and saddle us with the bill. I read the papers until I went cross-eyed and wrote repeatedly that yes, we'd assessed the house before entering and had brought the appropriate equipment. When I reached the end of the first page, I stopped to chew on my pen. This whole case was bizarre. Not only was it all but impossible for a mere ghost to cause so much damage, but the half-hobgoblin had appeared out of nowhere after avoiding the attuned senses of a trained necromancer. True, Colby wasn't the most skilled among the guild's number, but the second spirit hadn't acted at all like a confused, recently deceased ghost.

Moreover, the goblin had known my name. That, above all, was bad news.

My phone buzzed. Before I'd had the chance to read Vance's message, the doorbell rang downstairs.

"He could just teleport inside," said Isabel.

"He insists on doing it this way." Some women might find it romantic if they had a boyfriend who could literally appear right behind them whenever he wanted. Unfortunately, my experiences with the faeries had given me a permanent act-first-ask-questions-later response when people crept up on me, and after a couple of near-misses, Vance had switched to using the door to avoid an accidental impalement on the end of my blade.

I drank the rest of my coffee and went downstairs, ducking underneath Erwin the piskie. Given the manic way that he was bouncing off the walls, the bugger had got into the mulled wine again. Isabel and I had brought some home on Christmas Eve, not knowing it had ten times the effect on piskies, and we'd had to shut him out of the flat until he calmed down.

I walked down the sparsely carpeted hall to open the front door for Vance. "Hey."

"Hey yourself." He looked good. Okay, he always did. His long coat fit snugly across his well-muscled shoulders, while his neatly combed hair had grown a little, curling at the edges over his grey eyes. He was tall enough to block the cold air from getting inside, which was more than welcome. Pity he'd probably come with bad news.

Sure enough, Vance said, "I wanted to warn you. Lord Evander—"

"Wants to meet us." I groaned. "Has he found a way to blame me for last night yet?"

"Not yet."

That figured. He'd already left me an angry voicemail berating me for putting his apprentice in danger, as though he hadn't been the one to put Colby's name forward instead of a fully qualified necromancer. Arsehole. "You're really selling this meeting to me."

He wrapped an arm around my back. "You'll get the pleasure of my company as well."

"You're very pleasant company." I kissed him lightly. "But the necromancers aren't. What's Lord Evander saying about last night?"

"He's claiming the second ghost was outside of the necromancers' responsibilities, being a faerie."

"Seriously? I thought the rule of necromancers was that they dealt with all ghosts. Not just human ones."

At least according to Frank, the Guardian who kept me up to date with any developments on the other side of the veil. I wondered what *he'd* have to say, assuming Lord Evander had told him the details. Which was no guarantee.

"Yes," said Vance. "I persuaded him to add his signature to the forms, if you're done with them."

"Just about." I held up the wad of paper. "Can you double-check these? I made it clear enough that the ghost was responsible for the damage, but it's kinda hard to figure out a professional way to say that the ghost exploded." Honestly, ninety percent of the situations I ended up in were impossible to describe in a manner that would be acceptable in a professional setting.

Sometimes—okay, most of the time—I appreciated the benefits of working for the Mage Lords. I hadn't been above the poverty line long enough to have forgotten the struggle to make ends meet. Except all I really wanted was Vance, without the council attached.

Vance's eyes roved over the page. "No… this will do. The paperwork is a formality, nothing more. I already have the bank transfer set up."

"Formalities can get in the bin." Gratitude filled me, all the same. "Cheers. We didn't need a twenty grand bill for cleaning ectoplasm off the walls, and I know Lord Evander would rather eat grave dirt than admit his apprentice fucked up."

"You think Colby overlooked the second ghost out of incompetence?"

"I mean, it might have outwitted him instead." I shrugged. "Who the hell knows. How was your night?"

"You had a more exciting evening than me. I had to sit in on a hearing for someone who stole a witch's motorcycle. It backfired and he ended up with a nasty case of blisters."

I snorted. "That's why you never mess with a witch."

"Speaking of which, your trap nearly got me on the way in."

"It's meant to react to sudden movements."

Without the shifters living upstairs, Isabel and I owned the whole house, which left us entirely responsible for security. Considering we'd had dead bodies and murderous thorns show up outside in recent months, you might wonder why we hadn't moved, but my tendency to attract fae-related trouble would follow me even if we went to the North Pole. Besides, thanks to some assistance from Vance, our wards were second only to those on the mages' manor. I smiled at him, my bad mood evaporating even with the knowledge that Lord Evander would doubtless be a total dick to us.

With Vance, there was no need to walk or take the bus. He took my arm and we vanished from the doorstep, reappearing on a country lane. He didn't strictly need to be touching me to transport us, but I took the opportunity to snuggle closer to him.

Vance trailed a hand through my hair. "You're friendly today."

"A half-hobgoblin ghost nearly stabbed me to death last night."

He stopped stroking my hair. "What?"

"Didn't you read the report?"

His thumb traced the edge of my cheek. "No. I only heard the basics from Lady Granville. I thought she'd told me everything important."

"I'm not exactly a priority with her."

He moved back, and his eyes darkened a little. "You should be."

I shrugged. "I'll get over it. Let's go see Lord Evander."

The necromancers' place, as always, resembled the backdrop for a low-budget horror movie. Soot-black bricks formed a squat building beside an iron gate. On my usual visits, I went through that gate and into the cemetery to a mausoleum in which I met with Frank the necromancer ghost. I'd only been inside their actual headquarters once. My conversations with Lord Evander tended to be brief and ended with him storming off in an insulted huff.

Vance didn't need to ring the doorbell. Lord Evander already waited outside, with Colby hovering beside him. The apprentice studied his feet, avoiding our eyes.

Here we go.

Lord Evander was a short, unimpressive man with one of those forgettable faces that probably wouldn't look much different as a ghost. His suit was more threadbare than the Mage Lord's and had what looked like ectoplasm on the sleeves.

"Having trouble with ghosts?" I asked cheerily. "Out of interest, do *you* know a formal way to say, 'the ghost exploded'? I spent an hour this morning trying to figure that one out."

A muscle ticked in his jaw. "I'll thank you not to mock me, Ivy Lane. I notice you didn't deign to return my call."

"Sorry, I'm already taken."

Vance gave me an exasperated look. Colby watched me in open horror, while his boss's expression suggested he wished he could pull out a spirit sensor and make *me* explode.

"You," he said, "are lucky not to be on the other side of that gate."

"You break my heart, Lord Evander." I stopped myself before I got carried away. "In all seriousness, you're the ghost expert in town. None of us could see what the hell was going on in that house until it was too late. Two ghosts in a single human residence strikes me as serious enough to merit a proper inspection, doesn't it?"

"A half-faerie ghost isn't my responsibility."

"Or mine, since I'm an ambassador for the living ones, not the dead," I reminded him. "The half-faeries' Chief will say the same."

Which meant the mages would have to clear up the mess. Or rather, the mages' freelancers. Moreover, Isabel and I would be on our own if another half-faerie ghost showed up.

"The spirit spoke your name, didn't it?"

Thanks for that one, Colby. "I guess I'm famous among dead faeries as well as living ones. Anyway, your apprentice is the one with the spirit sight, not me."

Lord Evander gave Colby a sideways look. "He said the second spirit was hiding upstairs and his injury made it quite impossible for him to have seen the newcomer. Moreover, you've claimed yourself to be an expert in *all* faeries in the past."

"When did I ever say that?" Not to my knowledge, I hadn't. "Half-faerie or not, the ghost had way more power than it should have been able to access away from the Ley Line."

"The guild has limited experience with half-faerie ghosts," he retaliated. "The few necromancers who have encountered them have no memory of the experience."

Him and his eternal grudge. Yes, two necromancers had had up close and personal encounters with half-blood ghosts who'd possessed them on the Ley Line and forced Vance and me to kill them in self-defence. There *had* been other necromancers present, but the veil had been stirred up so badly at the time that the spirits had been able to physically materialise and use their elemental magic. Mercifully, the spirit we'd encountered yesterday hadn't been quite *that* strong, but Lord Evander kind of had a point in that there were no established guidelines as far as half-faeries went.

"The laws regarding ghosts still stand, regardless of whether those spirits are human or otherwise," said Vance. "The case was dealt with, but if I were you, I'd come up with a solution if it happens again."

"I fail to see what more I could have done," said Lord Evander. "The ghosts have gone, the incident is behind us, and if you want to maintain our professional relationship, I'd suggest you take any remaining complaints to the half-faeries instead."

I gritted my teeth. He knew perfectly well that the Chief would send me back here, and I'd end up stuck in a cycle of passing messages between grumbling supernaturals who acted like two squabbling children. "I have a quicker solution. Why don't you and the Chief meet directly?"

Outrage crossed the necromancer's face. "You have some cheek—"

"I think that's an excellent idea," said Vance. "Maybe the two of you can come to an agreement."

I bit my lip to avoid laughing. I'd been trying to wind him up, but it actually wasn't a bad call to force the pair of them into the same room to work out their differences.

"Absolutely not!" Lord Evander all but yelled the words. "You'll speak to him, Ivy Lane, and if I hear you're damaging my reputation—"

I snorted. His reputation was already six feet under, pun intended. People only came to the guild for help because there was no alternative when you had a poltergeist wrecking your house. Everyone in town with the spirit sight joined the guild. No exceptions.

"Enough," Vance cut in. "Have you spoken to Lord Sydney?"

"No, but I will, and you'll wait until I do. I don't want to find you creeping around my cemetery."

"Perish the thought." It kind of figured that the one reliable necromancer I'd met would be a ghost himself, but I didn't mind waiting to speak to him. As the half-hobgoblin had been blasted with the spirit eradication device, he wasn't an imminent threat and might even have passed beyond the gates altogether. You couldn't *destroy* a ghost, because they didn't have a physical form. I'd never got a conclusive answer on where the ectoplasm came from, but the ghost was long gone regardless, and I doubted Frank would have seen him.

There was, however, someone who might have met the hobgoblin back when he was still alive.

"We'll speak to the Chief," Vance said, clearly thinking the same. "I'll just need you to sign here."

Lord Evander's eyes bulged as the Mage Lord presented him with the paperwork I'd filled out. "You dare to ask me for—"

"You did agree."

He had, and evidently his desire to be rid of us won out over his need to get one over on the Mage Lord. Lord Evander pulled out a pen, scribbled a signature on the page, and retreated into the doorway. "Now, get out."

"If there are any new developments, Lord Evander, I expect to receive a call from you," said Vance. "Thank you for your time."

"It's been scintillating." On days like this, I'd sell my super-powered sword to be rid of my connection to the necromancers. There were few perks, if any, to allying with those who dabbled in Death.

Vance and I disappeared before the necromancer could utter another word. I grinned up at him as we landed at the roadside. "You should put out an ad offering to help people escape dodgy situations with a dramatic exit."

He chuckled. "It wouldn't surprise me if you pushed Lord Evander into early retirement."

"How'd you figure out my evil plan?" I let go of his arm. "It'd be better for everyone if he *did* retire. I mean, anyone's better than him."

"Not necessarily," said Vance. "The local necromancers' guild has a history of poor leadership."

"So does this place." I gestured to the hedges bordering the road. "They haven't the benefit of a few hundred years of history, though, so it's a bit more understandable."

"Precisely," said Vance. "Chieftain Taive might be able to give us some direction, though he's also unlikely to accept responsibility for the spirit."

"Definitely not," I said. "I mean, it's possible that the half-faeries can see the ghosts of their own kind, but he won't know the rules on what happens after they die."

Death was a touchy subject here, as half-blooded faeries weren't born with immortality the way pure-blooded faeries were. Granted, even a pure Sidhe couldn't survive an iron sword to the heart, but they were wicked hard to kill and were immune to age and sickness. Unless they came to this realm or were exiled to the Grey Vale, but those exceptions were rarely spoken of either.

"No," Vance said. "I imagine he also won't like you reminding him of his own mortality."

"Definitely not." If I didn't proceed carefully, I risked killing all the progress I'd made towards reconciling his people and the mages. Which wasn't a whole lot, but nobody had murdered one another over the holidays, and I considered that a win. "I suppose it can't hurt to ask, though."

Someone must have answers. My magic might be powerful, but the dead were on another level. Almost in a literal sense.

Especially since one person on the other side would dearly love to drag me over to join him.

3

I'd only been to half-blood territory a handful of times, but they changed décor every visit and today was no exception. Winter was in full swing. Icicles hung from the gate, a coating of frost decorated the hedge, and someone had strung up fairy lights made of live piskies clutching luminescent charms in their spindly hands. Now there was a safety hazard if I ever saw one. The piskies themselves didn't look unhappy with the arrangement. One even waved at me. Weirdos.

Two guards wearing armour waited inside. The Chief had had enough of Vance and me casually walking into his territory, so he had twenty-four-hour guards stationed at intervals throughout. Their attire was a weird combination of medieval and modern, with lightweight grey plating over thick, plain dark-coloured clothes. Both were male and inhumanly pretty, their faces perfectly symmetrical in a way that was more unsettling than attractive. Which summed up the faeries, to be honest.

I waved at the guards. "Hey, Bob."

Two pairs of eyes narrowed at me. It was a running joke

30

only I found funny. Since every faerie guard here called me "the human" as though they didn't know my name, I'd taken to calling every single one of them "Bob," regardless of gender. It drove the Chief out of his mind.

"Mage Lord." The guards nodded to Vance and totally blanked me. Dicks. As they parted, I adjusted my position so that my sword jutted out of its sheath and exposed the faint glow of Winter magic. While they didn't flinch, some of their hostility melted into wariness. Wise of them.

Half the territory had been turned into a giant ice rink in place of its usual lawns, on which fae of all kinds glided with abandon. Ice-crowned trees lined the path, decorated by twinkling lights. Snow drifted through the air. Magically created or not, the cold burn against my cheeks felt real enough. The bitter air cut through my coat, and despite the openness, the whistling wind made me think of echoing corridors in ancient castles with dungeons extending deep underground. The guards, with their armour and weapons, didn't help that impression either.

I clenched and unclenched my fists, more to stop myself losing sensation in my fingers than anything else. The guards parted to allow us through into a small clearing between leafless trees etched in frost. The Chief stood in the centre, on a small hill which made him stand taller than me, though not as high as Vance's six-foot-two frame. Since my last visit, he'd acquired a new crown, tarnished silver patterned with leaves. Perhaps a Christmas present, though I didn't think the half-bloods typically went in for human holidays. Icicles hung from the sides, and his staff shimmered with green Summer magic.

He sneezed. So much for the intimidating impression. As a Summer faerie, he probably wasn't pleased with the state of his territory.

"A little chilly in here, isn't it?" Actually, I was freezing my arse off, and the other Seelie half-faeries probably were, too.

"Ivy Lane," he said in neutral tones. "Mage Lord. What do you want?"

"We're here because a half-faerie ghost tried to kill me last night."

The Chief's breath hissed out, clouding the air. "And what, precisely, do you expect me to do about that?"

I raised an eyebrow. "A half-faerie ghost is a rarity. One that can deal physical damage, even more so. In the past, that's only occurred when the veil was thinning."

He remained unmoved. "I am no necromancer. The veil holds no interest for me."

That figured. "The ghost was a half-goblin. Know any who died recently?"

"Yes." He ground out the word. "A half-hobgoblin died in our jail yesterday afternoon."

"In jail?" My mind raced. "But that means… wait. He took the drug, didn't he? He's one of the people you arrested for rampaging around the city a few months ago. Am I right?"

"If you'd allow me to speak," said the Chief. "Yes, he took the drug. He was one of the half-bloods who claimed to have no memory of anything he did under the drug's influence. I kept him jailed because he killed two people. Believe it or not, I do know how to police my own."

"Oh." That was actually a smart move, not one I'd have expected of him. "So… how did he die?"

"Another prisoner killed him. We keep them in separate cells, but the ones with stronger magic occasionally break out."

"You don't use iron cages?"

"We aren't barbaric." The Chief's eyes narrowed. "Iron poisoning is equivalent to torture in our eyes, and it would not have helped in this case. A small group of prisoners coordinated an escape attempt and freed other inmates in an attempt to cause a diversion. Three were killed before the guards subdued them."

"Damn." I looked at Vance. "None of them got away, did they?"

"No," the Chief said. "The survivors were rounded up and returned to their cells."

"Good," said Vance. "Have you considered the possibility the drug might be involved again?"

That's what I thought. Unfortunately.

"They didn't take any drugs," said the Chief. "We tested everyone in the jail after the incident, including the ones who died."

"Who did die?" I couldn't help asking.

"I'm not obliged to disclose the details."

"The ghost knew my name," I pointed out. "He didn't have anything in particular to say about me in jail, did he?"

"I'm not in charge of the prison."

"Then take me to someone who is."

"Need I remind you of your agreement with the mage guild?" said Vance. "If we believe one of yours to be acting in a manner that places the rest of the supernatural community in danger, we will take immediate action."

"I haven't the slightest idea what you're accusing me of," said the Chief. "I wasn't at the jail. If you want to talk to the guards who were present, it's your prerogative."

"Where is the jail?" I didn't expect a reply, but he jerked his head northward.

"Follow the path to the left out of the clearing," said the Chief. "I can't promise the guards will be accommodating."

"I'm sure they'll be just as friendly as you are." I shifted on my feet, once again revealing my sword's dazzling blue glow. "Pleasure seeing you, Chieftain Taive."

"Consider our agreement," Vance added, sweeping after

me. He might upstage me with dramatic exits, but my new magic sent the half-faeries into retreat and even the Chief's ogre guards gave me a wide berth.

"Left," I muttered, turning down the path and rubbing my hands together to get some feeling back into my fingertips. I wished I had a long coat like Vance did. "What d'you reckon he's put in charge of watching the jail? Ogres, trolls, or chimeras?"

"Probably not a chimera," said Vance.

"What're the odds that the people involved in this are some of the same prisoners who helped Calder?" I asked. "Not sure on our odds of getting their cooperation."

"I think they'd talk to you."

"Why, because I'm so diplomatic?"

"No, threatening."

"Hello, Mr I-summon-swords-from-thin-air?"

He gave me a sideways grin. "As to the guards, I suspect a subtler tactic might work better."

"Depends who he has guarding the place."

If Unseelie territory was this cold, they could keep it. My feet, ears and nose were completely numb, and my boots crunched in the snow padding the way along the narrow path. Trees crowded either side, gnarled bark resembling monstrous faces. The presence of my sword and Vance's iron blade kept anything nasty from touching us, but the wildness of the area set my spine prickling. "You don't think he's sending us into a trap, do you?"

"He wouldn't dare," Vance said tightly. "He knows the two of us can take him to pieces, and so do the rest of the faeries who live here."

"Not necessarily." I didn't *think* any of the pure faeries lived here with the half-bloods, but that ghost hadn't been scared of me in the least.

A keening wail struck up, piercing my eardrums. "Ow."

"What's that?" Vance didn't stop walking, but he lifted his hand-and-a-half sword higher, his gaze roving over the trees.

I pulled my own sword out. "Haven't a clue."

The noise went on, high and sad, like a dirge crossed with an opera singer, albeit several miles off key. Coldness slid through me, under skin, under bone.

"Who's there?" Vance stalked down the path, and we both came to a halt when we saw the faerie standing in front of us like a statue. A statue with a hell of a mouth on her. The awful song poured from her throat, battering at me like a solid force. My magic formed a shield in front of me, but even then, I had to force my legs to stay in position.

Vance surveyed the faerie, seemingly unaffected by the blast of power emanating from her god-awful voice. "What manner of faerie are you?"

I knew. "You're a banshee?"

Or half-banshee. The wailing stopped as the woman—girl, really—noticed our presence. She was all of sixteen, though a few inches taller than me. Maybe five-eight or so. Her black hair spilled to her shoulders, her full lips pouted, and she had the sort of face that would make most human men fall at her feet. If they hadn't already passed out from hearing her singing.

"What are you doing?" I asked her.

"Death," she said, ominously.

"What about it?" The words came out through frosted lips. Damn, she packed a magical punch. If she was half-banshee, I didn't want to meet the real deal.

"Someone here will die." She cast a dramatic look over her shoulder. A squat building stood at the path's end, covered in a thick layer of snow. Creeping trees formed a circle around its edges, offering a claustrophobic feel.

"Is... that the jail?" No shit, Ivy. "Didn't someone already die?"

"Yesterday," said Vance. I was impressed at how steady his tone was, but his shifter heritage did give him some level of resistance to faerie mind tricks.

"Unless you're running behind schedule," I added.

"Are you insulting me, human?" hissed the half-banshee.

"Nope. And I have a name. Ivy. What's yours?"

"Alison," said the banshee. "Would you like a taste of my death magic?"

"Got plenty of death magic right here," I said. "We're here to speak to the guards running this place about yesterday's incident."

"*I'm* the guard."

She had to be joking. "What do you do, keep the prisoners contained by threatening to sing at them?"

"No." She spun to me in an elegant whirl, affecting a dramatic tone. "My song is a warning that someone will soon die."

The coldness intensified, the air thickening. "If that was a threat," said Vance, "I'd consider who you're speaking to."

"My apologies, Mage Lord. I meant no disrespect." There was nothing remotely respectful in her tone.

I cleared my throat. "And me?"

"I've heard about you, Ivy Lane," she said. "Death has marked you."

"Who's going to die?" *Please say me.* When I passed over the veil, that was death in a sense, and a million times better than another murder.

"I cannot say who the victim will be," she said. "Someone nearby will die, within the next three days."

"If your prisoners are planning another breakout, maybe you need to look at your security.'

Her hands warped and twisted, turning into black talons. "I will not tolerate mockery from humans."

Vance stepped forward. "You're required to answer our

questions. A half-faerie who died here yesterday attacked Ivy, and we'd like to know who he was."

I clenched my hand over my sword hilt. "Who let them out? Did you kill everyone responsible?"

"Yes." She lifted her taloned hands, revealing hints of dried blood. "I took the lives of the conspirators myself."

"And did any of them mention magical drugs?" Every one of my instincts went into overdrive just looking at the banshee. If she hadn't stated otherwise, I'd have suspected *her* of instigating a jailbreak and laughing at the mass slaughter of humans.

"No, but they didn't have much to say." A laugh issued from her mouth, but mercifully, it didn't turn into a song.

"We have reason to believe the incident was linked to the events three months ago," said Vance. "The Chief told us nobody in the jail remembered anything of the night they were drugged, but if they've been planning a jailbreak, it's plain that they aren't willing to adhere to the laws."

"I took care of them." The banshee lifted her talon to her mouth. Her tongue flicked out, lapping at the blood. Ew. "Ivy Lane, perhaps my song is for you."

I drew my sword in a spray of blue light. Energy surged up and smacked into her talons, though I'd purposefully held back on unleashing a stronger assault.

She danced back a step and eyed me with reproach. "What was that for?"

"Being creepy and weird." And the implied threat. "Does the Chief know you eat his prisoners?"

She responded with a shriek that hit me head-on and sent me staggering sideways into Vance. He took my arm, and the banshee's cries vanished on the breeze that swept us away.

"Whoa." I stepped away from him and rubbed my burning ears. We'd landed outside the hedges bordering half-blood territory. "That was a hell of an encore."

"Yes." Vance's eyes flashed light grey, and the tremor in the air was a warning hint that the banshee had escaped lightly. "My apologies. I rather think that if we'd stayed, I would have violated our peace treaty with my own hand."

"Not if I got there first." I walked around the hedges towards the gate. "Oi! Chief! Get some new guards."

"He's not there," said Vance.

I scowled. "What kind of person leaves a death faerie in charge of a prison?"

"A half-banshee," said Vance. "They're from Winter, correct? But you told me only the exiles fed on death."

Even after three months together, Vance hadn't heard all my tales about my stint in Faerie, but I had to admit banshees weren't a group I had extensive experience with.

"Yeah, banshees don't feed on death energy," I said. "They just have the impulse to scream whenever someone's going to die. I didn't realise the half-human sort were that powerful."

"I forgot she wasn't a pure faerie," he said. "She looked like one."

I raised a brow. "I thought you were immune to her charms."

"The singing rather spoiled the effect. And the talons."

"Lucky you've never heard me sing."

I spoke lightly, but the chilling effect of the banshee's words hadn't eased yet. *Someone will die. Within three days.* She might have meant anyone in the jail, even in the territory as a whole... but my mind kept jumping over to Vance.

The half-hobgoblin had seemingly been acting alone, but he hadn't been the only person to die in that jail, and we hadn't learned the identities of the others. I bloody well hoped they'd gone to the other side of the veil without a fuss.

"Anyway." I shook myself as if to dislodge all thoughts of death, banshees included. "What now?"

Vance pulled out his phone. "Lady Granville's called a meeting in ten minutes. I imagine she'll want to go through the paperwork on last night's case."

"Great. Another formality?" She'd probe every word I'd written on the page and try to twist them against me, but Vance and Lord Evander had already signed the forms, which meant this would be a colossal waste of time.

"Unfortunately yes," said Vance. "She wasn't happy with you last night."

"So, another day ending in 'y'." I gave an eye-roll. "Don't worry, I'll behave myself."

He nodded. "We have the gala tonight, and then—"

"Shit."

"What?"

"The gala. I forgot."

He looked at me. "You didn't have other plans, did you?"

"A date with you."

The corner of his mouth turned up. "The gala counts as a date."

"Not when other people are there."

Call me petty, but we'd hardly had any real dates since before Christmas. The manor was always packed with mages I didn't know, and Vance was so busy organising ways to keep them occupied that we only had alone time after dark. Admittedly, I had nothing to complain about in that department, but an evening away from the constant posturing of the other mages would have been nice.

"We're closed to clients today because of the gala, if you want to stay after the meeting. We might have some time for training before the guests arrive."

"Training?" I arched an eyebrow.

"Use your own definition." His teeth grazed my neck, nipping at my earlobe. "Enough incentive to sit in on a meeting with Lady Granville?"

"You aren't distracting me."

"Really."

My shoulders slumped. "Yeah, all right. On the condition that you and I get some time alone before the gala and I get Drake back for burying me in snow the other day."

The Mage Lord grinned at me. "That can be arranged."

4

Five minutes into the meeting and I was reminded of why I preferred using my sword to solve disagreements instead. I'd never been in the same room as so many obnoxious dickheads, and I'd worked for the bloody mercenary guild for ten years.

"If a more experienced necromancer had accompanied you, this would never have happened," said Lady Granville. Today she was clad in an expensive suit the colour of mould and with an expression to match. "They should have been the ones who took on this case, not you and the witch."

"The witch happens to be the Laurel Coven's Second." I'd managed to hold my tongue throughout Lady Granville's lecture on inappropriate conduct, but she knew perfectly well who Isabel was. Her name was on our joint contract, for god's sake.

I pointedly ignored the disapproving stares from the other council members. Even Vance was in uptight Mage Lord mode, though admittedly Lady Granville had read him the riot act, too, for letting us take on a case last night without full council approval. Kind of unfair, not to mention ridiculous. Vance was technically the one in charge, but Lady Granville's ambitions to take Vance's position as head of the council were widely known. Small wonder she didn't like me.

Nobody discussed the events of how Vance had taken leadership openly—Vance himself had summed it up in the cryptic words *I killed the last guy*—but by reading between the lines, I'd inferred that Lord Carlisle had originally been next in line to take the Mage Lord title but had ceded the position to Vance due to being close to retirement himself. The plain, sixty-something man had struck me as another out-of-touch aristocrat who'd got his position on connections alone, but he'd once been a formidable air mage, and I'd somewhat warmed towards him when I realised he was the one who'd given Vance a shot at the head title.

Since Vance had been the youngest on the council at the time and the newest member, Lady Granville felt like she'd been cheated, and Lady Penrose shared that opinion. The latter was around the same age, mid-forties, and wore a pair of thick-framed glasses perched on the bridge of her nose that I could have sworn she intentionally angled so that they amplified her glare whenever she looked at me. Lady Penrose had middling talents as a kinetic and Lady Granville was an earth mage, but both of them preferred to fight with words over actions. Mostly with me.

"Also, I agree that the more senior necromancers should have been present," I said in an attempt to placate them. "They were occupied with other clients, not unlike the mages."

The mages themselves were out of most people's budgets, and Lady Granville had all but laughed when I'd suggested lowering their fees. Poverty wasn't as glaringly bad as it had been in the first few years after the invasion, but there were still far too many people who couldn't afford to hire a mage even in an emergency. While I was willing to allow that a few hundred mages couldn't help everyone in a city of over a million, too many were unwilling to even try. The only Mage Lord aside from Vance I got along with was Drake, who at least seemed to find meetings as dull as I did.

"Sounds like the necromancers have an undead problem." Drake lounged in his seat. In a room full of stiff-backed people in suits, he and I stuck out like sore thumbs. "Someone had to take on the case."

"Exactly," I said. "That spirit was a nasty piece of work. Besides, Mrs Bennet called my agency directly."

I wasn't entirely sure how I'd ended up defending the necromancers, but if Lady Granville started bitching at Lord Evander next, I was the one who'd end up back at the top of his shit list, and he'd never offer his signature to protect me from paying fees from the next client whose house got trashed by ghosts.

"Then you should have sent her to us."

"There was a ghost destroying her property. If she'd left the house, she wouldn't have had anything to come back to." Now I was defending the shrieking old woman? Whatever next?

"And we don't stand for insubordination," Lady Granville added.

My hands clenched at my sides. "I followed the mages' guidelines to the letter. I think we need to discuss the pertinent issue at hand, which is that there was a half-faerie ghost with unknown abilities inside someone's home. As leaders of the supernatural community, the Mage Lords are responsible for assessing these situations for the sake of keeping the peace."

I was fairly proud of that one, but Lady Granville remained unmoved. "Assessing the situation is not the same as taking unapproved visits to half-blood territory."

"That was my idea," Vance cut in. "Moreover, we discovered that the ghost Ivy encountered last night was murdered in the half-faeries' jail yesterday. That certainly warrants further investigation, as there may be others in the same position."

A murmur ran down the table.

"You questioned the other half-bloods, I'm sure?" said Lady Granville.

"We spoke to the Chief." I looked at Vance. "And the… guard. At the prison." No need to mention the 'half-banshee' part.

"And?" she pressed.

"All the prisoners involved in the attempted coup were dead," I replied.

She tutted. "Convenient. I've long believed that allowing the beasts to police their own means inevitable violence. I'm glad no humans were hurt."

Yeah, right. "They aren't all beasts."

And now she'd successfully made me take the side of the half-faeries. At this rate, I'd be arguing for all the local spirits to have the right to meander around on this side of the veil without being banished, but her complete inability to see anyone outside of her tiny bubble as worthy of consideration made me seriously wonder how half the planet had been killed off in the invasion and she'd somehow walked away unscathed. If you asked me, she was living proof that the universe didn't play fair in the slightest.

"They certainly aren't human."

Oh, boy. This was one of our most frequent arguments. Sure, I strongly disliked the Chief, and most of the half-bloods I'd met had been hostile at best, but I didn't think they deserved to be left out of laws defining what counted as human. Shifters weren't, and they transformed into animals every month at the full moon. Though with Lady Granville's track record, she'd change that too, given the chance.

"Maybe not," I allowed, "but the ghosts were equally dangerous to the other half-faeries, and I'd like to know why one showed up in a regular human's house. Someone without magic at all."

"I believe that is irrelevant." And just like that, Lady Granville slammed a lid on that subject. "The other issue I wished to discuss is the matter of certain recent, ah, *incidents* that have caught the attention of other mages across the country. I'm sure some of you have questions, too."

She addressed the visiting mages from outside, who sat in a cluster at the opposite end of the table.

Vance spoke up first. "I believe I've already answered those questions to their satisfaction. Correct?"

The other mages nodded, and I bit back a laugh at Lady Granville's deflated expression. Honestly, Vance had probably exchanged more words with the other regional mages in the past few months than Lady Granville had in a lifetime.

"No." Lady Granville attempted to regain control. "We've had a number of other queries, particularly about the, ah, *creature* that recently appeared, near the Ley Line."

My heart sank. The giant dragon, supposedly the shifters' god, had escaped imprisonment thanks to the Lady of the Tree and had very nearly obliterated everyone in this room. And probably the rest of the country, too. I didn't know, because I'd managed to lure the creature into the Grey Vale and put it under a powerful sleeping spell. Courtesy of my recently acquired talismans, I could speak Invocations, immensely powerful words known only to the Sidhe. In the Grey Vale, those words had the ability to both create and destroy. The dragon might be contained, but the talismans were a different story, and I'd bet them both that I knew exactly what she intended to say next.

Sure enough… "And there's the matter of a certain object that currently resides in our storeroom. Keeping an unknown faerie talisman among valuable mage artefacts is against all our policies."

"You want me to move the life-drinker?" Okay, that was a new one. I'd thought she and the rest of the council had long exhausted all their questions on the talismans months ago, but it figured that she'd revive the subject in the hopes of winning our visitors over to her side. "There's nowhere with better security than the mages' stores."

"Undead were found on the property this morning," said Lady Granville.

Vance looked at her sharply. "Nobody informed me of this."

"You were paying a visit to half-blood territory at the time." Lady Granville surveyed the council. "We found the undead inside the building."

A chill took hold of me like grasping fingers. "I thought the storeroom was thoroughly warded."

"It is," said Lady Granville. "The undead were destroyed before they were able to reach any of the rooms. However, that they were present at all is a concerning sign."

"Yeah," I muttered. "There's nowhere else we can put the talisman without risking it being found by more powerful forces than undead. And we don't want it in the manor."

"The manor's security was breached by the faeries, too."

My heart plunged. "What—recently?"

"No, of course not," Vance said. "I believe she is referring to the incident with the thorns, after which we thoroughly redid our wards. I've explained at length."

"So did I, but I can do it again." Damn her for making me panic. Fucking thorns. "We redoubled the wards and threw in some of the Laurel Coven's most effective spells for warding off trespassers."

"Effective in what way?"

She really wanted me to spell it out? "Isabel makes trip-wire spells that cause trespassers to develop painful sores in… sensitive areas."

Drake laughed loudly. Nobody else did.

"C'mon, it's genius," he said to Lady Granville. "Have you seen a single trespasser since then?"

"That's enough," she said sharply. "Mere *pranks* will not dissuade those who wish to see us destroyed."

"No, but it'll give them a bad day." Drake continued to laugh. "Not that undead can feel any pain. Want me to burn them?"

"Yes, I would like to look at these dead myself," Vance cut in. "Are the remains still outside the storeroom?"

"No," she said. "The rain washed away all traces."

Really. More like she'd removed them herself, without telling Vance. "Then there's no reason to touch the talisman."

"Nevertheless, I believe the mage councils across the country should have been consulted before it was put into one of our depositories."

Vance met her steely gaze with calmness. "The rest of the council members would have voted in favour. Like Ivy said, there's no safer place than the storeroom."

"Exactly," I said to Lady Granville. "We sealed the talisman somewhere nobody else can pick it up by mistake. What's the problem?"

"I'm told you made considerable use of its power yourself."

Great. To no surprise, all eyes landed on me. Drake started to speak then stopped when I shot him a warning look. Of all the people who knew of my faerie magic, Drake was the person most likely to run his mouth off. That tendency was highly amusing on occasion—like when he'd told me half the mage council members' closely guarded secrets while inebriated on New Year's Eve—but not when I was on the receiving end.

"I made use of the talisman's power to bind that creature." I'd already told her a dozen times, but with half the room comprised of newcomers who hadn't heard yet, I'd had to repeat myself a lot recently. "If you're suggesting I'm working against the council, you're mistaken. I don't want power. That's why I gave up the talisman."

"Ivy has already given her story," said Vance. "If you have issues to raise regarding the talisman, you will require permission from both of us in order to act."

"Once you surrender an artefact to the mages' storeroom, it becomes our property by default," said Lady Granville.

I waved farewell to diplomacy. "It's a powerful faerie sword nobody but me can handle. I wouldn't try moving it without asking me."

A chill swept through the room. Vance rose to his feet, glaring at Lady Granville. "She's right, and we won't speak of this again. If anyone else attacks the storeroom, tell me before making decisions."

Most of the other mages shrank away from him. Irritation prickled my spine. I hadn't been allowed to bring my sword to the meeting, and besides, I'd never get away with the same strategy. Being head mage had its perks, but it was stark as day that Lady Granville wanted to sit where Vance did, and that she was ready to pull out all the stops to do so.

"This meeting is over," said Vance. "You may leave."

Gladly. I walked with him out of the room, Lady Granville's stare boring holes into my back.

"That went well," I muttered when we were out of earshot of the room. "If her priority is our security, I'm a leprechaun. She wants that talisman under her own beady eyes."

"She won't make the decision without consulting me,"

said Vance, as we climbed the thickly carpeted stairs down to the lowest floor.

"I want to be consulted, too." I walked alongside him past the open door to the armoury, noticing with amusement that Drake had drawn smiley faces on all the training dummies again. "I was dead serious. If one of the other mages touches that sword, it might blow their hands off. Not to mention moving it around would attract the attention of every faerie on both sides of the grave."

"I won't let it happen," said Vance. "She's all bluster."

"She's trying to dig up more dirt on me than that giant pit on shifter territory." The real kick in the face was that I'd made a genuine effort to toe the line. I'd started to revise my attitude towards the mages after years of resentment, but in situations like this, old habits dug their heels in. "This feels… personal. As if she knows she doesn't have the full picture."

"Of what?"

We rounded the corner into the main ground-floor corridor that led to the conservatory. "You know. My magic. The huge target stuck on my head."

The ghost who'd promised to kill me and return to life.

"That's your business." Vance's tone softened, and then he scowled when Drake sidled over to us.

"What're you two whispering about?" He tilted his head on one side. "Is it to do with how you're the only person who can handle that sword?"

"Please don't tell whichever random woman you hook up with tonight."

"That's mean." Drake put on a wounded look.

"Yeah, it was a little," I relented. "But it's true. I can't believe you told what's-her-name that I was a faerie on Christmas Eve."

"I did?" His forehead scrunched up. "Oh. I said you were *like* a faerie… I get your point."

"If I wanted the whole planet to know, I'd interview myself on the mages' radio station." The mages actually did have their own station that they used to inform the public about ongoing emergencies, and I fully intended to make use of it the next time a rogue Sidhe went on the rampage in the city.

"That'd be weird, interviewing yourself. Oh, all right, I get it." Drake scooted away from the dangerous look on Vance's face. "I won't tell anyone. I can keep a secret, believe it or not."

Vance made a sceptical noise but didn't pursue the issue.

"Anyway, thanks for telling Lady Granville that we have tripwires outside that make intruders come out in boils." Drake snickered. "Please keep coming to meetings."

"Ha ha," I said. "Is nobody else concerned that she might be planning…?"

"Planning what?" Drake conjured a flame to his palms and made it dance in midair. "She's all talk. Unlike us. She knows we can bury her alive."

"Speaking of burials." I gestured to the snow-covered back garden on the other side of the conservatory's glass windows. Despite the rest of the country being under a constant raincloud, the mages' garden had been transformed due to some frost mages who'd got bored on Christmas Eve. "You owe me a rematch."

Vance frowned. "We don't have time."

"Guests won't start arriving until this evening," said Drake. "Tell you what, we'll make it a contest. Loser has to clean up after the party tonight."

———

As it turned out, having the magic of a Winter Sidhe Lord had little advantage in a snowball fight. I limped back into the manor from the garden later, soaked in snow that instantly evaporated when I crossed the threshold of the conservatory. Drake's ability as a fire mage repelled snow, and he'd even beat out Vance when our three-person combat round turned into a contest as to who could bury someone in the most snow.

Spoiler: not me.

I tugged on my hair, which now stood on end like I'd walked over a tripwire spell. "How am I supposed to greet the guests like this?"

"It's a new style," said Drake. "You don't need to do anything but stand on the side and look pretty."

I gave him the finger. "I'm not the Mage Lord's *pet*."

"Of course you aren't," said Vance.

Noticing me shivering, he conjured a mug of hot chocolate and handed it to me. Often, there were some serious perks to dating the Mage Lord. I carried the mug to the table and chairs in the conservatory's corner, where Vance conjured up two plates piled with toasted sandwiches.

"There. This is now a lunch date."

"No, it isn't," said Drake. "The first guests will be here soon, and it's my duty to stop you two from getting distracted."

Vance shot him an irritated look. "Don't you have somewhere to be?"

"Yes. Annoying the crap out of you two." Drake stole one of the sandwiches from my plate. I glared at him, and he smiled, perching on one of the other chairs. "What? If it wasn't me, it'd be someone else."

I shrugged and grabbed a sandwich. He had a point there. Considering Vance could teleport at will, it was infuriating how often people managed to interrupt us when things were getting hot and heavy to drag him off to Mage Lord responsibilities while acting like I was a piece of furniture.

Still. The perks outweighed the downsides, and Vance didn't care if half the Grey Vale wanted my blood or that most of the council hated my guts. He wanted *me*, complications included, and that was reason enough to tolerate the general annoyance of not getting a moment's peace.

Sure enough, as I was stirring the dregs of my hot chocolate, Wanda ran into the conservatory. "My grandmother's here."

"She is?" I'd never seen Vance snap into Mage Lord mode so quickly. When he reached the doorway, he paused and looked back at me. "It's probably best that you stay here, unless she wants to talk to you."

"She asked for you," Wanda told Vance. "I didn't know she was coming."

"Lady Harper does have a habit of showing up unannounced." Vance followed her out of the room, leaving me staring after the pair of them.

Drake stood, too. "I'm going to… er, hide. Lady Harper doesn't like me."

"Hey!" I called after him, but he was already running off as though pursued by a poltergeist. "What's the problem?"

"Lady Harper strongly disapproves of the Sidhe," growled a voice, making me jump a foot in the air. "She will also not approve of you keeping one of their artefacts in the house."

"Dammit, don't scare me like that, Quentin." The small faerie had slipped past me to clear the plates from the table. He came up to my knees, built like a twig with knobbly tanned skin and large round eyes. I didn't exactly get along with the taciturn brownie servant of the Colton family, but he'd been forced—reluctantly—to accept my presence here. "And don't you start. I'm not leaving my talisman at home."

What's his *problem?* Everyone sure was twitchy today. It was true that the talismans carried inherent risks, but I was pretty sure the brownie was just trying to freak me out. He made no secret of his disapproval of my own jumpiness around faeries, as though it was my own fault that after spending three years as the Sidhe Lord Avalin's prisoner, I had an instinctive flinch response to the fae invading my personal space. Living in the same house as one had somewhat inured me to their presence—Erwin the piskie had been in my flat for years—but Vance's family servant made me edgy even when he wasn't sneaking up on me. Brownies were supposed to be inconspicuous household helpers, but Quentin was a little too shrewd and intelligent for my liking, and always seemed to be lurking around corners when Vance and I were discussing sensitive issues. Like my magic. And the many enemies I had lurking in the Grey Vale.

The brownie disappeared without a word when Vance came back into the conservatory. All traces of calm had vanished from his expression.

"Change of plans," he said. "Lady Harper insists on meeting you."

"Lady Harper? I thought I'd met all the local Mage Lords."

"She's retired," explained Vance. "She stepped in after the invasion because four of the five Mage Lords were dead and the city badly needed leadership. Two years later, she retired to the countryside. She's eighty-five and hates politics, so she has good reason."

"Fair enough," I said. "What's special about her?"

"She trained me."

"Whoa, really? She taught you to be a scary badass?"

"She also taught me how to play the piano."

This, I hadn't heard. "You're not having me on, are you?"

"Of course not. She's Wanda's grandmother."

"Wait, is she the scary lady?" I'd heard mention of the mythical retired master mage a few times, but I hadn't made the connection with our newest visitor.

"Yes, the scary lady. She wants to talk to you alone."

"Okay." We crossed the conservatory to the main corridor and reached Vance's office. He stepped to one side, wearing an expression more suited to someone walking into a fight to the death than a harmless chat with a retired Mage Lord.

Damn. He was rattled. Scary lady couldn't be that scary, right?

I pushed open the door and entered Vance's office. I didn't quite know what I'd expected to find on the other side, but the old woman sitting in the seat behind the cherrywood desk—Vance's chair, in fact—didn't strike me as too impressive at first glance. Her grey hair was cut to chin length, her glassy blue eyes deep-set above her wrinkled cheeks. She wore a long travelling cloak and held a paperback open in one gnarled hand.

I positioned myself in front of the desk, trying to catch her eye over the open book she held. Did she not realise I'd walked in?

I cleared my throat. "Hi. I'm Ivy."

She put down the book and locked me with a stare that made me feel like she'd stripped several layers of skin from me. My spine stiffened automatically, and my instinctive reaction was to check my weapon. Which, of course, I didn't have.

"You're not a talker." Her voice was rough but strong. "Good. It'll make this easier. I want you to stay away from Vance Colton."

"What?"

"You heard me, didn't you?"

I had. I just hadn't expected anything that... direct. "What's your problem with me?"

"Nothing in particular. I'm old and you're annoying."

I gaped at her, not entirely sure if she was being serious. "Uh... thanks? I'm not going anywhere. I work for the mages."

"You're not one."

"Vance employed me. Take it up with him."

"He's short-sighted when it comes to you." She leaned forward in her seat. "I can't see why. You're nothing special. Plain girl, no magic."

"I have magic." I'd have offered to give a demonstration, but she didn't have the Sight, and I had the suspicion that this was not a woman who feared the Sidhe's magic. "Maybe not the sort you're used to, but I do."

"If that's the case"—her wrinkled hands rose up, palms out—"defend yourself."

The air tightened, leaving me gasping to draw in a breath through lungs that no longer seemed to be working. Blue light filtered over my vision as my magic reacted, fuelled by my panic, yet my shield had no effect.

Holy shit, I was in trouble.

My body lifted, my feet leaving the floor as though drawn upward by an invisible force. I hovered above the plush carpet, no more in control of myself than a puppet.

Stop it, I tried to say, but my voice had fled along with all the air in the room. My vision swam. Magic gathered around me in thick, angry clouds, forming a shield, but the choking sensation remained. She was too strong, and whatever she was doing to stifle my breath would surely make me pass out at some point. It was a wonder I hadn't already, unless my magic had stepped in to heal some of the damage. I couldn't tell, but my rational mind told me that she wasn't trying to kill me, and that Vance would never have let me talk to her alone if that was her intention. This was a test… and I was losing.

"Defend yourself," she repeated. "You're not worthy to stand alongside the mage council."

Screw you. Fine. I'd give her everything I had.

I ignored the burning sensation in my lungs and concentrated on letting my emotions feed the magic in my hands. I hadn't used it to its full extent since my duel to the death with the Lady of the Tree. It wasn't as strong away from the Ley Line and without my talisman, but she was no Sidhe Lord. I wouldn't lose.

I splayed my hands, turning the shield into a forward assault. Magic hummed through me, strong even without my sword nearby, and as blue energy shot from my palms, air rushed back into my lungs.

An instant later, the attack dissolved into smoke, and a vice gripped my chest again. *What the hell?* She'd blocked me, but for a second, my attack had worked.

I launched into another. And another. Too angry to aim, I threw a wave of magic at her, but she blocked every single time.

Jesus. What the hell kind of power does she have? She'd trained Vance, but she wasn't a displacer, nor one of the more standard elemental mages. She definitely had some kind of control element, though, given how she'd locked my body down. The casual manner in which she deflected my attacks suggested some kind of shielding, too, but not one visible to me.

Think, Ivy. If her magic itself was both shield and sword, she could only use it for one purpose at a time. Vance had implied most mages had that limitation. When my body was locked down, her defences were wide open. Of course, that didn't mean a thing when I was more focused on not passing out than on anything else, but plainly my own shield was worthless. I'd have to go on the permanent offensive.

The other aspect I'd forgotten... she *couldn't* see my magic. Except when I used an obvious frontal assault.

I willed the blue clouds surging in the air to rise upward, taking aim not at her, but at the bookshelf directly behind her.

As my attack struck, the shelf began to topple. My feet hit the ground as magic rushed through me, tingling like live wires underneath my skin. My lungs expanded, taking in air. Through blurred vision, I watched the bookshelf freeze mid-fall. She hadn't so much as turned her head, nor did she move as the shelf returned to its previous position. She wielded her magic like a separate entity altogether.

"Pathetic."

Sweat ran down my forehead and back, like I'd run for miles. I swallowed a couple of times. My throat felt like sandpaper. I readied myself to shield again, but she sat back down in the desk chair. Was that the end of our bout?

"What the hell did you do to me?" I asked hoarsely.

"I intended to see what you were made of." She gave me that disdainful look again. "I saw."

I blinked to clear my blurred vision, fighting the urge to give her the finger. "If you ever did that to Vance, I'm surprised he didn't have you thrown out."

She'd trained him. That implied... okay, I wouldn't even go there.

"Lady Granville says you're insubordinate."

"She's right." I clenched my fingers and sucked in air, willing my legs to stop trembling. "Are you this nice to every new mage you meet?"

"You aren't a mage," said Lady Harper. "The mage council was set up to protect the supernatural community at large. Since you first set foot in here, you've nearly started two wars with the faeries, caused untold damage when you decided to take on an ancient entity on the Ley Line, and stolen directly from the Sidhe Lords themselves. Bringing you into meetings is both dangerous and irresponsible."

"Did you tell Vance that?" *He told her about the god?* It seemed impossible *not* to tell this woman anything she wanted to know, but I was starting to see why the mages had brought her back in after the invasion. The woman would scare the shit out of anyone, even the Sidhe. "Because he's already given his approval, and Lady Granville has no business challenging her superior."

"You don't strike me as the type who needs a bodyguard," she said. "Nor are you a simple airhead or a foolish little girl looking for the Mage Lord's approval."

"Wow." I waited for the backhanded edge of that compliment to hit. Sure enough—

"However, I fail to see why he'd pick you as a match. Even his own council is out looking for a weak link to exploit, a way to undercut him. You're the weak link, Ivy. You have no respect for our rules."

I folded my arms. "I'm with Vance because I want to be with him, not the council. They can stuff it."

"Do you want me to inform Lady Granville of that?"

"Go right ahead." Nobody got to call me a weak link. "Sounds to me like you're trying to undermine Vance yourself, if you're having clandestine meetings with the woman who wants to steal his title."

"You have no understanding of how we operate around here." Her mocking tone crawled under my skin. "He won't choose you, Ivy. It's only fair that you accept that as soon as possible, for both of your sakes. If you want him to keep his position, you'll leave him alone."

"Oh, I understand how you operate." She wouldn't get me that easily. "I've been dragged into enough of your petty debates over the past few months to know that."

"Then you'll understand that in the end, the council comes first. He's nearly given his life for the mages, too many times to count. Has he ever done the same for you?"

"Yes." I spoke clearly. "And I've done the same. The point is that both of us understand that there are forces outside of the mages that would be happy to see all of us dead, and that if you really want to keep the peace, looking the other way is no solution."

"Isn't it?" Now she looked amused, but the glint in her eyes told me she could do worse than choke the air from me if I pushed any further, and that she'd dearly enjoy the experience if I took the bait.

Instead, I gave her my best stone-cold mercenary glare before I left. "Whatever game you're playing, you haven't won. I won't be staying away from Vance."

5

Once outside, I sagged against the wall, taking quick breaths to loosen the tight feeling in my chest. My whole body felt drained, and I hardly believed I'd been overpowered so easily. Granted, she *had* once been a Mage Lord, and as was abundantly clear, I hadn't been practising my magic nearly enough in the past few weeks. I might have said that it was hardly worth wasting a Sidhe Lord's magic on trivialities, but in truth, I'd underestimated her. I'd never expected to have to wield the extent of my abilities against a human.

The blow to my pride hurt more than the physical damage. As did the emotional bludgeoning. Over the last few months, I'd finally made strides in healing the damage faeries had done to me a decade ago, but just as the wounds were knitting together, Lady Harper's attack had torn the stitches wide open.

"Ivy?" Vance approached me, concern in his expression. "Are you all right?"

I pushed away from the wall and gave him a smile that

was more of a grimace. "I'm good. I want to be like her when I'm older."

I spoke because I knew she was listening from the other side of the door, but she was also an undisputable badass. Who wouldn't want that power?

"She does leave quite the impression."

"Yeah. Tell me about it." I fell into step with him as we walked away from the office. "She wanted me to stay away from you. I couldn't figure out why."

I glanced at him. His mouth pulled into a frown I hadn't seen for a while. "She may have thought you were after my inheritance. Or planning to murder me. Possibly both."

We reached the wide-open doors to the great hall. Inside, Quentin and the apprentice mages were setting up tables around the hall's edges for the gala, but I was more concerned by Vance's alarming casualness in the face of a potential attempt on his life.

"Seriously?" I raised a brow. "What the hell did you tell her about me?"

"I didn't, until today," said Vance. "She hasn't come here for months."

"You're actually scared of her, aren't you?" I squinted at him. "Wait. If you didn't tell her anything before today, how'd she come out with an extensive list of everything I've done to screw up since I walked into your life?"

"She's a breaker, Ivy," said Vance. "She can cut into your mind and extract any memory she wants to."

My mouth fell open. "What? That's a thing?"

"A rare ability," he said. "Hers is one of the strongest there is, which is why she was chosen to train me."

My skin crawled. "She got all that from my *head*?"

Even the faeries hadn't crossed that boundary. I might have been their prisoner, but my mind had always been my own.

"Not direct mind-reading," Vance clarified. "It's not like she can walk into a room and instantly read the thoughts of everyone present. She needs to have a hold over you first, and then she can send your mind subtle directions. Often without you noticing."

"Like telling my body not to move?"

"She did that?"

"Yeah." I didn't much feel like discussing my humiliation. "She pinned me like a butterfly and... fuck."

While I'd been flailing and struggling to breathe, she'd ripped out my thoughts, a violation I'd never imagined I'd experience in my life. How had Vance grown up in the same house with her and not strangled her in her sleep?

His arm came around my back. "She must have thought you a serious threat. I shouldn't have sent you in there alone."

I stepped away from him, my insides pitching downward. "No... I'm glad you did."

A lie. The first I'd told in a while, but my mind was a tempest, and I frankly didn't know whether to give Vance a warning that he had a wild chimera sitting in his office or get the hell out of there before she called me back for Round Two.

"It's a rare ability," he said. "And not one many other mages have."

"Thank fuck for that." I shuddered. "It's a good job she's retired, if she's capable of making anyone who annoys her jump off a cliff."

At least Lady Granville, for all her bluster, had an easy-to-understand ability, though any mage could be deadly when pushed.

Vance's frown remained in place. "In theory, but nobody gets onto the mage council by abusing their power. The first lesson all new mages learn is when it's appropriate to use their ability and when to restrain themselves."

"Guess I'm used to mercenaries," I said. "Give any one of them a mage's ability and they'd burn the city down."

"Precisely why we bring any new mage in for training as soon as possible," said Vance. "The majority of us are born into it, so we learn early on the limits of our powers and the inherent responsibilities they carry."

"I did wonder who trained you. So she thinks I want... this?" I waved my hands vaguely at the hall. The polished floor reflected warm light from the chandelier dominating the high ceiling, and silver tinsel encircled a towering Christmas tree in the corner. "She actually thinks I want to steal your inheritance?"

I'd have laughed at the absurdity of the suggestion if I hadn't still been so shaken up. I'd never wanted to be part of the mages' society, and I'd be equally as happy with Vance if we lived in a run-down apartment in the mercenary district.

"I don't know what she's thinking," said Vance. "But I'm a Mage Lord. My first instinct always has to be to assume somebody wants a favour from me or to stab me in the back. You're the first woman I've dated since I became head mage."

"What, really?"

"Most Mage Lords have let someone slip through their defences. I didn't intend to be one of them."

Probably not, now I thought about it. Drake had told me he and Vance had spent their first few weeks as leaders of the mage council avoiding assassination attempts. Apparently, the attempts had stopped after Vance did something 'fucking scary'. Drake refused to tell me what, exactly, he'd done, but I hazarded a guess that it accounted for the rumours I'd heard of the Mage Lord keeping a row of troll heads in his office. According to Vance, Drake himself had started that one.

"What made you change your mind?" I asked, genuinely curious.

"You insulted me on more than one occasion, threatened my guards, dripped blood all over the floor and brazenly refused to cooperate. There was little chance you were the slightest bit interested in my position or reputation."

"You aren't wrong there."

"See what I mean?" He smiled. "It's refreshing not to have to wonder if you'll stab me in the back."

"Is that why you picked me, then? I'm not a mage, so there's no chance of me butting into your political games?"

"You're also quite attractive."

I poked him in the chest. "Seriously. I'm starting to feel like I should have stayed in half-blood district and sung a duet with the banshee instead."

"I don't know if it's any consolation, but Lady Harper scared off a dozen of my potential matches before they even met her."

"No, that doesn't make me feel better." A dozen? I could count my own past serious relationships on one hand. "I don't need to know people are queuing up at the door for a chance to get into the Mage Lord's—"

"I said potential matches, not serious considerations."

"Serious considerations." I snorted, despite myself. "What did you do, write a list of the pros and cons of every woman who showed an interest?"

"No, but I can make a list of your positive attributes if it'll put you at ease."

"Not particularly."

"Or…" He pulled me against him, and his mouth closed over mine, which did a pretty effective job of masking the aftereffects of Lady Harper's attack. "Or does that work instead?"

"Yeah, that works," I said breathlessly, this time in a good way. "Please tell me she isn't coming to the party. Because if she is, I might suddenly have an urgent appointment elsewhere. Like, on the other side of town. Don't take it personally."

"Sorry." His expression turned conflicted. "You aren't the only person to have that reaction to meeting her. She's the most revered—and feared—mage around, even though she's retired. But she won't be at the gala. She hates parties."

"Guess we have that in common." When the doorbell rang, I smothered a sigh. "Man, that's fucked."

"Get ready." He ran a hand over my shoulder blades. "I want to see you in that new dress."

"Which one?"

"Take your pick." His fingers brushed the nape of my neck. "And I'll thoroughly make it up to you later."

"I'll hold you to that." I leaned into him, and the doorbell rang again. I groaned. "Right, right, I'll go and get ready."

While I headed upstairs, Vance went to start showing the guests in. As for me, I faced a new challenge: making myself presentable. I glared at my reflection in Vance's ceiling-high three-way mirror, adjusting my dress straps to cover the red imprint of the mage mark on my shoulder, a connection to Vance if we were ever separated like we'd been in Faerie. The mirrors reflected Vance's bedroom back at me, from the elaborately decorated four-poster bed to the velvet curtains covering the glass doors to the balcony.

I'd never particularly cared how I looked—my experience with the faeries had taught me being inconspicuous was best —but finding an outfit that complemented my scars was a hair-tearing exercise. I wore a dress about once a month, when I didn't expect to need to run or fight. As for heels, forget it. With my hair properly combed and free of the usual gunk, I cleaned up okay, but showing my face in front of the mages, exposed without any weapons, was scarier than going up against a newly awoken shifter god.

The curtains fluttered in the breeze and Vance appeared

behind me. His reflection in profile looked as handsome as ever: clean-shaven jawline, hair combed to the side, tailored suit fitted to show off his athletic build. My heart skipped a little.

"Thought you were showing the guests in," I said.

"I was." His grey eyes gleamed. "You look stunning." He released my hair from the pins holding it up. "I like your hair down. I don't see you wear it like this often."

"Because it'd get in the way in a fight. Same reason I don't wear these." I flicked the bright gold earrings dangling from each lobe.

He ran a finger up my ear, making warmth pool inside me. "Relax. I think you're stunning in leather and denim, too."

"And covered in blood?"

"Of course. You're a difficult woman to compliment."

"I just have a highly reactive bullshit detector."

His hands moved to my waist, leaving a trail of fire through the thin fabric of my dress. "I think I've proved my opinion of you. As to the others, don't worry about what they think. They're slow to accept change."

Easy for him to say. He'd been born into this world. I'd done my best to assimilate, and succeeded somewhat, but Lady Granville, and most of the council, did their best to make me feel like an outsider. Having had an improvement in fortunes lately didn't mean I'd magically jumped to their class level. Polite social niceties went over my head. Petty arguments had me wanting to pull out my sword. And Lady Harper was the latest in a string of people who'd made it clear that some would never accept me as one of their own.

"Yeah, okay." I hitched on a smile. "Let's go see what's going on downstairs."

At least a hundred mages had gathered in the great hall, which had been fully transformed into party mode. Tinsel encircled the posts supporting the high ceiling, and glittering lights shone all over the huge Christmas tree, changing colours every minute from blue to green to red. Fake snowflakes scattered amongst the crowd like confetti. Probably Wanda's doing. I reached out a hand and caught one, and the snowflake fizzled out on contact with my fingertip.

Being under so many eyes made my spine prickle. Unconcerned, Vance strode casually towards Drake and a group of other mages. I followed, declining to pick up one of the glasses of champagne laid out on the nearby table. I wobbled on my heels too much already to trust myself with alcohol. *Calm down,* I told myself, rearranging my shoulder bag so I wouldn't feel the weight of the dagger hidden inside it, and wishing I'd worn flat shoes rather than strappy sandals.

Even here, I was a target.

The Mage Lords were in charge of maintaining order amongst the supernatural communities, but they knew how to throw a damn good party, too. At first, I'd been consumed with dread at every event, convinced I'd get thrown out as an interloper. By now, I'd realised half the guests were on my level of the social ladder, having charmed or talked their way in, or been invited in exchange for some favour or other. A few witches and even the odd half-faerie wandered amongst the crowd, though I didn't see any necromancers or shifters. Everyone was overwhelmingly polite, but I tallied up no fewer than twelve thinly veiled insults towards me in the first ten minutes. Nobody dared insult Vance. He didn't even need to use his mage abilities to scare people.

While Vance went to show more guests in, I joined Wanda and some other mages at a table near the back, including Rod and Bailey, who I'd interacted with a fair bit over the past few months. If I didn't need another reason to despise Lady Granville, her attitude towards their relation-ship was enough all on its own.

"You met Lady Harper?" asked Bailey.

"Yeah." So much for avoiding the subject. "Scary woman."

"She's terrifying, isn't she?" asked Wanda. "I don't tell people we're related usually unless they ask." Wanda was pretty even-tempered for a mage, which made her connection with Lady Harper even more bizarre.

Bailey grimaced. "I don't blame you. We were stuck in the same room for fifteen minutes once, and believe me, I counted every second. I tried to start a conversation with her about books and she acted like I'd dropped an earwig on her head."

"She was reading a book when I walked into the office," I admitted. "It felt like a statement. Like I wasn't important enough to pay attention to."

"No, she does that to everyone." Rod gave a shudder. "Creepy. What did she do, interrogate you?"

"Yeah." I didn't much feel like going into detail on our encounter, at least not tonight. "I mean, if even Drake's scared of her, she's got to be terrifying. Where is he?"

"You need to ask?" said Wanda. "He's been flirting with a woman from out of town for the past hour."

"I did wonder where he went after he ran off earlier." I picked up a strawberry from the bowl on the table. Only the Mage Lords could get them out of season. The sweet taste reminded me of another world, the one before the invasion. "Doesn't he worry that any of the women he flirts with will stab him in the back?"

"Oh, it's happened." Wanda grimaced. "Almost literally, in one case. I think my grandmother regrets ever putting him forward as a council member."

"So why do it in the first place?"

Wanda shrugged. "Drake is Vance's best friend. The

second-in-command needs to be someone the head mage trusts. There was a lot of turbulence before Vance stepped in a year ago."

Huh. Interesting. Not for the first time, Vance's words when I'd asked how he'd become head mage came back to me —*I killed the last guy.* He'd never told me who, exactly, or why.

"Turbulence?" I asked casually. "Does it have to do with how Vance became head mage?"

"I... can't really talk about it." Wanda stood quickly. "Speaking of my grandmother, I need to check the sound-proofing spells on her room. She'll scream the place down if the party wakes her up."

"Hey, you don't have to go," I said. "Never mind. Forget I asked."

I started to climb out of my seat and stopped when a familiar figure glided past. Ralph, Vance's quarter-faerie guard. He seemed to be doing his best to avoid attention, slipping through the crowd and lingering behind different groups of people. Eavesdropping? Ralph had taken up guard duty outside the manor less often since he'd fallen under the influence of the drug Calder had used on the half-faeries, but he never missed the opportunity to take jabs at me whenever we crossed paths.

"Wise move," Bailey said, watching Wanda's retreat. "We don't need Lady Harper coming in here and turning us all into statues for partying too loudly."

"No." My own attention was on Ralph, who continued his circuit of the room. "I'll be right back."

I spotted Vance making his way through the crowd and walked over to him. He slid an arm around my waist and steered me onto the dance floor. I still didn't like dancing, but I didn't object to Vance pulling me into his orbit, close enough to feel his warmth against my skin and inhale his cool, masculine scent.

"Enjoying the party?"

"Sure," I lied.

"What is it?"

I scanned the crowd for the other half-faeries, recognisable by their oddly unreal beauty and the shimmer of magic around them. "Ralph's skulking around. Thought it was weird."

"Oh, I asked him to," said Vance. "He's listening in on the other guests in case anyone's planning any subterfuge. Half the mages here are hoping to get onto the council at the elections in a few weeks. It's been a while since so many have been in the same room."

"Does Lady Harper think any of *them* are planning to murder you?" My hand twitched towards my bag, which I'd left half-zipped at an angle to make it easy to grab my dagger. This was why I didn't do parties. Nobody looked like they might be plotting against us, but that was the point, wasn't it?

"Not tonight," said Vance. "The wards keep out anyone intending immediate harm."

"Not… tonight." I found myself inching closer to him, scanning the crowd again. With my faerie magic, I was fairly sure I could deflect any kind of attack from here, but then again, I'd been sure of myself when I'd faced Lady Harper, too.

His hand rested at the base of my spine. "Don't worry, I have the best security in the city."

"Me?"

That got me a grin. "Trust me, we're safer here than anywhere else. Sorry I alarmed you."

"I'd rather know in advance if anyone here's planning an ambush."

"They wouldn't dare touch either of us." His tone didn't change much, but I detected the don't-fuck-with-me vibe that indicated he wouldn't be above blasting the roof off if someone attacked one of us.

"Good." I relaxed into step with him.

"Believe me," he said, his voice dropping low, seductive, "if I wasn't the host, I'd move us out of this room in a second, but unfortunately, Drake needs to have several eyes on him at all times."

"I don't doubt that." But the last twenty-four hours had been a reminder of just how many potential enemies we had out there. Even on the other side of the grave.

Nope. Don't think about ghosts, either.

My eyes drifted over the crowd and snagged on a faint blue light behind the tall window overlooking the lawn.

Faerie magic?

As the dance finished and I stepped away from Vance, a figure slipped ahead of me. Damn, faeries moved fast. In the time it took me to turn my back, Ralph had gone through the doors, and the blue glow was no longer present.

"Mage Lord!" A group of diplomats descended on us.

I gave Vance a look that communicated: *I want out.* Vance gave the slightest nod, and I made my way towards the door.

Ralph had turned the corner in the corridor, heading towards the conservatory. Weird. Nobody was in that area of the manor. Everyone was in the hall, as far as I knew. Was he following the light?

I kept a hand on my shoulder bag as I trod after Ralph— then walked *into* him. He'd stopped dead in the middle of the conservatory, and the collision took both of us off our feet. My elbows grazed the tiled floor, my heeled shoes tangling in my dress as we fell into a heap.

Baring his teeth in a snarl, Ralph wriggled out from underneath me and tried to pin me down. I might be without my sword, but I still had my magic. Blue light flared around my hands as I flipped him over and held him onto the floor.

"What the hell are you doing?" he yelled.

"You attacked me." I tightened my grip with one hand and used the other to retrieve the dagger I'd dropped. "Why are you in here?"

"None of your business."

My blade nicked the skin of his neck.

His blue eyes widened. "You're out of your mind!"

"What did you expect me to do? You attacked me."

"You ran into me," he retaliated. "I thought you were an assassin. Let me go!"

I released my hold, marginally. "What were you even doing in here?"

"Nothing. What're you accusing me of?"

"Sneaking around and acting suspicious," I said. "Call me paranoid, but too many faeries have tried to kill me recently."

"I'm not a faerie."

"So what's with the skulking around?"

His alabaster-pale face gleamed in the bright light, his eyes wide. Scared, and not of me. "Thought I saw someone outside."

"A faerie?" Tension gripped my spine. Now we'd left the warmth of the hall behind, the chill from outside seeped through the glass-fronted windows and brought me out in goosebumps.

"Never mind." He slumped against the floor. "I bet it was you I saw. Your reflection."

I stilled. "You're aware I have Winter magic, aren't you?"

"Yeah, like I said. The light was you."

"You saw it too?" Damn. I hadn't imagined it. The light had been too far away to have possibly come from me. "I saw blue light outside. That's why I was following you."

"What?" His voice was too high for his fear to be an act.

"No, really." I loosened my hold, removing my dagger

from his neck. "Why here, though? Didn't you see the light outside on the front lawn?"

"It went that way." He pointed to the right. "I thought it might be circling the manor. That's why I came back here."

"And did you see anything?" I rose upward to squint outside, but the only light came from the reflection of moonlight on the snowy lawn, glittering like spider-silk.

"Not before you jumped me."

"Then why are you so freaked out?" I retained a one-handed grip on him. "Should I ask Vance?"

"I didn't do anything!" His voice hitched up an octave. "Let me go."

"What's going on?" Vance's voice echoed through the empty conservatory.

I released him and climbed to my feet. "Just a friendly chat."

"She attacked me!" said Ralph.

"We attacked each other," I explained in response to Vance's raised eyebrow. "I followed him in here because he sneaked out of the hall and was acting suspiciously."

"Since when is walking in the corridor suspicious?" Ralph rubbed his neck, sliding to his feet in a fluid motion that only faerie magic could accomplish.

"When everyone else is in the hall?" I dusted my dress off and stashed my dagger back in my shoulder bag. "He says he saw something weird outside. Won't tell me what it was."

Vance levelled his gaze onto Ralph. "Is that true?"

"I said I don't know what I saw," said Ralph. "It's dark out there. It looked like a person, but it might have been *her* reflection. Probably was. She jumped me before I could take a proper look."

"Are you certain?" asked Vance.

"Positive."

"Then go."

Brushing dust from his black suit, Ralph slipped out of the conservatory, leaving us alone.

"Don't," I said.

"I wasn't going to blame you." Vance's eyes were on the snow-covered lawn. "I know you wouldn't pick a fight for no reason. Did you see anything outside?"

"Didn't have a chance to look, but I thought I saw something in the front window. Faerie magic."

He turned to me. "Faerie magic? Inside the manor?"

"No, outside." I shifted on my feet, my ankles protesting at the movement. Damn those heels. "Blue light, and it wasn't a reflection. Magic can't get past the boundaries, can it?"

"The wards specifically keep out anything intending harm," said Vance. "I will order a search of the manor, however."

"Don't make a big deal of it," I said quickly. "I might have been mistaken, but if Ralph saw it, too…"

He inclined his head. "Yes, you're right to be suspicious. You and he both have the Sight."

"We do." As much as he might deny his faerie heritage, he and I shared the same window into a world that went unseen to most people. "I don't like that he was skulking around. I thought he was going to try to strangle me back then. I know I took him by surprise, but still."

"Like I said, he's listening out for useful information because I trust him," said Vance. "He isn't working against the mages. He dislikes the faeries, too, and his human family disowned him, so we're all he has."

"Wait, they did?" Harsh, but not a reason to unequivocally trust someone as a spy. "How'd he wind up here?"

"By application, like most of our staff." He moved closer to the windows overlooking the lawn. "I picked him myself, as the Mage Lords took me in after the invasion in the same way."

"What?" I blinked in confusion. "You own this house. Right? Didn't you inherit it?"

"Technically, yes, but there were certain individuals at the time who believed handing the mages' headquarters over to a child was a foolish move on my parents' part. They thought I should live with my uncle."

"Oh. *Oh.*" His uncle hated the shifters *and* the mages. That would have gone down well. "You were what, ten years old? They really tried to take the house away from you?"

"I never wanted it," said Vance quietly. "Not then. But my uncle closed the door in my face. Lady Harper offered to mentor me, and the other Mage Lords quickly backed down."

So I wasn't the only one who'd been screwed over by former Mage Lords. I never would have guessed it'd happen to Vance, of all people, and it made me grudgingly move Lady Harper one step lower on my list of enemies. "Jesus. Sorry."

"It's old history. Besides, those Mage Lords didn't last long. This house is designated as a safe zone... so nothing dangerous can possibly have passed our wards."

He peered outside. The snow-covered lawns gleamed under the moonlight, but no blue glow remained. I would have assumed my mind had been playing tricks on me, but Ralph had seen the light, too, and after Vance's explanation, I was more inclined to believe in his innocence.

The intruder, though? If Ralph hadn't been mistaken, if he'd actually seen a person outside, they sure as hell weren't there now. My Sight would reveal anything concealed by glamour.

Except, perhaps, a ghost.

Goosebumps prickled my arms and legs, and not just from the cold air seeping into the conservatory and chilling my bare skin. The whole manor was covered in glyphs built into the very bricks, and iron foundations surrounded the extensive grounds. I wouldn't have thought even a spirit could surpass them. Right?

"The guests will notice our absence," said Vance. "I'll order some of my most trusted mages to run the search."

"I'd volunteer, but not in these bloody heels." I was pretty sure I had blisters after being on my feet for so long. "There are guests here with faerie magic. Maybe it was one of them I saw."

"Maybe." Vance took one last look outside and moved closer to me, his warmth blocking out the chill. "You're safe here."

"Even with all the backstabbing mages in the hall?"

"Even then."

I looked out the window again. A normal night, crowned with stars. No signs of foul play. Suppressing the knot of unease in my chest, I turned and walked back to the party with Vance.

6

"Ivy!" Isabel's voice chirped out of the phone. "We've got a client."

"What?" I yawned, half asleep. It'd been a late night after the party, even though Vance had taken pity on me and made Drake retract the bet we'd made on yesterday's snowball fight so I didn't have to clean up. The guests took forever to leave, and my face still hurt from wearing a false smile for so many hours. Not to mention the blisters on my feet.

"A client," Isabel said. "Another ghost case."

I groaned and rubbed my eyes. "What time is it?"

"Nine o'clock. I've been holding the fort in the office. I thought you'd have a late night."

"You weren't wrong." I looked over at Vance. He was awake before me, as usual, seated at the desk with a neat stack of papers in front of him.

"They'll be back in an hour, if you can drag yourself away from Vance."

"I'll be there." I clicked off the phone and went searching

for my clothes. Before I'd moved a metre, they appeared on the bed, along with… "Is this a healing spell?"

"You were limping last night," said Vance.

I smiled. "You're too observant for your own good."

"You tortured yourself with those heels to keep my guests happy."

"I doubt most of them noticed." I activated the spell, sighing in relief when the sting of my blisters faded.

Once I was showered and dressed, I joined Vance at the desk dominating the left side of the room. It was large enough to accommodate both Vance's paperwork and a plate of pancakes heaped with more fresh strawberries next to a mug of coffee. I could definitely get used to living the high life with the Mage Lord.

"Was that Isabel?" he asked me.

"Yeah." I took a bite of pancake. "Another client wanting us to handle a ghost. I should have asked why they didn't hire the necromancers instead, but I can guess the answer. What're those papers for?"

"Council meetings, mostly."

"Wait, do they know about last night?" I turned to face him. "The council, I mean. Did you tell them what I saw… or thought I saw?"

"No. I told the guards I wanted to run a general security check. There was no reason to draw attention."

"Good." I didn't need to get a reputation among the mages for jumping at shadows. "I don't think anyone saw except for Ralph and me, and I should have told you before I went looking. Or someone who doesn't have the Sight."

"Don't worry about it. Lady Granville's paranoid about our security, so I thought it'd be best to anticipate any possible problems."

"Like ghosts."

He looked at me. "You think he saw a ghost?"

"Can ghosts bypass wards?"

"It depends on the ward, I imagine." His forehead creased. "Only necromantic circles can properly contain a spirit, but ghosts are usually tied to one place regardless."

"Like where they died." Hence why home intrusions were rare, and they rarely haunted total strangers. "Frankly, I'm more worried Lady Granville will find out and use it as an excuse to blame me for something else."

"She won't," he said. "She doesn't know about last night, but she made her position on our involvement in ghost-related cases clear."

I groaned. "I don't have time to grovel before her every single time I want to take on a case."

"You don't have to," he said. "I'll handle it. Just give me a copy of the contract and I'll put it through."

"And deal with another interrogation." I stabbed my fork into a strawberry and imagined it was Lady Granville's face. "You'd think she'd have better things to do with her time."

"Yes. I do wish Lord Evander would get his act together."

"Tell me about it." I finished eating my pancake. "Our client's probably after an exorcism, too. Maybe the ghosts heard me complaining about the lack of clients and decided to oblige."

"Be careful," he said.

"Will do." I put down my fork and stood. "Drop me in the corridor. I don't want to freak out our clients."

He took my arm. "Should I call you in a few hours?"

"I'll let you know what I'm doing," I told him. "Oh, and if you have time, can you check in with the Chief? I want to know if… if the banshee was right."

The Chief wasn't a big fan of technology and didn't have a mobile phone or any way of keeping in contact, so one of us would have to go there in person. I didn't want to hope anyone had died at the jail last night, but it was better than most alternatives.

"Of course."

We landed in the upstairs corridor of my flat, where I kissed Vance goodbye and walked into the office. Isabel stood behind the desk, while in front was a guy around my age, pale and shaggy-haired, and a short Asian woman with a nasty scar across one ear that looked as though she'd tangled with a goblin at some point. Both were lean and tough-looking, wearing daggers strapped to their legs and arms, and clothed in tattered jeans and thick leather jackets. Mercenaries.

"You're Ivy Lane?" The guy had that unshaven, in-need-of-a-haircut look some people found attractive. "The one who walked out on Larsen?"

"That's me."

From his tone, he disbelieved that I'd left of my own volition, as opposed to being fired.

I drew myself up to my full height. Since I was five-four, five-six with heels, I generally needed to display my sword to make an impression. "I'm Isabel's partner. You wanted our help?"

"If you can offer us anything," said the woman in doubtful tones. "I'm Charlie. This is Rex. We live in mercenary district, and there's... something inside our apartment."

"All the signs suggest it's a spirit," Isabel added. "Or something invisible, at any rate."

"And you couldn't catch it?"

"No." The guy's hand twitched towards one of his knives. "Damn thing moved too quickly, and our weapons didn't make a dent in it."

"So you came to us and not the necromancers... why?"

"Because the necromancers aren't taking on clients," said Charlie. "I'm told you performed an exorcism the other day."

"Yeah, I did." *They aren't taking on clients at all? Really?*

I didn't ask why they hadn't hired the mages, though. Their threadbare clothes and second-hand daggers spoke for themselves. I'd been in their position not so long ago.

"Did you want us to call the necromancers, or just do an evaluation? We can't go up against a spirit without the proper equipment."

"Er, actually, we have some," said Isabel. "I called them, and Lord Evander agreed to loan us some gear, on the condition that we return it straight to him afterwards. Sounds like his people are dealing with a major case of undead today."

Or a major case of I-don't-give-a-shit. I'd ask why Lord Evander had trusted her with his equipment when he hated me so much, but not in front of our clients.

"Was that a yes?" asked Rex.

I turned to him. "I'll get my weapons first, then we'll go and handle this spirit."

"You can't kill it with any regular weapon," said Charlie. "We tried everything. Swords, daggers, a machete…"

I resisted the impulse to roll my eyes. Mercenaries' default response to anything hostile was to try to stick a knife in it. Not that I was one to talk.

It'd been a while since I'd last taken the bus. More people avoided me than usual when Isabel and I paid for our tickets and sat down, probably due to my sword. Most couldn't see that it flared blue whenever a half-faerie got on the bus, luckily, but the faeries sure as hell could, and to my own eyes, the faint blue glow of magic wreathing my body was noticeable even in my reflection in the bus's window.

"What the hell are the necromancers doing?" I asked Isabel in an undertone. "Why'd Lord Evander hand his equipment over to you?"

"The undead," said Isabel. "Apparently the guild spent the

whole of last night chasing zombies and they're still cleaning up the mess."

Last night. When a spirit had appeared at the manor… if I believed Ralph.

"Lord Evander was a complete shit to me yesterday," I said. "Why trust *us* with the equipment? How'd you convince him?"

"Well, he lent the equipment to the coven, not to me. I didn't mention you'd be involved."

"Oh."

"Yeah." She grimaced. "He's a fool not to acknowledge you're probably better at banishing the dead than half his necromancers."

"Some dead," I corrected. "My only experience with banishing ghosts was the other night, and it didn't end so well."

"Hope today goes better," Isabel said. "What did Lord Evander say when you spoke?"

"That his people aren't responsible for faerie ghosts. The Chief said the same." I filled her in on everything she'd missed after my return to the mages, including the encounter with the banshee. Since my sword successfully deterred anyone from sitting near us on the bus, I didn't worry we might be overheard beneath the roar of the engine and the intermittent thuds when we ran over a pothole.

"Damn, Ivy," said Isabel. "There I was thinking you just went for a quick rendezvous with Lord Evander before the gala so you could get him to sign those forms."

"The bloody forms." I heaved a sigh. "Vance really pulled through for me on that one, but if this case goes tits-up, he won't be able to perform a miracle twice."

Her brow wrinkled. "What did you learn about that ghost, then? The half-faerie one?"

"Only that he claimed to be under the drug's influence

when Calder tried to blow up the town. He was killed in the fighting during the attempted jailbreak."

"That's it? No more details?"

"That was when the banshee attacked us and kinda killed the conversation."

"Oh."

"Yeah. I know. I need to check back with the Chief at some point today. And Vance. And Lord Evander."

"I think the Mage Lord's influence is rubbing off on you," said Isabel. "You know you can't teleport like he can, right? And even he can't be in three places at once."

"Ha ha." I yawned, wishing I'd grabbed more coffee to go. "Honestly, it feels like the instant I let my attention focus on one problem, another appears behind me and thwacks me on the head."

"They're not all your responsibility," said Isabel. "Even the mages."

"I know." *But the banshee said someone would die. And I'd like to make sure it isn't Vance or me.*

I forced the thoughts from my head. Creepy death faeries and their weird predictions weren't as important as getting rid of this spirit.

We hopped off the bus in one of the more run-down mercenary districts. Blocks of flats crowded both sides of the road, the sort that had barely been returned to habitable quality following the invasion and that boasted the cheapest rent in the city as recompense for neighbouring with monsters.

I'd taken part in many a mercenary mission in this very area, where a ghost was the least deadly enemy one might encounter. At least a disembodied spirit couldn't rip out your insides and leave you to rot in an alley. Even the clean-up crew rarely showed up this close to the canal, and while half the inhabitants were mercs themselves, only problems big enough to attract widespread public complaint were brought to the attention of the guild. Through gaps in the dingy apartment blocks, the water flowed sluggishly. I drew my sword, its glow a clear warning to any nasties that might be lurking in the alleys between buildings and cracks in the pavement. Isabel and I walked behind the couple and tried not to breathe in the stench that hung in the air like miasma.

"I'd still rather be here than in a meeting with Lady Granville," I remarked to Isabel.

"That bad?" she said sympathetically. I hadn't given her the details of yesterday's meeting yet—or what had followed.

"Yeah." We crossed the pothole-strewn road to the buildings that backed onto the canal. "It's like she compiles a list of ways to piss me off before each meeting. Between her and the scary mage who showed up yesterday and tried to choke me, I'm kinda glad to be away from the manor today."

"Wait, *who* tried to choke you?"

"Lady Harper." I had to tell her eventually. "Vance's guardian… sort of. I don't know how it works with the mages."

Isabel gaped at me. "You met Lady Harper?"

"You know her?" That, I hadn't expected.

"She used to be the adviser to the coven."

"The coven?" I echoed. "She's a mage, though. A bloody powerful one at that."

"Before my time, but I think she's the reason the mages have an unlimited supply of the coven's high-grade spells."

"She didn't strike me as the selfless type." I lowered my voice in case the mercs might be listening in. "She cracked my mind open to read my thoughts, to make sure I wasn't plotting against Vance."

Isabel tripped over the jagged edge of a piece of shattered pavement. "She broke into your *mind*? Is that even legal?"

"Maybe she's the one who wrote the lawbook. Who

knows." I gave a shudder. "I never thought I'd meet anyone scarier than Vance, but she trained him, so…"

"What did *he* have to say about that?"

"He wasn't overly thrilled that she told me to stay away from him."

"She told you that? Does she have authority over his life?"

"No, but she did raise him, because he lost his parents in the invasion." I lifted my shoulder in a shrug, feeling spots of rain against my face that promised to turn into drizzle later. "I told her no way in hell and Vance backed me up, so we're good."

In theory. I'd never doubted I'd have to fight to prove my value to the mages, but it was another blow altogether to realise that Lady Harper didn't believe I was worthy to stand beside Vance as a partner. Thinking of how she'd called me a weak link made me all the more determined not to screw up this case.

The couple led us to one of the apartment buildings and buzzed their way into a dingy corridor that smelled of days-old rotting food and cigarette smoke. There were no working lights inside and the elevator was broken, so we had to make our way up two flights of stairs with the aid of a light spell Isabel had brought with her. The corridor was a hazardous game of leaping over cracks and hoping we didn't fall through the floor. Something clawed stuck its head through a particularly large hole and snapped its teeth at us. The mercenary woman stabbed it in the eye with a jagged knife, and it retreated, blood spattering the floorboards.

As I'd suspected, they took care of their own here. It must dent their pride to have to call for our help over a disembodied intruder.

The inside of the one-bedroom apartment reminded me of a troll's lair. Trophies hung on the walls, ranging from shrivelled heads to curved teeth and unidentifiable claws.

Rows of bloody footprints decorated the threadbare carpet, and the only furniture aside from the sunken old double bed was a set of shelves displaying weapons rather than books. The flickering light illuminated a set of bloodstained swords that might fetch a good price on the market. Honestly, if they sold the lot, they might have been able to afford a better flat, but mercs often had a bizarre sense of sentimental value attached to their weapons.

A rattling sounded from behind the shelves.

"Just a mouse," said Rex. "Not fae, I don't think."

Isabel gave the wobbly shelf a wary look and moved aside. Like me, I'd bet she was thinking of how even our arsehole of a landlord had never let our flat get into this stage of neglect. Admittedly, he'd nearly thrown me out on the streets the time I'd come in covered in redcap entrails, but at least being flatmates with Isabel ensured a never-ending supply of cleansing spells.

The only spells on the shelves here were healing concoctions, and the cheap and nasty homemade sort. The jagged scar on the woman's ear told me they'd been in situations that called for a super-strength healing spell but hadn't had one to hand. Not unlike me, when I'd been in Faerie.

Isabel cleared her throat. "Where's the ghost?"

"We don't know," said Rex. "It woke us up early this morning by ripping cupboard doors off." He indicated the dark area of the kitchenette, which I gathered was the origin of the smell of mould. Two wooden cupboard doors lay in splintered pieces on the floor.

"We thought it was some kind of fae at first," said Charlie. "But we tore the place up and there's nothing."

"I called the necromancers," added Rex. "Their assistant said they were busy. He gave us your number instead."

"Colby?" I guessed. "Nice of him to volunteer us."

Rex gave me a suspicious look. "Is there a ghost in here or not? Can you tell?"

"I brought a sensor." Isabel put down the rucksack she'd brought with her and unzipped the top, reaching inside to retrieve Colby's spirit sensor. Dried ectoplasm still coated the top, and I fervently hoped that we wouldn't need to use the emergency button this time around.

I surveyed the room. "Best place for a trapping circle's probably by the door. There's no other way to escape, since the window's boarded up."

"Can't ghosts float through walls?" asked Rex.

"In theory, but they tend to stick to one place, and we can secure the room once we figure out where it is."

"Thought you could see it."

"No," said Isabel. "I told you before that we're borrowing the necromancers' equipment. Anyone can use this sensor, though."

The pair of them watched as she crossed the room and held up the device, waiting for a flashing light to tell us where to go. *Where's the little bastard hiding?*

"Maybe it ran off," Charlie said hopefully, watching us. "Can they do that?"

Time for Necromancy 101 again. "Sometimes, but if a ghost cares enough to stick around, they're as persistent as dry rot. They usually tend to attach themselves to a place which was important to them in life. Somewhere they lived once. Or died in." I figured they could handle the honest response.

"We moved into this apartment last year," said Charlie. "Nothing strange appeared in the ads."

"People don't usually advertise ghosts," I said.

"Very funny, you are," he said.

"Do you know if anyone was killed here at any point?"

"No clue."

Great. Typical mercs. Both of them had their weapons out, for all the good that'd do against a spectre with the strength to tear off cupboard doors. That level of viciousness was rare even for a poltergeist, whose usual repertoire of pranks was limited to knocking things over. Poltergeist or not, I fervently hoped that this ghost was human, if just because of the sheer number of trophies displayed on the shelves. Troll teeth, a redcap's hat... even a handful of hairs that might have been pulled out of a kelpie's tail.

"This isn't reacting." Isabel poked the sensor into the room's distant corner. "It might've left the apartment..."

"Or be hiding." That was the problem. The ten percent efficiency rate meant that the sensor was very unlikely to pick up on the spirit before it exposed itself.

And if it is a half-faerie ghost...

I pulled out my sword a little more to reveal the blue glow around its edges. If the ghost was a half-faerie, I'd rather it punched me in the face right away than have to stand here for hours waiting for the inevitable ambush.

"Found it?" Rex brandished his dagger at the wall. "Tell me where to stab."

"That won't work."

A chill lifted the hair from my scalp and bit at my arms underneath my leather jacket. My sword's blue glow brightened noticeably. *Oh, hell.*

I caught Isabel's eye. "We can do this without pinning down its exact location. I'll use the salt."

I pulled out my newly refilled saltshaker, and the two mercs looked at me as though I'd retrieved a fluffy kitten from my pocket.

"Salt?" said Rex in a sceptical tone. "Salt scares off ghosts?"

"Don't ask me why." I walked to Isabel's side. "Maybe it's

because salt destroys undead. And ghosts, if they materialise, but usually it just scares them off."

Isabel reached into the rucksack again and got out the trapping spell and another salt canister, handing me the latter. "Here. I'll handle the trap."

"Gotcha." I held the salt canisters awkwardly in one hand. "We'll seal the room's edges first so it can't pass through the walls. That is, if it hasn't already."

"There's no one living in the next apartment," said Rex. "They say the last dude fell through the floor."

Seriously? "Thought you said no one died here."

"I said no one was murdered here."

"People die around here all the time," added Charlie.

"You might have mentioned that," I said. "Whatever the cause of death, multiple casualties make a place more likely to turn into a target for spectral activity."

"How was I meant to know?" said Rex defensively. "I'm not a necromancer. Don't know anyone who's been haunted before either."

"Yes, well, ghosts don't usually come back. Luckily for you."

I made my way around the edge of the flat with the salt-shakers, sealing off the bathroom and the kitchenette first so that the ghost would be confined to this room. If it hadn't already left. The creaking noises in the worn floorboards did nothing to soothe my frazzled nerves.

I finished encircling the room with salt and waited for Isabel to set up an illusion over the trap. She'd positioned it in the centre, beside the shattered cupboard doors. I pocketed one saltshaker and reached for my blade. *Come out and play, spirit.*

The floorboards gave an alarming creak beneath my feet, then folded inward, pulling me into darkness.

7

Isabel shouted my name. A yell jammed in my chest as my hands scrabbled to get a grip on the sides of the splintering floorboards. My fall slowed as sharpness dug into my legs, suggesting the boards had only half-collapsed, but the continuous creaking warned me that wouldn't last for long.

Isabel began to run towards me and then let out a startled yell when her body flew sideways, as though tossed by an invisible force.

"Isabel!"

She'd managed to land on her feet, but the floorboards around me gave another loud creak. Swearing, I half pulled myself out, calling on the faerie magic to boost my speed and balance. The salt container had rolled to the side, spilling half its contents onto the bloodstained carpet. The two mercs stood frozen against one of the trophy cases, mouths slack, eyes focused on the spot from which Isabel had been thrown. *Yeah, there's our spirit.*

I grabbed for the saltshaker, but it rolled underneath the bed, out of reach.

"Isabel, the trap," I yelled, scooping a handful of salt from the floor. We'd sealed the spirit inside this room, but there were entirely too many potential hazards in addition to the actual weapons. And I'd thought Mrs Bennet's antique china was bad enough.

The shelf behind the mercenaries wobbled, ominously. I grabbed my sword. "Both of you get away from that."

"Huh?" Rex's confusion turned to panic when a dagger lifted itself to point at the back of his head. "Help!"

Charlie's eyes bulged. "Help him!"

Throwing myself across the room, I shot magic through my palms at the shelves. The heavy wooden structure fell forwards and knocked the knife askew. I hurtled beneath and snatched the weapon out of the air, but my fingers met an unseen resistance. Was the spirit still *holding* the knife?

I tugged again, harder, and the knife came away in my hand. My sword slashed at the spot where the weapon had hovered but passed through empty air.

"I thought you said you couldn't see the spirit!" Rex gaped at the wrecked shelves, one hand on the back of his head. His face had paled as it dawned on him how close he'd come to joining the ghost on the other side.

"Saw the knife," I said, which was technically true.

"How the hell did you move so fast?" Charlie demanded. "Thought you were a witch."

"Speed enhancing rune." I fell back on my usual excuse. "Isabel, why isn't that sensor working?"

"No clue." She'd crouched down, frantically going through her backpack. "The trapping circle—"

"Think we'll need the emergency button instead." There were too many dangerous instruments in the room to risk the spirit roaming around for any longer.

"Not when we don't know where the ghost is."

I threw a handful of salt at the pile of weapons that had

collapsed with the shelves, hoping that would deter the spirit from trying another assault, but there were countless other sharp objects within reach. "Give me the sensor. Maybe I can—"

Sudden cold laughter echoed around the room. I froze, as did Isabel. The tracker gave one long beep.

Then the ceiling came down.

A faint creaking noise was our only warning before the broken light fell, bringing a shower of plaster and wood. I whipped my sword out, magic flaring through my palms and forming a shield above our heads. The haze of shimmering blue light pressed against the mass of plaster and wood, but both mercenaries continued to whimper hysterically.

"Relax, I'm holding it." I did anything but relax as I held the shield in place. "Get out. Isabel, you too. I'll take it down."

Isabel gave me a frightened look but didn't argue. The mercs both gawped at my hands, which I held palm-up to focus on the layer of blue energy that formed the only defence between us and the falling heap of plaster and wood. What they saw instead of the vibrant glow of my magic, I had no idea, but rivulets of sweat ran down my neck from the effort. I'd never maintained a shield for this long before.

"I can't hold it forever," I snapped at the mercenaries. "Get out if you want to live."

They obliged. When they were outside, Isabel shut the door on them and began sprinkling salt on the floor in a circle around herself.

"I told you to run with them."

"I'm not leaving you alone in here." She put down the salt-shaker and opened the rucksack. "I'll get the trap set up."

My shoulders slumped. "Okay. I'll take the sensor, then."

Still holding the shield in place, I backed towards the door until we both stood out of the path of the collapsing ceiling.

Then I braced myself and let go. The ceiling came down in a room-shaking crash that sent a wave of dust over our heads. I coughed, my eyes watering, arms raised to protect myself and Isabel from the onslaught of debris. Slowly I lowered my hands, still coughing, dust hazing my vision.

Isabel groaned behind me. "I hope nobody was upstairs."

"Me too." A huge chunk of ceiling had come down, but there didn't appear to be anyone in the wreckage, human or otherwise. "Can you pass me the sensor?"

She did so. The red light flashed, albeit weakly. *Took long enough.*

I pointed my sword ahead of me into the haze of plaster dust. The faint blue glow pushed the shadows away—and illuminated the smiling face of a ghost.

I jerked back. "What the fuck?"

"Did I startle you, Ivy Lane?" asked the ghost.

It's not him. Of course it wasn't Calder, but the male half-faerie had the same look: icy blue eyes, eerily handsome features, chin-length silver hair transparent in ghost form. Hands clenched, I moved in front of Isabel.

"Ivy? What's going on?"

Oh, hell. The ghost must have used glamour to ensure only I saw him.

"Glamour," I said. "Another half-faerie. Don't move from the door."

I advanced towards the spirit, my sword outstretched and the sensor in my other hand. The spirit's eyes glowed blue, the same colour as my sword. Winter.

"Bye bye." I hit the sensor's button.

The ghostly figure should have exploded into ectoplasm. Instead, he disappeared.

"Huh?"

"Ivy, what's going on?" Isabel whimpered. "I can't see anything."

"Is the trap set up?" I asked in an undertone. "Because the exterminator didn't work."

"It's done, but… shit, Ivy. It didn't work?"

"Maybe it's out of battery life." Just what we needed. "I'll lure the ghost into the trap myself."

"Be careful." I heard her sharp inhale when I stepped forward, moving closer to the collapsed ceiling. I was reasonably confident that my magic would protect me from another onslaught, but that didn't extend to anyone else in the building, nor Isabel either.

"What's your deal?" I asked the empty shadows. "How'd you avoid the sensor?"

I pointed the sensor at the spot where I thought the ghost should be, and an invisible force seized my hand, as though someone was trying to grab my fingers and pry them loose from the sensor. *Holy crap.* The dagger hadn't been a one-off. Someone had given this ghost a serious power boost.

Fortunately, I was stronger. I wrenched my hand away and drove my blade upward through thin air. As I'd hoped, the unseen grip on the sensor disappeared. Even ghosts had an instinctive response when you ran them through with a sword.

The ghost popped back into existence, hovering a foot off the ground. "Nice try."

"Okay, here's how this is going to go," I said. "You're going to get into the trap, and the necromancers will take you for a one-way trip past the veil. Deal?"

The ghost's fist went through my chest.

Even though I *knew,* rationally, a ghost couldn't harm me, my body flinched of its own accord. A piece of wood crashed into the back of my head, and I swore explosively as a series of pretty lights shone before my eyes.

"Quit it." I swiped at the air, but the ghost vanished again.

Dammit. My talisman's power came from death, which

ought to give me some edge over the spirit. Maybe if I went into Death, I'd be able to take it by surprise… but there was no way in hell I'd take the risk.

My head throbbed. The bloody ghost had likely hidden somewhere within the ruin of the collapsed ceiling, and I was not in the mood to play hide-and-seek.

"Hey." The blue glow from my sword illuminated the room. "Know what this is? Know where it comes from?"

A knife threw itself at me. I deflected it with a shield, my veins humming with magic. The light grew brighter, but the ghost remained unseen.

Think, Ivy. Ghosts usually had one good boost of energy and that was it. The pauses between attacks suggested the spirit was conserving his strength, but if I provoked him into a full attack, maybe I'd be in with a chance of tiring it out enough to get it into the trapping spell.

"Well, this is disappointing." I moved forwards, lifting my blade. "I expected a better effort, since you took the trouble to drag us out here. Any reason you picked this place to terrorise? We both know I'm your real target. Seems a waste of energy to smash up people's homes instead."

"You don't know anything, Ivy Lane," said the cold male voice. "You were supposed to die."

"Yeah, no," I said. "Who told you that?"

"You wouldn't know." The ghost appeared, his transparent form haloed in the same blueness as my sword. "You never asked our names. We were always nothing to you. You sacrificed all of us for your own sake. Until he saved us."

Ice flooded my veins. "Calder?"

"He's coming for you, Ivy."

"He's dead," I informed him. "So are you."

"Not for long."

The ghost's hand shot out. I held my sword up, and the

blue glow caused the spirit to recoil. *It's scared of Avalin's magic.*

"Is Calder with you?" I asked, my voice all but drowned out by the hum of magic in my veins.

"He will be." The spirit kept a wary distance from my weapon, and I pushed against the air, hoping to drive him away from the collapsed ceiling. "The dead won't rest for much longer… except for you."

"Care to elaborate?" My hands numbed. I *hoped* it was just the cold presence of death, not Winter magic. Because if the ghost had his magic back…

The floor shook again. I braced my feet, but the shaking forced me to lower my sword to stabilise myself.

The ghost once again lunged forward and drove a transparent fist into my chest. Ice flooded me, locked my body into place. Even my sword stilled as a chill like death's own touch gripped me by the throat.

"Stop that." Growling between my teeth, I drew upon the pain and fear, both mine and the ghost's, and the glow of the magic in my hands brightened.

My shield flared back to life and the ghost flew across the room into the wreckage of the collapsed ceiling. But the trap was behind me, and the only way for me to get to the ghost's other side was to leap over the ruins and hope I didn't end up buried alive.

My humming magical shield bolstered my nerves. *Fine, then.*

I jumped high, over the pile of splintered wood and plaster. When my feet touched down behind the ghost, he pivoted towards the door. Which was where I wanted the spirit to be—except if the ghost could evade a sensor, would Isabel's trap even work?

"Ivy?" Isabel called to me. "My god. It's so cold in here."

"I know." In another leap, I cleared the wreckage and

thrust upwards, my blade piercing the ghost's chest. Magic poured out of the blade, fuelled by fear and anger deeper than I'd expect from a mere ghost. I could almost taste his own fury on my tongue as the sword vibrated in my hands and blue light flared out. "Just *die.*"

The ghost shattered like glass.

I stared, jaw hanging open. Lowered my blade. Blessed silence fell over the room. The ghost had gone.

"Ivy." Isabel gaped at me from beside the trap. "You okay? Did the ghost… leave?"

"Yeah." I shook my head, my body numb. Not just with cold, but shock. I'd never made a ghost explode with my bare hands before. *What the hell was that?*

Isabel's hand grabbed my wrist, tugging me towards the door. "Jesus, Ivy, you're cold as ice."

"Probably because the ghost of a Winter faerie just punched me in the chest." I kept my sword in one hand and handed Isabel the now useless sensor. "Let's get out of here."

"Ivy…" Her gaze travelled over room. "Are you *sure* the ghost is gone?"

"Apparently I'm a human exterminator now." I gave a quiet laugh. "I didn't know I could do that."

"You said… the ghost wanted to target you."

"I figured as much when he said my name." I shuddered. "And confirmed my guess when he mentioned…" The name stuck in my throat, but I forced it out. Calder."

The one ghost who hated me enough that he'd tear open the veil and return to life if he held the means in his hands. Both of the half-faerie spirits I'd encountered had known him when he was alive Let's face it, this whole situation had Calder's ghostly fingerprints all over it.

"Shit," said Isabel quietly. "Okay. We need to get *out,* first. Before the bloody building falls down. This place isn't safe."

"No kidding," I murmured, opening the door.

As expected, we found the two mercs cowering in the corridor outside.

"What the hell?" whimpered Rex. "What did you do? Our flat's in ruins."

"You're lucky to be alive," I retaliated. "The ghost's gone."

I'd shattered it with my sword, blasted it with death energy. What I'd done shouldn't be possible with the veil intact. Then again, the ghost shouldn't have been able to physically touch me either.

Ten minutes of navigating staircases later, the four of us stood outside in the cold air. The building didn't *look* like it was about to fall apart—any more than it had before the ghost showed up, anyway—but I put as much distance between us and the door as possible.

"Tell your landlord what happened," I told the mercs. Seeing their scepticism, I changed tack. "All right, the damages'll be covered by the necromancer guild or the mages, depending on who I can get to cooperate. I'll make some calls. Oh, and you can check in at the mercenary guild if you need somewhere immediate to stay, but I expect you know that already."

I'd used that tactic myself, many times.

"You'll really call the necromancers?" asked Charlie.

"Of course. I used to work with Larsen. Wouldn't want any merc living out on the streets. It's not pretty out there."

"Not pretty here either." Rex pulled out his phone. "I'll call Larsen."

"Thanks," Charlie added. "For whatever you did."

"Any time," I lied. I *hoped* this was the last time I'd have to fight a ghost as powerful as that one.

As for my magic? The last time I'd used it to kill a spirit had been when I'd stabbed a wraith impersonating Avalin. In the Grey Vale.

Right. Call Vance first.

I hit the call button and heard nothing but a dial tone. "Must be dealing with clients."

"Vance?" Isabel guessed. "Where *are* the necromancers? They've never let a ghost incident slide with no investigation before. Let alone one on this scale."

"Exactly," I said. "I don't give a flying fuck what Lord Evander said. These spirits are getting a power boost from somewhere, and unless they want everyone in the city to know how incompetent they are, they'll have to listen to me this time."

"You're going to their headquarters?"

"I have to." I turned back to the mercs. "Will you be okay? I'd help, but I can't personally arrange to have your possessions replaced. Like I said, speak to Larsen if you need anywhere to stay."

"'S'okay," said Charlie. "Place was a shithole anyway."

That was true.

As we walked away, my phone buzzed in my hand. I breathed out when I saw the name. "Vance?"

"Ivy," said Vance. "Ralph's dead."

8

I stared at the phone, then lifted it upward to my ear. "What?"

That couldn't be right. I must have misheard him.

"Ralph," Vance said. "We found him outside the gates. He was killed a couple of hours ago at most."

"Shit," I whispered, moving away from the mercs, who watched me with curious expressions. "Vance, a ghost showed up, another half-faerie. He pretty much said the pair of them knew one another, and that—that Calder gave the orders. I think they distracted the necromancers on purpose."

And purposefully created a diversion so I wouldn't be at the manor when they attacked.

Vance swore quietly. "He wasn't killed by a ghost. He was savaged by some kind of beast. A hellhound, I suspect."

My grip on the phone grew sweaty. "Calder used them last time."

We'd never accounted for all of them, but they'd been hiding on the Ley Line, out of sight unless someone called them to attack.

"He did." I heard Vance's sharp exhale. "That said, Lady Granville has appointed herself chief investigator of the murder."

"And she's qualified to investigate a murder committed by a hellhound?" I walked faster, not wanting to risk anyone hearing a single word of this. "I doubt she'd ever believe that someone dead is the instigator either."

"Not without evidence. Did the ghost you encountered offer you any clues about last night? Any connection to what you saw at the manor?"

Oh. He meant the blue light I'd seen outside. "No. He laughed at me and tried to kill me. What are you doing now?"

"Lady Granville has taken Ralph's death as a threat to all the mages. She's called a meeting."

"Get a tracking spell at the site of the attack." The part of me used to handling a crisis took over. I didn't know Ralph, nor had I particularly liked him, but I'd dealt with plenty of murder cases before. "Or I'll do it, if you're tied up."

"We already did," Vance told me. "The tracking spells were inconclusive, but I believe the attackers came from the usual place."

"The Ley Line." I swore. "And if there was a ghost there giving the orders, no tracker would pick up on them."

That the mages couldn't see through glamour either had made them doubly unprepared for the attack. Except Ralph *could* see through glamour. Maybe that was why he'd been the target.

"Exactly," said Vance. "However, Lady Granville requested that I ask you to come here at once."

"Seriously?" The timing was far from ideal, but—wait. "Did you say she *asked* you to bring me there? Has she finally realised I'm qualified in that area?"

An ominous pause followed. "Two witnesses saw you

leave the hall after Ralph last night. She wants to question you."

"Fuck me sideways."

On a less serious occasion, Vance might have turned that comment into something suggestive. Instead, he said, "Come as fast as you can. I'd rather not leave the council in this state."

More like he didn't want to risk another murder happening when he wasn't present, but this was ridiculous. I couldn't be a suspect, not even in Lady Granville's disapproving eyes. She was just fucking with me. Right?

"Sure," I said. "I'll be there."

"Ivy?" Isabel caught me up. "You look like you've seen a… this is a bad time for jokes, isn't it?"

"You could say that. I think I just got blamed for a murder."

Isabel's eyes went wide. "What?"

"Ralph. He's dead."

Her mouth parted. "Who? The faerie guard at the manor who kept arguing with you?"

"Quarter faerie." My mind raced. Ralph was only a part-time security guard, not a powerful mage. Why kill him? *Because he saw something he shouldn't have?*

It did no help to let my paranoia have free rein, so I tried to summon up sympathy for Ralph instead. I wouldn't wish a hellhound's teeth on anyone, no matter how obnoxious they might have been. Isabel had nearly died from a single bite.

"Ivy." Isabel eyed me with concern. "Why would anyone in their right mind blame *you* for his death?"

I winced. "He was acting weird last night, and I followed him out of the party. When they found his body, someone told tales on me to Lady Granville, and here we are."

"Why'd you follow him in the first place?"

"We both thought we saw faerie magic, or… something." I

wished I'd stayed put, but that wouldn't have made any difference to Ralph's fate. "It disappeared when we tried to get a closer look, but he thought it might be... well, a ghost."

"Really?"

"Yeah, but you know, I have spirits on the brain, so I told myself I was imagining things." I shook my head. "Whatever it was, it vanished before I got there, but that's not the important part. Lady Granville's taking control of the investigation and she wants to interrogate me as a suspect."

"She can't possibly suspect you," Isabel protested. "Vance..."

"Oh, he'll knock her off her high horse, but she's derailing the actual investigation with this bullshit." My hands curled into fists. "I'll set her straight."

Isabel's mouth turned down at the corners. "I expect the mages already have enough tracking spells, but if they need anything from me..."

"The trackers didn't work, but you know, ghosts are kinda immune. And none of the mages have the Sight."

Isabel nodded and adjusted her rucksack on her shoulders. "I'll call the necromancers while you're tied up and explain the damage. Maybe bring in the coven, but I'll try to avoid mentioning your name."

"Not sure that's possible." And now I had to find yet another way to explain a ghostly explosion in an office-appropriate manner. "But thanks. You should get away from here before Larsen shows up. He won't be happy I told the mercs to ask for help finding a new place to live."

"If he refuses, they have our number," said Isabel. "Are you sure you'll be okay? I know Vance will be there, but a murder accusation... it's absurd. How can any of the mages think you'd kill someone in cold blood?"

"I hated the guy," I admitted. "That probably didn't help.

But Lady Granville's out to get me, and this gave her the excuse she needed."

"How…?" she faltered. "How did he die?"

"According to Vance, Ralph was savaged by some kind of animal." I took in a breath. "You know what that usually means. And… and you know who used hellhounds last time."

Isabel gave a grim nod. "I'll get more supplies from the coven and ask them to back me up against the necromancers. Anything else?"

"Just tell the necromancers that the ghosts we've run into are way overpowered. They shouldn't be that strong away from the Ley Line—and being half-fae and not human is irrelevant." Not necessarily true, but I needed to clear my name before I dealt with another round of scepticism from Lord Evander.

"Then I'll speak to them," Isabel said, her jaw set. "If they aren't at the guild, I'll get on the phone and leave them a message every other minute until they answer."

"That'd be great. I need to go. Text me if anything happens." I took off at a fast stride, and when I hit the street corner, I broke into a run.

Too restless to wait for the bus, I sprinted past the stop. Trains had once regularly passed through this part of the suburbs, but the first place the invasion hit had caused a shockwave of destruction across the railway lines. Skeletal carcasses of old trains still sat on the rails, teeming with monsters. I kept my sword out as I passed by the high fence beside a broken-down station, already regretting the decision to run off alone. Not so much out of fear, but because I didn't have *time* to be ambushed.

As I crossed the bridge over the canal, a dark, heavy shape lumbered into view. Most trolls lived under hills, not bridges, but there was the occasional specimen who played up to stereotypes. Here, the shallow water heaved sluggishly along, weighed down by garbage and the rotten bodies of the unfortunate souls dragged under the surface. The troll didn't look much better, its lumpy body dyed blackish grey by the filthy water. I approached slowly, raising my sword.

"Get out the way," I told the troll.

The beast tilted its head, regarding me with eyes like pools of black tar.

"Can we do this later?"

I wasn't about to jump in the canal for a swim, so I kept walking. The troll didn't move until I was within a metre. The stench rolling off it made my eyes water. Screwing my eyes up, I lifted my sword and formed my magic into a shield. Then I ran at the beast, slicing my blade along the lumpy skin of its arm.

I averted my face from the spray of blood, but it never came. I skidded past, ducking the troll's swinging club. Its slow reactions were typical, but despite the gaping wound in its arm, not a drop of blood spilled. *Huh?*

The troll swung again. I ducked, somewhat hindered by the narrow bridge, and drove my blade under its armpit. The troll's heavy body slumped sideways, and as I'd hoped, it lost its balance, tumbling off the bridge into the filthy water.

"Don't say I didn't warn you." I shook my blade, expecting to scatter droplets of blood, but not so much as a crimson smear stained the surface. How could there be no blood? I'd definitely stabbed the creature.

My phone began buzzing again. I swore and shoved the sword back into its sheath. I'd worry about trolls that didn't bleed when cut later. I had to be present at my own trial.

9

I ran to a halt outside the manor's gates, spying the crumbling remains of a tracking spell nearby. At least Lady Granville hadn't dug her heels in and stopped anyone from taking meaningful action, but trackers were no use against disembodied spirits. The spell's remnants stirred in the breeze, and my nose caught the faint hint of a cleansing spell. *Is this where the murder took place?*

My skin prickled. A cleansing spell wouldn't remove any hints of faerie magic that might have lingered, and if the murder had taken place only a couple of hours prior, there ought to be traces. Obviously, the mages wouldn't be able to see them... but *I* could.

I squinted, concentrating hard, willing my eyes to see what my mind refused to believe in. The trick to seeing through faerie glamour was to never look directly at it. I'd learned through observing half-faeries on the streets that even the most powerful glamours were never precise enough to hold up when I observed them through my peripheral vision.

As I tilted my head, the faintest hint of blue faerie magic

came into view, becoming more distinct by the second. The light formed a glimmering trail from the manor's gate, which I followed, one hand on my sword and one eye on the road. Few people drove this way. The entire area belonged to the mages, and though it hadn't been cordoned off, someone had applied cleansing spells at intervals.

The spells had removed the blood, but not the trail of vibrant blue leading to the street's corner. When I neared, my own magic flared up, and I swallowed bile at the sudden sharp taste of panic and fear on my tongue. The residual echoes of someone's death.

Ralph had died here, but someone had carried him to the manor and left his body outside. The killer, or someone else? No traces of blood remained on the pavement, but my Sight showed the vibrant trail the killer had left, and the lingering remnants of Ralph's panic mingled with the glow around my own blade.

Movement from the direction of the manor reminded me I shouldn't be here. I saw a cloaked figure crossing the garden through the hedge and fervently hoped it was Vance.

Quickly, I retraced my steps to the gate and released a sigh of relief when I saw Vance waiting on the other side. "Ivy. I thought I saw you walk past."

"Yeah." I entered the garden, all the remaining traces of magic vanishing behind the neatly clipped hedges. "Did Lady Granville?"

"No, but she's taking no prisoners today. Try not to provoke her."

"Got it." It was obvious from his tone that this was no time for levity or verbal games. I'd give her the facts, straight-up, and she could do with them what she would. "She can't seriously think I killed Ralph. I have no motive."

"I know." He glanced behind him at the gate. "Did you find anything?"

Vance knew me well enough to guess I'd been searching outside before I approached the manor. "A trail of faerie magic. The murder didn't take place outside the gates, but over there." I pointed. "Someone carried the body here to the manor… did you know?"

Vance's mouth tightened. "Don't say that in the meeting."

"Wasn't planning to." My heart rate kicked up. "They're already waiting? Is anyone else on the suspect list?"

You'd think the sheer number of visitors would have pushed me out of consideration, but almost all the other non-mages had left after the party. The only people from outside the city were mages, whose status alone protected them from being accused. The sheer injustice burned inside me like a brand.

We reached the front door. I took in a breath, steeling myself. "I'm going in with the assumption that I'll get to walk out of here today and not in handcuffs. Fair warning, if not, there's going to be a problem."

"You won't be arrested." He rested a hand on my shoulder. "I'm here."

I wished I shared his confidence. Lady Granville would leap at the chance to punish both of us at once for getting in the way of her ambitions, and even Vance's Mage Lord status had its limits.

Partway down the hallway, an obvious question hit me. "Is Lady Harper around? Can't she read my mind and prove my innocence?" Not that I exactly relished the idea of another grilling, but between that and being jailed for murder, I'd suffer the humiliation.

"No. She isn't around."

"Fuck." My hands clenched. "Well. It was worth a shot."

He kept one arm around my shoulders as we walked upstairs to the meeting room. Then he released me and pushed open the door. Lady Granville waited expectantly at the table, around which the rest of the mage council had gathered.

"There you are, Ivy." Her tone was that of a teacher whose pupil had shown up halfway through a lesson. "We've been waiting for you for quite some time."

"I was on a job." *Okay. Play nice.* "I left before Ralph died. I didn't see who was responsible."

"That remains to be seen." She beckoned me to sit down in a vacant chair. I forced a neutral expression as I took a seat between her and Drake. Even the fire mage looked unusually sombre.

"Where exactly where you today?" asked Lady Granville.

I surreptitiously adjusted my sword so it wasn't poking out of the sheath. White bits of plaster scattered where I sat, a reminder that I was still covered in dust. You'd think the universe might have given me a break after the ghost had thrown me through the floorboards and dumped a ceiling on my head, but no such luck.

"On a case in mercenary district," I told her. "Ask Isabel. I've been with her since I left the manor this morning. We were hired to deal with a ghost inside one of the apartment blocks. I can give more details of the mission if need be."

"What time did you leave?"

"Around nine thirty. Vance took me directly home. I never even stepped outside the manor doors."

"A ghost," she repeated. "A different client to the last one? Did you inform the mages?"

"I was going to bring a copy of the contract, but I was on my way home when I got the call from Vance," I said. "The case was via an independent client. The coven liaised with the necromancers to borrow some equipment and we went there immediately after signing the contract."

None of that was against the rules, but I hadn't reckoned on having to recount the entire case in front of a bunch of strangers, especially when I didn't fully understand everything that had taken place myself. I sure as hell wouldn't mention the part where I'd made the ghost explode with my own hands and not a sensor.

"And?" she pressed. "What then?"

"We banished the ghost." No need to get into specifics. "I got the call from Vance when I was outside and came here as soon as I could."

"That was…" She checked her watch. "Nearly an hour ago."

My jaw twitched in annoyance. "Yes. I was on the other side of town. Listen, I'm not the killer. I'll be honest and say Ralph and I weren't friends, but I'd have had nothing to gain from senselessly murdering him. And I haven't seen a hellhound since I killed Calder." Which didn't mean much, but I could hardly tell Lady Granville that the main person I suspected was *dead*.

"You're the only person here to have had contact with hellhounds," she said.

"Contact?" Did she mean when I'd stuck my sword in them? I doubted it. "They attacked and nearly killed my best friend a few months ago, if that's what you mean. They're wild animals."

"They obey commands," she said. "According to our records, they have a single master at any given time, and if you're telling the truth, the previous one is dead."

Had she seriously delved into research on the fae for the purposes of proving my guilt? "Yes, because I killed him. Your tracking spells will have shown you the hellhounds' location, which was a long way from where I spent the morning."

"Yes." Her blue eyes were flinty. "Everyone who used a tracking spell gave the same report. The origin is at the Ley Line, where you've been known to operate from."

She made me sound like an evil mastermind. "Operate? It's a place where powerful magic can avoid detection. Calder concealed the hellhounds there when he summoned them. As far as I know, only Sidhe, or half-Sidhe, can give them orders."

Given what my magic had been capable of in the past, maybe I *could* control hellhounds, but at this rate I'd find myself in the mages' jail before I could test that claim.

"Then who do you propose is giving them orders, if not yourself?"

"I don't know. Calder's dead. Velkas is, too." I needed to find another direction. "We could... well, we could ask Ralph's ghost. He's half—no, three quarters human. The necromancers should be able to reach him and ask if he remembers his death."

"She has a point," Drake ventured. "That isn't against our procedures. We've consulted the necromancers before."

"And tell them we allowed someone on our staff to be murdered within full view of our headquarters?" asked Lady Granville. "No. I won't allow it."

My mouth parted. "The necromancers can keep a secret. It's pretty much in their job description."

"They're failing at their duties," said Lady Granville. "They've been struggling to keep the undead from rising for weeks. Today is the final straw."

"For what?" I hadn't the faintest idea what she was implying. "You want Lord Evander to step down? I suppose he deserves it, but I'm pretty sure the mages don't get to make that call."

"We don't have authority over the necromancers," said Lady Granville. "We do, however, have the means to sever our relations with them."

"What would that achieve?" Vance cut in. "I'm no friend

of Lord Evander's, but it seems to me that turning on our allies at a time like this is the height of folly."

Thanks for that, Vance. "Exactly. Someone as good as declared war on the mages, and sending our allies away will only make things worse."

"You aren't a voice on this council," said Lady Granville. "You've done everything to implicate yourself in Ralph's death."

"I offered you a solution," I corrected. "Speaking to his ghost would clear up the matter. No disputing that."

But Lady Granville thrived on certainty and clear-cut answers. Rules were black and white for her. Grey areas, like the dead, or the faeries, didn't even register as legitimate sources of information.

"I disagree," she said. "Assuming the necromancers were able to reach him—which I very much doubt—there's nothing to say that Ralph would be a reliable witness to his own demise."

Not inaccurate, given my general experience of ghosts. They tended to forget the details of their deaths upon the shock of entering the afterlife, but summoning his spirit would be a damn sight more useful than sitting through a pointless interrogation. "Regardless, if hellhounds were indeed responsible for his murder, I'd be more than happy to hunt them down myself."

"Out of the question," she said. "This is undeniably the faeries' work, and you're known to be their ally."

I twitched in my seat, my sword brushing against my shin. "I'm the only person in this room who can *see* faerie magic. Moreover, I've been attacked by two ghosts in the last two days, and both were half-faeries. Hardly allies."

"That has nothing to do with this outrageous murder," said Lady Granville.

"Need I remind you that I was the one who recommended inviting Ivy here to consult with the mage council?" Vance said. "She has more experience hunting faeries than anyone else here."

"I have the Sight," I added. "That means I can see and hear things other humans can't. If I take a position on the search team, I stand a good chance of finding whoever did this."

Whichever side of the grave they might be on.

"We have no need of any more assistance," she said dismissively. "We've already identified the creature responsible, and all that remains is for us to track it down."

Good luck doing that without the Sight. My thoughts jumped back to the flaring beacon on the road's corner, the proof that someone had carried the body to the gates... but what had Ralph been doing over there in the first place?

"Were there other guards outside?" I caught Vance's eye, and he inclined his head. "Who was the last person to see Ralph alive?"

"That's a good question," Drake said. "What did the guards have to say for themselves?"

"I already spoke to both of them." Lady Granville's nostrils flared. "They didn't see Ralph leave the manor."

"You'd think one of them would have heard a hellhound attack on the doorstep." My suspicions multiplied. "Someone should question them again."

"As I told you, Ivy, I am in charge of the investigation."

"It seems pertinent to know what the guards were doing immediately before Ralph's death," Vance interjected. "I believe we should ask them some more questions."

At a guess, Lady Granville had dragged everyone in here instead of properly speaking to the guards. While I might have suspected her of purposefully sabotaging our attempts to find the killer, her own ambition was motive enough to ensure that the person who went to jail for the crime was the one who was the biggest threat to her plans, as opposed to the actual murderer.

Lady Granville's mouth thinned. "Very well. Lord Carlisle, will you speak to the guards? Ask Lady Harper to help, if she is amenable. I shall join you after I finish ascertaining Ivy's innocence."

"Lady Harper has already declined to be involved," said Lord Carlisle in his gravelly voice.

"She has," Lady Penrose agreed. "With your permission, I shall accompany Lord Carlisle."

"Very well." She sat back, while I suppressed the urge to follow. I wanted to speak to the guards myself, to find out how the faeries had slipped their attention, but Lady Granville flat-out refused to let me leave the room. Instead, she subjected me to yet more questions, each more pointless than the last.

By the time Lord Carlisle and Lady Penrose returned, I'd burned through the remnants of my patience. Drake, too, kept fidgeting, his knee jiggling the table and occasionally knocking piles of paperwork askew. The twitch in Lady Granville's door betrayed her annoyance, but I was the focus of her ire, and not a word I spoke was enough to assuage her suspicions.

Lord Carlisle took his seat again. "The two guards who were supposed to be outside this morning slept through their shift."

"Really?" Vance frowned at him. "That's certainly not what they said when we spoke earlier."

"Should we talk to them, too?" Drake rose upright, hopefully.

"No," Lady Granville said. "What was their story?"

"They claimed to be suffering from memory loss." Lord Carlisle's gaze slid to Vance. "Perhaps understandable after gala last night."

"They were hungover?" I asked, disbelieving. "Though… memory loss also sounds like the effect of a potion or spell."

"I was careful to appoint guards who behaved responsibly last night," Vance said. "I spoke to them after the party's end as well as this morning."

"They were bewitched, then?" Drake's usual grin disappeared. "They weren't drugged, were they?"

"Faerie mind tricks," I guessed. "Glamours can affect all the senses, not just sight."

"We shall see." Lady Granville outright ignored me. "I'll question them myself."

"So will I." Vance rose to his feet, too. "We'll get this situation cleared up."

"And Ivy will stay here," said Lady Granville. "I believe Lord Carlisle and Lady Penrose will want to hear everything they missed while they were downstairs."

"They didn't miss anything." She was spouting utter bullshit, but to my indignation, Vance didn't leap to my defence.

"Very well." He locked eyes with me briefly before he addressed the remaining mages. "However, I don't believe for a second the guilty party is present in this building."

He left, as did Lady Granville. Rationally, I knew he wanted to speak to the guards before Lady Granville swept his authority out from underneath him, but damn, *I* was the one with the Sight. I knew glamours. I caught Drake's eye, hoping he'd 'accidentally' set a pile of paperwork on fire and set off the sprinkler system so I could get the hell out of here. He didn't look overly thrilled at Vance's departure either, but the instant the door closed, a blinding glow made me jump out of my seat.

My sword had ignited, reacting to a threat. *Faeries.*

I leapt back as something whizzed past my face and burst into sparkling fragments above the table. At once, every single mage slumped in their seats, with the exception of Drake and me.

I stared in bemusement. The glitter had suggested a witch spell, but my sword's reaction said otherwise. Heart racing, I looked at Drake, who cracked up laughing inexplicably. Then a pointy-eared figure ran into the room.

I gaped at him. "Quentin?"

"Come with me, human, before the others notice."

"Did you just knock out two council members?" Not just them. Everyone at the table was unconscious. Since when had he had that kind of power at his fingertips?

"On the Mage Lord's orders," the brownie said in his gravelly voice.

"What?" I swivelled to Drake. "What the fuck was that?"

"Vance," he said between laughs. "I hope you did the same to Lady Granville, Quentin. Cheers."

"I didn't." Quentin beckoned with an impatient hand. "Lady Granville is in charge of the investigation, and the Mage Lord decided it was simpler to let her think she's had her way so we can find the killer as soon as possible."

Oh. "You want me to sneak out, investigate on my own, and come back before they realise I'm gone?"

"Yes."

"This is brilliant." Drake snickered. "Vance is bloody devious when he wants to be."

"Couldn't he have told me first?" Honestly. "He's the Mage Lord. If he wanted, he could overturn every one of Lady Granville's attempts to derail the investigation."

"Not without significant delays that might prevent him from catching the culprit behind Ralph's death," said Quentin.

"And what happens when Lady Granville comes back in here to find everyone unconscious?"

"You'll be back before she is," said Quentin. "At least, if you have any kind of sense, you will."

"Noted." I took in a breath. "You'd better cover for me, Quentin, otherwise they'll hang me out to dry."

I left the room, but when Drake tried to follow, the brownie barred the way. "Stay here and make sure the council members don't stir. They shouldn't remember any of this when they wake up."

"What?" Drake's face fell. "You expect me to stay in the same room as two sleeping Mage Lords and *not* draw dicks on their faces?"

I closed the door on his complaints and followed Quentin to a back staircase. Even now, I still got lost on a regular basis whenever I ventured away from the rooms in the manor I used the most often, and it came as something of a surprise to find an exit I'd never seen before. The brownie opened the door onto an alleyway bordered by a brick wall.

"Come back in through the same route," he told me. "There are guards in both the front and back gardens, but this entrance is for staff only."

Erm... isn't he *the only permanent staff?* "Quentin, why are you doing this? Did *you* see anything last night?"

"Such as?"

"Faerie magic," I said. "Both Ralph and I thought we saw a blue glow outside, but it vanished before we could get a closer look."

"I was occupied with the guests," he growled. "However, that's reason enough for you to hurry."

"Right, right." I slipped out the side door and made my careful way down the alley. I wished I'd brought one of Isabel's shadow spells, but at least Vance and Quentin would keep the others distracted. And if Wanda looked out the window, I trusted that she'd cover for me, too.

I slowed my pace as I neared the street corner. The blue

glow remained, but the trail of faerie magic ceased as suddenly as though the person who'd used it had vanished into thin air. Which, if they were a ghost, was not out of the realm of possibility.

All right. Vance and I hadn't discussed a plan, but I had infinitely more options here than trapped in a council room. Whipping a tracking spell from my pocket, I crouched down.

Green light flared, circling the spot where the faerie magic had coalesced. The cleansing spells had scrubbed all traces of blood from the scene, so this would be less effective than usual, but a glimpse into Ralph's death might be enough to point me to the culprit.

I leaned forward, my vision tunnelling and all colour leaching from my surroundings. It was always disorientating to see the same place at a different time and date, without any colour or sound. A cloaked figure passed by, making me jump, but it was only a mage. Which meant I wasn't seeing Ralph's death, but whatever had occurred right after. The cloaked figure was unrecognisable from the back view, walking from the corner to the spot where blue light shone in a halo.

Another figure watched from near the light, unnoticed by the mage. *A spirit?*

I squinted, trying to see, but the dazzling light made it difficult to see if the second figure was transparent. An instant later, the vision faded out. Goosebumps prickled at my arms. Had I seen a ghost? The mage in the vision sure as hell hadn't, but there was one way to check.

Vance would be less than thrilled that my first instinct was to take a jaunt into the afterlife, but the other mages had trampled all over the crime scene and scrubbed the place for good measure. I could try another tracking spell at a different spot, but there wasn't time to pick my way across every inch of the road until I found somewhere untouched by Lady Granville and her allies' meddling.

So be it. I returned to the alley alongside the manor and positioned myself out of sight of any windows. Then I closed my eyes and willed myself to shift into Death.

The crossing was smoother than I'd expected considering how far I was from the Ley Line. All bodily sensations vanished as grey smoke overlaid my vision and formed a uniform landscape, unbroken save for the faint outlines of other spirits.

Except there weren't any. Not a single spirit drifted past. It was a ghost town. Minus the town. And the ghosts. *Okay, that doesn't work, Ivy.*

"Frank?" I asked uncertainly. My voice didn't echo, but the area in front of me rippled as though I'd blown out a breath into frigid winter air.

Where is he? Death wasn't a physical plane, so my body would remain in the alleyway no matter how far my spirit moved. Necromancers could theoretically bring their physical bodies along for the ride, but the mere act of crossing into Death without a summoning circle was considered suicidal. My magic, which directly bound me to Death, made me an exception. I wasn't too worried I might get stuck here, but where were the other ghosts?

"Frank?" I'd run into him every time I'd crossed over the veil, so he must be somewhere nearby, but I saw no signs of anyone.

"Ivy?" That wasn't Frank. The female voice came from about a metre away, and as I drifted that way, I spied a semi-transparent figure hovering, her features revealing themselves the longer I watched her. Long, curly hair, pointed ears, and a faint green glow that could only mean faerie magic.

My heart sank. Which made no sense because I didn't have one. "Alain?"

"Did you—did you die, too?" she asked tremulously. She reached for my hand, but her fingers passed right through mine. "Have you seen Lucas?"

"You're dead." No shit, Ivy. Lucas, I recalled, was her boyfriend, the charming individual who'd once set a kelpie on me and had later fallen under the influence of a certain drug. Then he'd got locked up for... *oh, no. The deaths at the jail. Was he involved?*

Her face crumpled, her body blurring around the edges. "I had to try. He was innocent."

"You didn't try to break him out of jail. Did you?"

"He didn't mean to kill anyone," she whimpered. "But... *you* can't be dead. Are you?"

"I'm not." I didn't need to get into that, not now. "It's a long story. I was looking for someone else... but who killed you?"

"I don't know." She sobbed, her voice fading in and out, like a badly tuned radio. "I was at the jail, and next thing I knew, I was here."

Damn. "And Lucas?"

"I haven't been able to find him." She whimpered. "It's so unfair."

"You'll see him again." Pity rose inside me . "Find a necromancer. There's a guy called Frank over here. He'll take you to Lucas. Promise."

"I'd never believe a promise from you," she spat with sudden venom. "The necromancers will take me away from him forever."

"No, you'll move on together, like you're supposed to." I spoke in a firm tone despite my sympathy. We didn't need *another* half-faerie ghost lingering beyond the grave to cause trouble. "Someone will come and help you."

"I don't want to move on."

"Trust me, you do." As bad as I felt for her predicament, I had my doubts she was the one who'd set the hellhounds on Ralph, and there was only so long I could leave my own body vacantly standing around an alleyway until someone noticed. Or worse, Lady Granville figured out I'd slipped out of the manor. "I'm here to find someone who was murdered recently. A part-faerie guard who worked at the mages' headquarters. Did you see him?"

"I can't see *anyone* here," she wailed. "I'm stuck here forever, and it's *your* fault."

"Hey, *I* didn't kill you." I wouldn't get any more sense out of her. That much was abundantly clear. "What am I supposed to have done?"

"You killed Calder!"

His name echoed, shrill, and my heart plummeted. "Have… you seen him?"

"He's here, Ivy. He wants you."

"He can't have me." Fuck. My fears were right on the mark. I'd had a few months' reprieve, but my worst enemy was well and truly back. "Whereabouts is he hiding?"

A burning sensation rent through my shoulder. I fell, as though someone had yanked the ground out from underneath me, and slammed back into my body. Staggering against the alley wall, I pressed a hand to my shoulder, tugging down the sleeve. The glyph stood out in a blistering red circle like someone had pressed a brand to my skin.

Vance was being attacked. He'd called for my help.

10

The mark burned again, and alarm sang through my veins. Vance had never called for my help before, especially not when he'd gone to such lengths to stop Lady Granville from discovering my absence.

There was only one explanation: *faeries*.

I ran, feet smacking the pavement, my sword lighting the air. The blue glow enveloped me, and the glyph burned, almost like a compass dragging my body in the right direction. I'd never asked Vance how it'd felt when I'd done the same for him, but he had the advantage of being able to teleport to my side. I had to travel the slow way, even with the enhanced speed my magic gifted me.

My feet skimmed the pavement as I followed the invisible path west of the manor, towards half-blood territory then northward. My bafflement grew the longer I went without seeing Vance, my path carrying me through deserted streets lined with houses destroyed in the invasion. What was Vance doing all the way out here? From the size of the houses, this part of the city had once belonged to the mages, but now the large houses sported shattered windows and torn-up gardens.

Worry clawing at my chest, I glided down the street, then another, until the houses came to an abrupt end near a field I recognised as the location of the mages' depository.

Oh, no. Not too far from here was the building where I'd left the talisman. Why had he come here? Had there been another attack? I spied one of the mages' cars parked on a corner, and the burning sensation in my shoulder reached its peak when I came to a rusting metal gate. Graves lay beyond, albeit in a visibly more neglected state than the ones outside the necromancers' headquarters. Was this where the undead that had attacked the storeroom had come from?

More to the point, why would the mages have come here with a murderous ghost on the loose in the city? *Dammit, Lady Granville.* I *assumed* she was to blame, though I thought she'd refused point-blank to entertain the idea of the dead being involved in Ralph's murder.

Whatever was going on, the glyph on my shoulder didn't lie. Vance needed me.

The gate opened on a cemetery shrouded in darkness that went beyond any natural gloom. The pale light of the sun didn't touch this area at all, like a barrier lay between the cemetery and the overcast sky.

I'd only seen that kind of darkness in the Grey Vale.

I clenched my hand around my sword and stalked forwards as though I was the one doing the hunting and not the other way around.

I'll find you, Vance.

I held the sword high, willing its light to repel the darkness. It was the middle of the day. This level of dark wasn't natural, and not caused by the undead, either, though I was fairly sure they were responsible for the stench filling my nostrils the further I walked.

I nearly tripped over the first body. A mage lay sprawled, blood soaking his white shirt. He couldn't be older than twenty.

Someone will die. Within three days.

Oh, god.

A second body lay alongside him, a blond woman sprawled in such a position that suggested she'd thrown herself in front of the other guy to protect him, and with a similar stab wound in her chest. I'd never spoken to either of them before, but I'd seen them among Vance's security at the manor.

I couldn't tell if either was still breathing, but I grabbed a pair of healing spells from my jacket and threw one over each body. Then I let the light from my sword illuminate the path through the broken headstones. This place hadn't just been abandoned; it'd been desecrated. Recently. Thick black tendrils of plant spilled over the graves. *Ugh.* I'd spent an unpleasant night strung up by the feet when a strain of this particular plant had invaded Avalin's castle one of the times he'd gone away for a week, but I couldn't remember which fae they belonged to.

I walked further into the cemetery, my sword's blue glow alighting on a row of intact graves beside a small brick mausoleum.

I ran around the corner and smack into a tall figure. "I— *Vance.* Thank god. What happened?"

"Don't move, Ivy," he warned. "It's—"

"A trap," I finished.

A current of energy smacked into me with the force of a rampaging troll. The air left my lungs as I was flung backwards, but I flipped over and managed to land on my feet. My legs crouched at the impact, both hands gripping my sword.

A vaguely defined shape outlined in neon blue flew at me. I raised my sword, cutting through nothingness. *Another ghost?*

More than one. I counted at least five indistinct shapes floating above the graves, etched in blue light. Like me, when I passed into Death. Half-faeries.

One of them turned to me, outlined in blue, his face twisted into an angry snarl. Even blurred and indistinct, I recognised Alain's deceased arsehole of a boyfriend. So this was where Lucas was hanging out.

I raised my sword and willed the fear and panic rolling around the cemetery to flow into the blade. Energy surged out in a wave that struck the ghosts-head on. The spirit that had attacked me burst apart in a flare of blue light, and the others fled, shrieking, vanishing amid the graves.

"Nasty bugger." I lowered my sword. "That was a half-faerie ghost. Same thing happened to the one I killed earlier."

"Same... what?" He peered at the spot where the ghost had been. "I saw a flash of light."

"It exploded. The ghost did." I shuddered. "Not in an ecto-plasm-style way either. Figured that mentioning that in front of our intrepid investigator would make me look guiltier than I already did."

Which conjured up another array of questions. Starting with: "You used the glyph. I thought you were dying."

"Shouldn't I have?" His eyes flickered with concern. "When those spirits attacked, I assumed not having the Sight would get my people killed."

"No, you were right, I'm just surprised you wanted me to risk exposing myself." I scanned the nearby graves. "Unless you buried Lady Granville alive?"

"Not quite, but she came straight here when the guards from the manor recounted that they visited the cemetery earlier this morning. Their memories were defective, but Lady Harper was able to extract something of use."

"Lady *Harper?*" Horror rooted me to the spot. "Please tell me they volunteered willingly."

"Of course. I'd never have made the suggestion if she hadn't recanted her intention not to get involved."

"I should bloody well hope so," I said. "I notice she didn't volunteer to read *my* mind to prove my innocence. I left two unconscious Mage Lords in the council room, too. How much shit will I be in when I'm back?"

"None, if I have anything to do with it." He scanned the cemetery. "It helps now the ghosts have gone. There were undead everywhere, too. Some people got hurt."

"Yeah." I swallowed, thinking of the bodies I'd tripped over on the way in. "Thanks for calling me."

He grunted. "Only you would thank me for bringing you into a nest of undead."

"Well, when you put it like that..." I raised my sword, its blue light spilling over the surrounding graves and revealing a bloody trail leading up Vance's arm. "You're injured."

"I'll be fine. I'll get a healing spell."

"There were two people hurt over there." I watched the light of the spell ignite over his arm. "I used healing spells, but I don't know if I got here in time."

"The guards." Worry flickered in his eyes. "I'll check on them. The others..."

"Where's Lady Granville?" I took the lead. Someone had called those ghosts, and while I'd sent them packing, more of the thick black substance oozed between the graves and made it difficult to find a route through the darkness.

Vance moved to my side. "I couldn't see a thing past this point, but Drake's somewhere over there as well."

"Oh—right." I gestured at the oozing blackness. "You

probably can't see there's a nasty slimy plant all over everything either. Follow me and watch where I tread."

I focused on the blue glow of my sword, illuminating graves draped in slick blackness and not much else. My ears picked up on faint skittering noises, and I held out a hand for Vance to stop.

A semi-transparent shape rose from behind a gravestone, elongating as it straightened upright. Thick limbs supported a misshapen body and a lumpy head.

Sluagh. I had to think for a moment to remember the name. Not a species I'd seen in this realm before. Its form was partly physical, partly incorporeal, and resembled a cuddly toy that'd gone through one too many spin cycles. Except a hundred times more grotesque.

The sluagh's mouth opened and a flurry of spiders spilled out.

"Oh, lovely." I swept my blade through the oncoming horde, spraying blue-tinged blood into the blackness underneath our feet. Vance moved with a snarl, his own blade flashing out, though his inability to see his targets was a hindrance.

I stepped in front of him and sent a current of magic sweeping towards the sluagh. The creature dodged, sliding across the ground like the slimy plants it had doubtless conjured.

Vance's sword swiped surprisingly close to its target, but a physical weapon would have no effect on the creature in its semi-corporeal form. I'd have to wait until it solidified... or use magic.

Threads of darkness whipped out and flung me sideways. My back slammed into a headstone, and I fell onto my knees on wet grass. I brought my sword up, and a viscous black liquid spilled down the blade. I yanked the blade free and cut at the darkness again, this time slicing through empty air.

A pair of grasping hands latched onto my elbow. I struck out and bones shattered. Human hands meant undead. I lifted a hand and blasted magic over my shoulder without looking at them and kept my attention on the sluagh.

Vance's two swords appeared and disappeared, dealing blows both to the undead and the sluagh, but he had to use guesswork to find the latter, and the black substance seemed to have slowed his weapons down more than mine. Oily stickiness covered the blade's edge, but it was no hindrance to my speed. I sent a burst of magic outward at the sluagh, but the wave of energy passed right through its target.

What the hell? I'd never met a faerie my magic didn't affect before, but sluagh were death fae, which might give them some level of resistance. I struck out with my blade and sent a second wave of energy at the sluagh, but once again, my attack passed right through its semi-transparent body.

Come on. Hadn't I exploded a ghost with the same power? What was up with this faerie? Teeth gritted, I raised my blade and called upon the pain and fear I knew must be lurking under the surface of the graveyard.

A scream rang through my head. The blue light grew brighter even as I trembled at the horrible noise. Someone had been tortured here, the echo of their pain imprinted on the afterlife long after their death.

My shaking hands locked onto the sword's hilt, my own anger mingled with the echoing pain reverberating through the air. I leaped at the semi-transparent form of the sluagh, and my sword pierced its bulbous head. Spiders exploded from its mouth, but I ignored the unpleasant tickling sensation and fired magic into its open maw.

The sluagh's dark form collapsed back in on itself like a folding chair. The black substance covering the graves turned transparent as the power sustaining its growth faded, and the spiders vanished, too.

"That fucker was stronger than I expected." A gasp lodged in my throat when the blackness receded, revealing a body curled up beneath. Bright coppery hair stood out in the gloom. *Oh, no.*

"Drake?" I climbed over to him. "Shit."

Vance moved to my side, conjuring a healing spell. "He's alive."

Drake groaned, and I sagged against the nearest grave in relief. My hands were cold and clammy. I hadn't passed into Death, but I'd felt its presence through my sword. Someone who'd been killed here… by the Sidhe.

I swallowed hard. I'd deal with that later. "Drake? Did you follow me?"

"No, I followed Vance." As the healing spell's light faded, he sat up and rubbed his forehead. "I assumed you'd already be here, though."

"Unlike you, I listened to Quentin." I looked for Lady Granville, but no other bodies had been exposed when the fae plant receded.

Footsteps came from behind a tall headstone on the right. I moved closer, spying more undead lumbering over, unsteady on their skeletal feet. I reached for my container of salt.

Vance joined me. "Drake, stay there."

"Like I can move." He groaned again. "Feels like someone put their icy hands inside my body."

I get that feeling. "They're persistent, aren't they?"

I raised a hand to blast the undead, and the ground exploded. I reeled back as earth shot in every direction, along with bits of decomposing flesh.

"What is going on?" Lady Granville marched over to us. Her pinstripe suit was covered in soil and bits of zombie, and it took a moment for me to realise the ground moving had been due to her using earth magic. I'd never seen her mage abilities in action before.

"Erm…" I looked sheepishly at Vance, then back at Lady Granville. "Please tell me you didn't disturb the dead."

Had her earth magic been responsible for those zombies? Likely not, if they'd already been stirring, but I kind of wished she'd been buried underneath the faerie plant and not Drake.

"Ivy Lane," said Lady Granville. "You aren't supposed to be outside of the manor."

"I called her," Vance said, without missing a beat. "Given the danger, I decided it was in our interests to have an ally present with the ability to see our attackers where we could not."

"She saved my arse," Drake added, spitting out dirt. "You, however, nearly buried me alive."

"This is the fault of the necromancers," said Lady Granville, without so much as an apology. "Their job is to bind the dead."

"They're on the other side of the city," I reminded her. "I'll talk to Lord Evander—"

"No," said Lady Granville. "Someone at his guild is clearly working against us. None but a necromancer is capable of raising the dead."

"The undead are capable of raising themselves." Surely even she knew that. Didn't mean one of his other necromancers hadn't turned traitor like last time, but shunning their fellow supernaturals would only hurt the mages. I didn't know anyone else who could banish the dead… except for me, of course.

Lady Granville opened her mouth to argue, but Drake cut in. "Don't challenge us on this one. You're in over your head."

Unfortunately, the same might be said of the rest of us. I picked my way around the undead as we retraced our steps from the mausoleum, wondering if they were the same ones who'd attacked the storeroom. Some wore the tattered remains of what had once been cloaks, but others were decidedly *not* mages. One, a small figure with pointed ears, wore a faded cap stained in blood, hands twitching with the energy that fuelled the restless dead. A redcap, one of the fae drawn to sites of murder.

"Fuck me," I breathed. "Those aren't human dead."

"What?" Vance came to a sharp halt behind me. "What is it?"

"The undead." I gestured to the shredded remnants of zombies around us. "That's not a human. It's a redcap. Some of the others are fae, too."

Even Lady Granville stared at me in the ensuing silence.

"What?" Drake recovered first. "Our enemy ran out of humans and decided to resurrect faeries, too?"

"They shouldn't *exist*. At least, I've never seen one before." I backtracked. "I mean, pure faeries are immortal, but..."

My mind veered back to that troll on the bridge. It hadn't bled when I'd sliced it open. *No way.*

When nobody else spoke, I cleared my throat and tried to inject some calm into m voice. "I don't think it's a usual epidemic the necromancers are dealing with. I think undead fae are showing up as well as humans."

"You just said they're immortal," said Lady Granville, though with less of her usual bluster.

"Half-faeries can die like us, and so can pure faeries if they spend too long in this realm. Guess it makes sense they can come back as undead. Question is, who raised them in the first place?"

"There's one obvious answer."

"Not the necromancers. They don't know a thing about faeries. Lord Evander included." I could guarantee he would argue to the ends of the earth that it was impossible to raise a faerie from death. I almost hoped Lady Granville would call him and prove my point, not least because then they'd both be out of my hair. "A troll jumped me earlier, too, on the way to the manor. I cut it with my sword, and it didn't bleed. I'd never seen a half-faerie undead before, and I was in a hurry, so I didn't stop to look closer."

"Why?" Drake pulled a face. "I've never seen the point in raising people from death anyway, but a troll? They make terrible conversationalists when they're alive, let alone dead."

"I don't know what's going on." I *did* know this must be connected to the half-faerie ghosts I'd encountered—and to the one who might be giving them orders. "Let's get out of here first."

"Agreed," said Vance. "We can discuss our options when we're back at the manor."

At least I'd put my trial on hold for the time being, but on top of Ralph's murder, we had another mystery to solve... why would anyone raise faeries from the dead?

———

"Nobody is to act without consulting me first," Vance told the assembled mages as the afternoon's meeting finally drew to a close. "I will speak to Lord Evander myself. I'd strongly advise taking precautions if you leave the manor."

For once, nobody argued. I'd expected to face more back-lash for my disappearing act, but thanks to whatever trickery Quentin had used, the mages were convinced I'd run out of the meeting room from under their noses in pursuit of Vance and not that they'd been out cold at the time. I owed the brownie, majorly, for covering my tracks.

The other bright spot in my day was that Lord Evander had officially taken my spot at the top of the murder suspect list, and I'd faced the minimum of questions about how I'd ended up at the cemetery. Vance helped, of course, and he implied he'd called me on the phone rather than using a glyph to summon me to his side. The omission puzzled me a little, but I wouldn't complain about avoiding Lady Granville's judgement at my being bound so intimately to the Mage Lord that he could summon me to his side with a mere touch. It was none of her fucking business regardless.

Lady Granville gave me a filthy look as I stood up to leave, my jacket scattering soil and dead spiders on the table. She'd somehow had time to use a cleansing spell, but I'd been more concerned with helping Vance move the injured mages than with the state of my clothes. The two mages I'd found at the cemetery entrance had survived, though they hadn't woken up yet. Given that they were the same guards who'd had their minds scrambled by Lady Harper earlier, I expected they'd be shaken up for a while.

We hadn't come to any definite conclusions at the meeting, but Vance had arranged for a broadcast to be sent out on the mages' radio station informing the public that certain measures were in place to deal with rogue undead. He'd kept the content vague and hadn't mentioned that the faeries seemed to be rising from death and not just humans. I'd wanted to tell them the truth, but he'd rightly pointed out that if the fae were rising from death, they'd be more common in the areas of the city that people already knew to avoid. I conceded and left the room ahead of the others before Lady Granville changed her mind about interrogating me again.

I waited for Vance near his office in the main hallway. When he came downstairs, I beckoned to him. "Can we talk alone?"

"Sure." When he'd closed his office door behind us, he faced me with a worried frown. "I'm sorry I didn't tell you that I planned to get you out of that room. Or did you wonder why I called you to the cemetery using the glyph?"

"I'm glad you did," I said. "Given the ghosts. Some of them might have stuck around, but I guess it's too much to ask for the necromancers to hunt them down."

"No doubt," he said. "Given the undead fae, too… are you certain they were true fae?"

"As opposed to half-bloods?" I nodded. "Full-blooded faeries can die in this realm. They lose their immortality when they spend too long here. I don't think they can come back as ghosts, but before this morning, I wouldn't have said they could become undead either." I wiped my hands on my jeans, feeling the phantom shiver of death's touch on my bare skin.

Vance's gaze shadowed. "You've never seen one before?"

"What, undead? No, not in the Grey Vale." Given the number of beasts there that fed on corpses, the odds of a dead body lasting long enough to be revived were low. "Or ghosts? Only human ones. Any fae that die in there either disappear or turn into wraiths. I guess they're like ghosts, but not the sort we get here."

Avalin's ghostly echo had been more concentrated magic than a sentient being. As for human ghosts, I'd at least managed to get Helena out during my last trip over to the Vale. She was at peace now in the true afterlife, which brought me comfort enough to let go of the guilt of my role in her death.

Vance inclined his head. "I imagine fae undead have the same vulnerabilities as human ones."

"Salt," I agreed. "Is Lady Granville going to ease up on the bullshit now she has someone else to point the blame at? Because I have a plan, but it involves being left alone and allowed to do my own thing."

"She won't," said Vance. "She's not a fool, and you're the reason we got out of that cemetery. She won't forget that."

"Good, because I have enough enemies." Now we'd left the meeting, it was time to face the subject I'd been avoiding. "You should know… two ghosts so far have mentioned Calder's name. Including the one Isabel and I dealt with this morning."

Vance's shoulders stiffened. "Calder?"

My heart gave a spasm. "Yeah. One, I might have been able to ignore, but the second ghost, I knew when she was still alive. Alain. You know, the one whose boyfriend set a kelpie on me. Turns out she was one of the half-faeries who broke the others out of jail and ended up dead. So did her boyfriend. I saw him at the cemetery."

Vance's expression remained inscrutable. "What did she say?"

"About Calder?" Even now, his name left the taste of fear on my tongue. "She said it's my fault she died, because I killed Calder. Not sure on her logic, but my gut tells me he's behind this. He wants to return from death, like he promised."

Vance shook his head. "Even if he did somehow endure as a ghost, his power will be nonexistent, and his body was destroyed. I made sure of it."

"Oh, right." I relaxed, marginally. "Not having a body is bound to be an obstacle to returning from death, but he's still dangerous as a disembodied spirit, and nobody else will even believe he's a threat."

Vance's hand closed over mine. "I believe you. I won't deny the situation is worrying, to say the least, but we'll speak to the Chief tomorrow and see what he says."

"I doubt that'll have any more result than talking to the necromancers." I squeezed his hand back, though. "You know

Calder, though. That guy's persistent enough that if anyone *can* find a way to return from death, it'll be him."

"It's not possible to reunite a soul with a body once it's been severed," said Vance. "Lord Evander told me as much, and only necromancers have true power over death."

But that's not true. I do. To some extent, anyway. Calder, too, had inherited his magic from Avalin. "His magic… it's not exactly conventional."

"You sealed his magic, did you not?"

"Oh." It'd slipped my mind, but back when I'd duelled Calder, I'd spoken an Invocation to seal away all the magic he'd stirred up, therefore closing the door to Faerie he'd opened. If he wanted to try the same again, he'd have to start from scratch. "Wait. Someone tried to break into your depository, didn't they?"

Using the undead, in fact.

"The storeroom is sealed," Vance said. "The room cannot be breached from the outside, not even if trespassers get into the building itself."

"True." Only the Mage Lords could enter the room where I'd put both the Invocations and the second talisman I'd claimed, but that someone had tried to break in at all suggested Calder had a more sophisticated plan this time around.

"Ivy," said Vance. "I know you're worried about Calder, but I'd suggest going through the necromancers if you want to cross the veil again. At least use a summoning circle to anchor yourself. I don't want you to get into trouble over there where I can't help you."

His resigned tone dug inside my chest. Going into Death probably *was* the only way to get answers at this point, but given my shaky relationship with the necromancers, the odds of getting a tutor from among their ranks was next to zero.

Unless…

"Do you trust me?" I asked. "I need a favour."

"What kind of question is that? Of course I do. Just tell me what you need. As long as it doesn't involve winding up Lady Granville."

"Not her, but someone almost as unpleasant." I offered a smile. "Can you come with me to the necromancers' head-quarters?"

11

Isabel pounced on me when I walked through the door to our flat. "Are you okay?"

I ducked as a shrieking Erwin flew over my head. "I'm fine. You?"

"I haven't been able to get through to the necromancers, so I called the mages. Vance's receptionist told me you'd left."

"Huh. Didn't realise Wanda saw me," I said. "I kinda sneaked out, but it was Vance's idea. Certain other council members didn't want me investigating Ralph's death."

"Big mistake," said Isabel. "So what happened?"

"Long story," I said wearily. "Ending, as usual, with 'we're fucked'."

Erwin flew over my head again. "You smell of dead things, Ivy!"

"Yeah, sounds about right." I kicked off my boots and went to the kitchen to scrounge for some food. I hadn't eaten since breakfast and I'd run halfway across the city since then. Not to mention the hours-long interrogation. I threw together a sandwich and flung myself on the sofa to eat it while updating Isabel on the circumstances of Ralph's murder, my impromptu investigation, and the fight at the cemetery.

Isabel's eyes rounded at the mention of the undead faeries. "*How* can they be undead? They don't have souls, do they?"

"Apparently, that's not a requirement," I said through a mouthful of chicken and tomato. "What I'd like to know is if they rose of their own accord because the veil is fucked *again*, or if someone brought them back intentionally."

Her breath caught. "You don't think there's another necromancer turned traitor?"

"Perhaps." I swallowed my mouthful. "I don't know what to believe, which is why I want to get into their headquarters and see what's really going on. Vance and I are meeting in an hour. I want a shower first." I'd washed my hands, obviously, but my clothes were covered in grave dirt along with residual plaster dust from the mercenaries' flat.

"Good call." Isabel chewed on her lower lip. "I told those mercenaries that the necromancers would pay for damages, but I'm not sure we'll be able to keep that promise. I need to check in with them and see if they want their equipment back, too."

"Never mind the bloody equipment. We'll all need it the way things are going." I took another bite. "If you switch on the radio, there's a broadcast from the mages telling everyone to take precautions as though it's zombie night again. I'm not convinced it'll be enough. They opted not to mention some of the dead are fae."

"These wards are designed to dismember undead. That'll help." Isabel indicated her newest batch of elastic-band-shaped spells. "What's with the spiders?"

I looked down. Half a dozen dead spiders had fallen out of my coat. "The faerie at the cemetery." My skin itched. I didn't mind spiders too much—after my stint in Faerie, harmless insects were the least of my worries—but any trace of faeries in the flat were an unacceptable safety risk. "Better destroy them just in case."

"Good plan," said Isabel. "As for the necromancers, I can come with you and create a distraction if you need one."

"It's all right, Vance is taking me there," I said. "In case there are more undead wandering around outside."

"Didn't you say their headquarters was bound in iron?"

"Yeah, it is." Which ought to mean that the fae would stay away, dead or otherwise. "That doesn't keep out the human dead."

"This does." Isabel picked up a spare saltshaker from the coffee table. "Maybe we should cover ourselves in salt, to be on the safe side."

"That," I said, "is a terrible idea. Anyway, the headquarters itself was pretty much built as a stronghold for the zombie apocalypse. Nothing hostile can enter."

Isabel gave a wry smile. "Their ancestors must have been a thousand times more reliable than they are today."

"Yeah, they lost the plot a few generations back." I shook another spider out of my coat. "All right, you might as well come. Erwin, can you keep an eye out for undead near the flat while we're gone?"

The piskie flew overhead with a delighted scream. Isabel and I had experimented with putting him on guard duty, with less-than-stellar results, but at least we were reasonably certain any ghost would immediately run away when faced with his yelling.

"No bad faeries," Erwin proclaimed. "Bad faeries are all dead!"

"Yeah," I muttered. "That's kind of the problem."

———

Visiting the necromancers' headquarters under cover of dark was less than ideal with the memories of my last visit to a cemetery as fresh as the grave dirt stains on my boots, but dusk fell around four thirty in the afternoon in winter, and I wasn't inclined to delay until morning. Isabel rang the old-fashioned doorbell first, but nobody answered.

"I don't think anyone's in there." Isabel pressed an ear to the door and then shook her head. "They won't answer their phones, either. Seems weird that they haven't asked for their equipment back. I feel bad for those mercs, too. They'll have to wait for their compensation."

"Yeah." Unease slid down my spine, and the apparent emptiness of the cold, dark-walled building did nothing to ease my misgivings. "Right. We can either go into the mausoleum or the main building. I'd prefer the former, because at least I have permission to be in there, but it's also in the cemetery, and the last one I visited contained a plague of ghosts and a man-eating plant." Not to mention the sluagh.

"We're prepared." Isabel waved a jar of salt.

Vance lifted a hand, and the front door clicked open. "I think it's best if we go inside the main building, as it's better protected."

"What did you tell Lady Granville we were doing, anyway?"

"Nothing," he said. "This isn't related to the investigation into Ralph's death. I left Drake in charge of updating her, if she wants to know where I am."

"Nice one." I grinned. "You're banking on him annoying her so much that she won't ask him for updates, aren't you?"

"The thought did cross my mind."

We entered the gloomy hallway and followed the light of candles burning in old-fashioned sconces on the walls.

"Forgot how creepy this place is." Isabel shivered as we entered the main room.

Twelve candles were already positioned around the edges of the circle chalked upon the metal floor.

"How nice of them to set this up for us," I said through chattering teeth. It was markedly colder inside the building than outside, no doubt due to the close presence of the dead. The metal walls didn't help either, and nor did the high ceilings and the wide space.

Unlike the mages, the necromancers didn't leave their base under guard all the time because the building itself was a fortress. They were in no danger of being overrun, and I assumed most of their members didn't even live here at headquarters. But for nobody to be present at all was markedly strange.

Necromantic candles had no need for matches, and a simple touch conjured a white flame to each of the twelve. With three of us, we soon had the circle ready, and when I touched the last candle, their flames merged around the circle's edges. Blinking the glare from my eyes, I faced the grey smoke rising between the glowing lights. *Hope this works.*

"Frank?" I called. "Lord Frank Sydney."

Summoning an individual ghost required a bunch of complicated incantations, but a necromancer Guardian could bypass the usual methods, and Frank and I already knew one another besides. I shuffled my feet to stop my toes going numb, running my hand over the hilt of my sword and trying to ignore how the quietness and the icy chill in the air gave the place a haunted atmosphere without the need for any ghosts to be present.

When a transparent figure appeared within the circle, I sighed in relief. "There you are, Frank."

"Ivy Lane." Frank's tall body flickered like the image from

a faulty TV screen. "What are you doing in the main summoning chamber? Is that the Mage Lord?"

"Every necromancer in town's gone walkabout at the worst possible time," I said. "I went looking for you over the veil earlier, but I couldn't find you. What's going on?"

"Reanimates," said Frank. "A considerable number. They might not be threatening individually, but in large numbers as they are now, every single person able to fight is committed to taking them down."

"And ghosts?" I asked. "There seem to be plenty of them, too."

"We've never had so many spirits flat-out refuse to pass through the gates," he said. "What *are* you doing in there? Does Lord Evander know?"

"Never mind that. The spirits are refusing to pass through the gates?" My heart sank in my chest. "Are any of them half-faeries? Because I've had to deal with two this week and they were both way stronger than they should have been."

Frank swore. "I was afraid of that."

"Are they getting a boost from somewhere?" I pressed. "They're showing up in places they have no business being in, attacking regular humans, and…" *And they know my name. They're working for Calder.*

"Unfortunately, Lord Evander is correct when he claims that we don't have enough knowledge of the faeries to gauge how powerful their ghosts should be," he said. "Their rules are unknown."

"And fae undead?" I asked. "I got attacked by some of those, too. Faeries, pure or half, risen from the grave the same as a human undead."

I never thought it'd be possible to see a ghost go any paler, but Frank might have proved me wrong. His body flickered in and out of existence until I worried he'd disappear altogether. "Half-faerie undead? That's impossible."

"Sorry to be the bearer of bad news," I said. "Do you think a necromancer might be involved?"

"If they are, they've avoided capture. Certainly no necromancer would have the audacity to attempt a reanimation on a *faerie*." He drifted closer to the circle's edge, urgency filling his tone. "Are you absolutely certain they were undead?"

"They didn't bleed when I cut them. Does anyone outside the guild know how to reanimate a body?"

"It's not possible," said Frank. "To summon a reanimate… unless the veil is in a worse state than I thought, the necromancer must tie his or her life force to the undead they summon. No one other than one of us has the capability to do so. Given the state of things, I would guess that due to the upheaval with the veil, the undead are rising of their own accord."

"And that's giving the half-faerie ghosts a boost, too, right? One of them even used magic on me earlier. That only happened on the Ley Line before." Undead were different. It didn't take much for the dead to leave their graves. Fae undead were a new and unwelcome development, but ghosts were far more dangerous.

Frank paused as though thinking hard. "Ghosts are more likely to return if they died in a particularly violent manner and carry a strong presence in Death. However, essentially, the main feature of all ghosts is their will to survive even without their physical body. Whether they're a violent poltergeist or a persistent phantom, they *want* desperately to continue to exist."

"Sounds like the half-faeries," I said. "They're descended from people who can't die, and they had Calder feeding them lies about immortality for months last year. That's bound to make them reluctant to move on. But I also learned from the Chief of the half-faeries that the ghosts I encountered died on their own territory when someone attempted a prison break involving some of the faeries who took the drug during the incident a few months ago. Coincidence?"

"Doubtful." His mouth set in a grim line. "That is beyond the realm of my own knowledge, however. My work as a Guardian keeps me closer to the gates than to the waking world, and if the living necromancers haven't found the source of the trouble, there's very little I can do."

"Then why didn't you come when I crossed over into Death?" I asked. "I called your name and got punched by a ghost instead."

His eyes turned downward. "I was ordered to remain here."

"You're lying," said Vance suddenly from behind me. I jumped, having almost forgotten I wasn't alone in the room. "You're higher ranked than Lord Evander. He doesn't give you orders."

"No, he doesn't," I agreed. "Are the necromancers really that clueless about what's going on? The faeries have been here for over twenty years. You'd think they'd know if it was possible to reanimate one at the very least."

Frank hissed out a breath. "I might have no confidence in the guild's current leader, but the necromancers have more knowledge and experience with the dead than you do, Ivy. Remember that."

"Oh, I remember," I said. "Just like I remember that the half-faerie ghosts I ran into told me that Calder is behind this and is trying to find a way to come back to life."

"That," he said, "is impossible. When someone passes beyond the gate, there isn't a single force that can bring back a soul."

"His allies are Winter faeries. They have death magic of their own. Could that take the place of necromancy?" I hoped not, given that half the faeries in the Chief's territory were Unseelie.

"No," said Frank. "Aside, perhaps, for *your* magic."

Oh.

I knew it, said some small, quiet part of me. I'd known from the moment I'd stripped the power from Avalin's corpse, and those screaming voices of the dead had rung through my ears like a bell tolling my own demise. I'd known when I crossed the veil as easily as drawing a breath. And if I hadn't known then, I'd sure as hell known when I'd stabbed a ghost with my sword and shattered the spirit into pieces.

I could kill half-faerie ghosts because my sword—and my magic—belonged to Death. To the Grey Vale, which lay on Death's doorstep. True Winter magic was a different entity. Mine was something else.

"If you're wondering if I know more about your magic, I don't," said Frank. "I didn't lie when I said I'd never encountered such a phenomenon in my life. However, based on what you told me, somebody has found a way to give these half-faerie ghosts a temporary boost of spiritual energy, enough for them to leave the place they died and freely move through the veil."

"The cemetery," I said slowly. "That's a source of spiritual energy, isn't it?"

"We found no traces of necromantic equipment at the scene," said Vance. "But you seem to be implying that someone's bringing back the spirits without the need for traditional necromancy."

"None of this is in any way traditional," said Frank. "A spirit left untethered generally fades away of its own accord. For that not to be the case implies a disturbance in the veil, but there isn't one that we have been able to detect."

"Not being able to detect something doesn't mean it isn't there." I rubbed my cold hands together. "Calder had death magic. I know I sealed away all the power he drew on to break the veil open, but he's resourceful, and he's spoken to necromancers before. Through Velkas. What if he found..." *A way to come back. A way to drag me kicking and screaming into Death.* "You're the expert here. I know for a fact your people were involved with the faeries in the past. They built this place out of iron for a reason, didn't they?"

Frank's body went transparent. A swishing noise came from behind me, and I turned in time to see twin blades fly out of the air and land either side of Lord Evander, pinning him to the wall.

"What is the meaning of this?" bellowed the necromancers' leader.

Vance waved a hand and the blades released Lord Evander. He pushed away from the wall, glowering at us. He looked tired and angry, his suit covered in what I assumed was grave dirt.

"You *dare* to break into our home?" he spat. "I'd expect this behaviour from *you*, Ivy Lane, but the Mage Lord?"

Out of the corner of my eye, I saw Isabel shuffle backwards, hiding the bag of necromantic equipment behind her back.

"I came here to speak to Frank," I told him, to keep his attention off her. "Given that you're having trouble controlling your dead, I decided it'd be safer to do so in here than the mausoleum."

Lord Evander's angry glare slid to the Mage Lord. "You helped her break in?"

"She has an open invitation," said Vance. "As do I, technically."

"We're leaving anyway." The necromancers didn't have the answers, as was abundantly clear. "You know, you might at least have left *one* person behind. People have been trying to call you all day."

Lord Evander ignored me. "Lord Sydney, would you care to explain what you're doing?"

"She wanted to know where in damnation you all disappeared to," said Frank. "The mages have been attacked by the dead, and so have an alarming number of members of the public."

"The mages can handle themselves," he retaliated. "As to the public, we're spread too thin. Three of my people are missing, twelve are injured, and I've had enough of—"

"Missing?" Vance said sharply. "Since when?"

"Since this morning. What business is it of yours?"

"It's possible that a necromancer has gone rogue." I could tell it took effort for him not to add *again*.

"None of my people have gone rogue," snarled Lord Evander. "The three who disappeared were banishing the undead, not *summoning* anything."

"And everyone's been fully accounted for during every minute of the last week?" I asked. "I don't think so, somehow."

Even if there wasn't an actual rogue at work, someone had bewitched the mages' guards into abandoning their posts, and the necromancers didn't apply a fraction of the same effort to their security as the mages did.

"Look," I said cautiously when he gave me an ugly look in return. "Don't blow up at me, but I'm ninety percent sure I know who's behind this. Calder—the half-faerie I killed a few months ago—wants to come back from the dead. He's called the other half-faerie ghosts to rally around him and has given them a power boost."

"Calder," repeated Lord Evander. "Is he the one who cracked open the veil? I thought you killed him yourself."

"Well, yes, but he's not your average ghost. I think he's giving people orders from beyond the grave."

"What nonsense," said Lord Evander. "Your faeries are subject to the same rules as any other spirits."

"They're not *mine*," I said, bristling.

Vance gave him a warning look. "As Ivy said, we were leaving. I'd strongly suggest contacting myself and the mage council if any of your people encounter these half-faerie ghosts yourself."

And we left. Nobody spoke until Vance had transported us back into the living room of the flat and Isabel switched on the light, pulling a thick, heavy book from her pocket.

"What's that?" I asked.

"The necromancers' handbook. Updated edition."

"Did you steal it?"

Isabel gave me a faint smile. "Someone left a copy lying in a corner. I had a quick peek while you were talking to Frank. It contains detailed instructions on spirit summoning, and banishing, too. Might come in handy."

That'd teach me to underestimate my best friend. "You're amazing, you know that?"

She handed the book to me. "Here. You'll probably be able to make more sense of this than I can."

"Hope so." I hefted the thick book in my hands and turned to Vance, who had his phone out. Sending a message back to the manor, I guessed. "Is Drake holding the fort okay?"

"He challenged Lady Granville to a snowball fight."

"Ha."

"She doesn't know where we went, but I'd prefer to avoid her finding out about our breaking-and-entering."

"Yeah." I groaned. "You know, I completely forgot to ask Frank to look for Ralph's spirit like we said we would. We're never going to get invited back to the guild to try again."

"I doubt he'll have seen anything," said Vance. "He was killed by a hellhound. The person who gave orders likely wasn't nearby or didn't allow themselves to be seen."

"Spirit summoning isn't exactly reliable, anyway," said Isabel. "From what I saw in the book."

"No." I turned the textbook over in my hands, hoping whoever it belonged to wouldn't get into trouble for losing it. "What now? Should we act without the necromancers? Because they're more of a hindrance than a help, to be honest."

Admittedly, Lady Granville had said the same, but severing ties with the guild outright wasn't the same as borrowing one of their textbooks.

"For now," said Vance. "That there are missing necromancers reminds me of the last time some of their number went rogue. It's certainly a possibility."

"They might be avoiding Lord Evander." I smothered a sigh. "Or someone might have cast a spell on them, like those guards at the manor."

"Perhaps." Vance's mouth pinched. "If a ghost was responsible, we'll need to rethink the manor's defences to avoid future incidents."

"Yeah." How to stop a ghost from glamouring someone, though? Unless I stood guard myself twenty-four-seven, nobody with the Sight was outside the manor constantly. It was an obvious weak point.

I lifted the handbook and brushed dust from the surface. The necromancers' text might provide some answers, but if faerie ghosts had never been recorded in the guild's history, we were dealing with a problem that was simultaneously brand-new and also far older than the necromancers.

Older, perhaps, than Death itself.

"Found anything new?" asked Vance.

I sat on the bed with the necromancer handbook open in my lap, while he lay at my side, his arm curled around my back.

Luckily, nobody had accosted us back at the manor. We'd had dinner out on the balcony, cocooned in a spell that kept the cold air from reaching us. A while ago, I might have objected to Vance wasting the mages' spells on unnecessary extravagance, but after the day I'd had, I desperately needed some quiet time with Vance.

I showed him the yellowing pages. "I'm trying to figure out how Calder might have evaded banishment. He's got to still be somewhere on the first layer of the veil." *Or in the Vale*, I added silently, but I wouldn't find any mention of *that* in the necromancers' handbook.

Vance leaned over to see. "Yes… that's as much as they teach non-necromancers. There are two layers to the afterlife."

"Most spirits hang out on the first." I turned the page. "A

dead person—or half-faerie—is typically sent right through the gate to the second layer. Even the necromancers don't know what lies over there, but the process usually doesn't need to involve a necromancer at all."

"Yes, most spirits move on of their own accord." Vance nodded. "And if you ask a necromancer to recall a spirit, they can only do so if the ghost is on the veil's first layer. Hence why you can only contact the recently deceased."

"Unless they refuse to go through the gate." I didn't know if the book meant a literal gate or a metaphorical one. "Guardians are supposed to be powerful enough to drive out any stragglers, but Frank implied that a lot of them were lost during the invasion."

Vance gave another slow nod. "There was no system for dealing with a greater number of dead. Evidently, there still isn't."

"And Calder's digging his heels in and refusing to leave." My shoulders tensed. "How can he be that powerful? I sealed his magic. He should have nothing left."

"Spirits can be tricky," he said. "And despite the number of enemies he's made, Calder seems to have convinced some of his fellow ghosts to rally around him. No doubt many were his allies in life."

Yeah. I'd bet he'd visited the prisoners on half-blood territory and convinced them to instigate a jailbreak. And they'd obliged, getting themselves killed in the process.

"Alain isn't exactly an ally of his, but her boyfriend definitely is, and they both blame me for what I did to Calder." I clenched my hands to stop them trembling. "Why don't faeries know how to stay dead? Don't answer that. I know it's because faeries are immortal and their offspring have a permanent inferiority complex, but it's also fucking annoying."

"This is Calder we're speaking of," said Vance. "He's not a sophisticated thinker, and his plans have a tendency to backfire."

"On other people as well as on himself." I heaved a sigh. "At least Avalin had the decency to stay dead." His wraith notwithstanding.

"You mentioned your talisman destroyed the ghost that attacked you in that mercenary's flat?" he asked.

"Apparently my sword can kill dead people now." I gave a short laugh. "Not sure if it's because I can draw on the power of the dead and there's a lot of pissed-off ghosts around, but I kind of wish I had a normal power like throwing fire and lightning, or… okay, maybe not mind-reading."

"No." His fingers brushed the back of my neck. "I've had words with her."

I lifted my head. "And you didn't end up skewered to the wall?"

"No." He traced circles on my upper back, drawing a shiver to my skin. "She ought to have intervened on your behalf when Lady Granville made her accusation."

I shuddered for an entirely different reason. "She'd better be done trying to accuse me of murder."

"Lady Granville isn't a threat," said Vance. "My word overrides hers, and she's dropped all the accusations against you."

"Honestly, she's the least of my worries." I gestured to the textbook. "I feel like there's something I missed, but it's gonna take a while to read this cover to cover."

"Then we'll find it tomorrow." Vance reached and closed the book. "That's not pleasant bedtime reading."

I dragged a hand over my forehead. "Not like I can sleep when I know he's really out there. I wasn't being paranoid at all."

I'll kill your mage first.

Vance's calloused hand gently curled around my wrist. "We're safe in here."

"Sure we are. I have my sword." I leaned over and tapped the hilt where it rested against the bedside table. The light of the fire glinted off its shimmering length. "I haven't named it yet. Should probably do that before I kill Calder with it. For real, this time."

"Your old sword was named Irene…"

"It started as a joke. Irene. Iron. Get it?"

Vance groaned. I hit him in the arm. "I was sixteen. Anyway. This one's not iron, and Badass God-Killer is a bit of a mouthful. Any ideas?"

"I'll think about it," he said. "Is there anyone you particularly admire? Who won't mind having a sword named after them?"

"Isabel, but that'd get confusing fast." I might have widened my friend network since I'd befriended the mages, but I wouldn't say I was close to any of them. Not enough to name my faerie talisman after them, anyway. Wanda was an option, but like with Isabel, I interacted her too often, and she was far too mild-mannered to loan her name to a blood-thirsty weapon.

Maybe if I used a dead person instead of a living one… well, I certainly had no shortage of ghosts in my past. Even when I'd claimed the sword itself, I'd seen her. "Helena."

"Really?" he asked. "That's the name of one of our former Mage Lords. I think you'd have liked her."

"Did she kill dead people?"

"No."

"Or glow when there's an evil faerie nearby?" I put the book down and shifted to face him. "Helena… she was a friend of mine. We both got taken by Avalin, and I—left her behind."

She'd forgiven me, in the end, and I'd helped her escape the Vale and move on. I'd never be able to ask her for permission to use her name, but there were worse ways to live on than in the embodiment of revenge against the faeries who'd taken her life.

Vance drew his arm around me. "It wasn't your fault."

"No." I leaned into him. "You know, Avalin would *hate* that I named my sword after one of his prisoners."

"I bet." He pulled me closer, giving comfort from his warmness. "You don't have to think about the past."

"No." I ran a finger down the sword's hilt. "No, but I think she deserves the memorial. Helena it is."

The dead body lay strewn across the road, its head several feet away.

"At least someone took care of it without needing to call the necromancers," I remarked, trying not to breathe in the stench. Salt had been scattered in a long line in front of the houses on the road, and glass shards lay beside the body, indicating that someone had thrown a jar at the undead from an upstairs window. The salt had been delivered to every street on the orders of the mages, but Lord Evander still wasn't taking calls.

We neared half-blood territory, Vance holding out the spirit sensor he'd found in a cupboard at the manor. Given its ten percent accuracy rate, we'd have had more success flinging salt at thin air until we hit something, but there didn't seem to be any ghosts present here.

This was our third stop, after the mages' depository and another detour to the nearby cemetery to make sure no more undead had wandered out. All we'd found on the way were a bunch of dismembered undead, like this one. While all the main roads were lined with salt, we had to raise our voices to hear one another over the melody of angrily beeping horns and high-volume swearing from drivers trying to get past dismembered bodies that had piled up in the night. I carried as many saltshakers as I could fit into my pockets alongside my daggers, and my sword was strapped to my waist, its vibrant glow guaranteed to announce our arrival.

"We'll have to wait outside." Vance halted at the gates.

They swung open, revealing the Chief. As usual, he was crowned in silver and armoured in green and flanked by two armoured guards. *Here we go.*

"Mage Lord." The Chief jerked his head irritably at the spirit sensor. "What is that?"

"A ghost detector," said Vance. "Have you seen any undead on your territory?"

"Certainly not."

"Or hellhounds?" I walked in behind Vance and gave the guards a cheery wave. "Hey, Bob."

A muscle ticked in the Chief's jaw. "What are you doing here?"

"We'd like to take another look around the prison," I said. "The banshee told us that everyone involved in the breakout was killed, but thanks to her, we didn't get a good look inside."

"What banshee?"

I blinked. "Erm, your prison guard?"

"What nonsense are you speaking now? There are no banshees living on this territory."

Vance and I exchanged glances. Well, crap.

"A banshee showed up at the jail when we last visited." I searched his face and found nothing but confusion and irritation. "She also performed her horrific death song, which usually means someone's going to die, am I right?"

"Whoever that banshee is, she isn't one of mine," said the Chief.

"If that's true, a banshee is playing at being a security guard behind your back." As if this mess wasn't confusing enough already. "There weren't any other people around the jail. No other guards."

"Really."

"Yes. Why would I lie about that?" I folded my chilled arms. "She told us she's the one who killed your runaway prisoners and the people who tried to rescue them."

"What?" He swayed on the spot, his expression aghast. "I spoke to the guards an hour ago. Nobody mentioned seeing any kind of death fae. They assumed the prisoners killed one another during the breakout."

"Did it not strike you as suspicious that they were all killed by something with talons?" I queried.

"There were plenty of shapeshifter fae in the jail." He didn't meet my eyes. "This is… concerning."

"That I can agree with," said Vance. "With your permission, we'll go to the jail and talk to the guards—the *real* ones this time."

He didn't wait for an answer before transporting us to the path where we'd first encountered the banshee. Snow-encrusted gnarled trees crowded on either side, but no banshee barred the path to the jail, and its high wooden doors were guarded by two near-identical green-skinned ogres.

"Hiding, is she?" I muttered to Vance.

Our footsteps crunched through snow until we reached the jail. Seeing our approach, the ogres closed in and lifted their clubs. *So these guys are the normal security, are they?*

"Humans aren't allowed here," growled the ogre on the left.

"What are you doing here?" asked the second ogre. "You're… the Mage Lord."

At least they knew who Vance was.

"We have the Chief's permission to search the jail and speak to its prisoners," said Vance smoothly. "Would you mind letting us pass?"

"Not while you're carrying iron." The ogre on the left indicated my sword.

"It's not iron." I withdrew the blade, revealing the silvery-blue glow, and they both recoiled in shock.

"You carry a fae-forged sword?" said the ogre on the right.

"Yes, I do. We're here to question your prisoners, as several of them were murdered the other day." Though I wouldn't mind asking the ogres a couple of questions, too. "Out of interest, have either of you seen a banshee recently?"

The ogres regarded me blankly and shook their heads.

"And where were you during the attempted breakout?" Vance pressed. "Did someone tell you to abandon your post at any point?"

The leftmost ogre blinked at him. "What's it to you?"

"That means yes," I said. Evidently, Vance had come to the same conclusion as I had. "You weren't here when we last visited. Has anyone told you to leave the jail?"

"Chief's emissary did," said the first ogre. "Told us to take the evening off."

"No, he didn't," said the other.

"Yes, he did."

I watched with raised eyebrows. "Which of you is right?"

"I am." The first ogre shoved his companion so hard he fell flat on his back, and I stepped aside as his opponent punched him in the mouth and knocked out several teeth.

Vance beckoned, and the door to the jail sprang open. As I

followed him inside, one ogre bodily threw the other into a tree. I winced, ducking into the narrow entryway.

"It seems my guards weren't the only ones to be bewitched," said Vance quietly. "Moreover, the banshee is an impostor."

"I'd bet my sword she's the one manipulating people." I pulled my weapon out, casting a blue-tinted glow into the gloomy corridor. Cells lined both sides, some barely large enough to accommodate their hulking half-troll inhabitants.

"The half-faeries don't screw around with their punishments. It's bloody freezing in here."

My hands numbed on the sword's hilt, but I didn't dare put it away. Some of the prisoners stirred as we walked through the corridor, but most didn't seem to notice our presence.

"You." Vance pointed at a slumped figure. "Tell me what happened during the jailbreak the other day."

"You're not the Chief," said the guy. He looked about sixteen, dressed in a filthy T-shirt and jeans. "Wait. Mage Lord. I swear I didn't—who are you?" He goggled at my sword.

"Didn't what?" I enquired. "Go on."

"I don't deserve this," said the guy petulantly. "I hit him because he insulted me. I shouldn't be locked up with murderers. I'm innocent—"

"Did you ever meet Calder?" I interrupted.

"Who?"

That settled that, then.

A strangled yell came in from outside. I tensed, before remembering the ogres we'd left clobbering each other on the doorstep.

"I don't care who you are or why you're here," said Vance. "Several of your fellow prisoners died in the jailbreak. I want you to tell me what happened."

"I didn't see. It went dark, and then there was this awful singing. Or screaming. couldn't tell which." The kid gave a violent shudder. "When the lights came back on, the Chief showed up and had someone haul the bodies away."

"I see." Vance moved to the next cell.

Three questionings later, we had our story straight. The people who'd broken into the jail, including Alain, hadn't said a word about their intentions to the other prisoners, but they'd freed only a select handful of people, Lucas included. Nobody had seen how the intruders had died, but I could hazard a guess.

"The banshee." I walked to the doors with Vance. "I don't know if she murdered them out of boredom or what. I mean, if she's the one who distracted the guards, it makes no sense for her to kill her own allies during their escape."

"Doesn't it?" he queried. "Or were they of more use dead than alive?"

"That's not a nice sentiment. At all." But unfortunately fitting for the banshee… and Calder, too. "Where is she now, though?"

"Hiding, no doubt," Vance said tightly. "I doubt we'll find her even if we upend the whole territory, not if she's managed to sneak in and out without the Chief's awareness."

"And Calder?" I spoke half to myself. "Does *he* want to be found?"

"I doubt the answers lie here," said Vance. "It sounds like the jailbreak was led by people like Alain, who wanted to free loved ones from perceived injustices. However, the Chief has a glaring hole in his security."

"What does he expect?" I followed him outside to a flurry of thumps and growls. The ogres weren't having the best of mornings. "It'd save on time if we made the enemy come to us rather than combing the whole city. Maybe I should walk into the middle of a field wearing a sign that says, 'bite me' and see if more hellhounds show up. Or faerie undead, if they're his latest allies."

Vance's forehead pinched. "If what Calder did with the drug is an example, the minor faerie undead might be a test. Like the way he tested the drug on piskies first, then the Trials."

I blinked. "I was joking. I mean, it's equally possible that the fae undead rose of their own accord due to the veil being fucked up."

"All instances of undead so far have involved humans alone, but there's no shortage of fae who've died within the city, too."

That was true enough. But then, why would Calder have used them as a test? For what purpose?

"He can't have summoned them himself." Though as far as I knew, nobody had found those missing necromancers. Fresh goosebumps peppered my arms. "I'd say we should go back to the cemetery and look around, but if there was any evidence to show who raised them from death, Lady Granville probably destroyed it when she dug up the place."

"Exactly." Irritation flickered in his eyes. "I was sure we'd find something in here."

I racked my thoughts. "I killed an undead troll on the canal bridge. It might still be there."

"The canal?"

"Yeah, miles away from here," I replied. "It's right near where the last ghost showed up, in mercenary district."

"That's worth checking out," he agreed. "I'll take us there."

We vanished once again, trading the cool yet clean scent of Winter territory for the pungent stench of the canal. Dilapidated tower blocks overlooked the murky waters, and I stood on tiptoe, scanning the area to get my bearings. "This way."

Vance followed my lead, likely less familiar with the area

than I was. My thoughts roiled. Why would Calder raise the dead? Undead bodies weren't of any use on their own, without their spirits, were they?

But his body was destroyed…

I halted in my steps. "Please tell me he isn't trying to see if it's possible to raise a faerie from the dead before attempting to take a body of his own."

Vance gave me a sharp look. "You think so?"

"No. I have no idea." I gave a head-shake. "I'm just throwing out theories. I can't think of any other reason why he'd be experimenting with raising undead, unless he's lonely and needs a friend. I can't imagine the ghosts are good company, but undead are even worse. If it was possible to reunite a soul with a body, the necromancers would know, but they're adamant that it isn't."

Vance fell into step with me as we resumed walking. "Dangerous experiments with the boundaries of life and death certainly sounds like Calder."

"Yeah." I grimaced. "He's certainly inventive, but he's also impatient. I doubt he'll wait until he has a body again before unleashing his plan. Soon as he has a way to kill me, he will."

Recognising the bridge, I veered in that direction. The water was barely existent on our left side, foul-smelling sludge lapping against the banks amid piles of junk people had thrown into the canal. A mass of everyday rubbish and discarded old furniture piled high enough to dam the canal's flow. On the other side, the water had backlogged until it spilled over the edges.

"The troll came from that side." I indicated the heap of wrecked sofas and splintered pieces of wood. Now I looked closer, the area below the bridge did somewhat resemble a troll's lair.

Vance held out the fountain-pen-shaped device that detected life forms, but no response came. "Nothing living in there, but it doesn't work on the dead. Do you want to go in?"

"Yeah. You should stay out here and make sure nothing ambushes us."

Based on my experience with this canal, there were all kinds of nasties lurking around. Undead trolls were far from the worst I'd seen.

I kept my sword out and jumped, landing precariously on a large chunk of debris that might have once been a piece of wall or ceiling. As it wobbled, I climbed to the next piece, as though I was navigating a precarious sea of stepping stones.

Amid the wreckage, I spied a chunk of wood propped up to resemble a door. When I pulled it open, the stench of rot poured out. I held my breath, my eyes watering, and climbed in.

My feet wobbled on the uneven slabs of wood arranged to make up the cave's interior, illuminated in my sword's blue light. The troll wasn't here, though its collection of junk remained. Trolls were hoarders, and this one apparently had a thing for shiny purple objects. I even spotted what looked like one of Isabel's glitter spells among the general debris.

The smell grew worse as I navigated the heaps of discarded clothes and broken household objects the troll had presumably pulled out of the canal. Children's toys, broken pens, plastic boxes… dead rats.

Wait a minute.

A chill ran down my back. I crouched down beside the small heap of dismembered rodents and saw the chalked remains of a summoning circle.

Oh, hell.

Necromancy. The person who'd raised the troll from the dead had been here.

The smell, however, didn't come from the dead rats. I

straightened up and walked to the back of the cave where it joined with a smaller cave.

With a scraping noise, a human-sized body fell from above, thumping onto the ground. I jerked back, choking on a scream as a pair of sightless eyes stared into mine. The bodies had been shoved roughly onto a shelf above the entryway, torn and mangled, but still recognisably human. They hadn't gone pleasantly. An arm stripped of most of its flesh flopped downward, clothed in the fabric of a black necromancer cloak.

Heart in my throat, I grabbed a cleansing spell from my pocket and threw it over the chalked circle. That ought to deal with any lingering necromantic aftereffects hanging about the place—but what if there were others, buried beneath the piles of junk?

"Ivy?" Vance called to me. "Are you all right in there?"

"I think I found the missing necromancers," I called to Vance.

A roaring sounded from somewhere above, rattling my eardrums. That wasn't a troll, but I'd heard the sound before.

"Get off the bridge!" I yelled at Vance as I ran out of the troll's nest. Ascending the pile of junk, I leapt for solid ground and landed on the bank.

I staggered against Vance as the wave crashed down over the bridge and splattered both of us with filthy water. Vance swore, conjuring a blade in his hands and slashing at the tentacle that followed the wave. A foul stench spilled out as his blade severed it in two.

I drew my own blade, facing this new monstrosity. Decomposing tentacles splayed out of the water, trailing decay and viscera. *Okay, that's foul.*

Vance's sword cleaved through tentacles at the same time, while I cut down another. Two more rose in its place, and four replaced the two Vance had cut down. Grim realisation sank in.

"I think," I said, "this is the same hydra I killed last year. Someone raised its rotting corpse from the dead."

"What?" Vance conjured a second blade and sliced through more tentacles. Chunks of decomposing flesh rained down on the bank, but each tentacle sprouted a clone before its rotting remains hit the ground.

"Seriously?" I drove my sword into another tentacle. "What kind of depraved fucker brings back a dead hydra?"

"I warned you, Ivy Lane," whispered a voice.

13

The eerie voice slid through my bones, but I didn't slow. When another tentacle lashed at my feet, I swung my blade and sent a blast of magic for good measure. The tentacle burst apart and a colossal serpentine head reared upward from the water. Two rows of curved fangs protruded from a mouth stretched over half its head, while its eyes were tiny, more the size of pennies.

Fuck me, I forgot how big that thing was.

I blasted the serpent's head with magic and it exploded into a haze of decaying flesh, but a second reptilian head loomed behind, letting out a bone-shaking roar. Vance lifted a hand, and a large salt canister appeared in midair, upending itself over the monster. The beast recoiled violently, shedding flakes of scaly skin as the salt burned through its undead flesh like a quick-acting virus.

"As if it wasn't already persistent enough." I raised my blade. "Vance, did you hear that voice?"

"No…"

"I thought not." I dodged a swiping tentacle, reaching into

my pocket for one of the saltshakers I carried. "A ghost just spoke to me. Well, more threatened me."

"A ghost." Vance paused. "Not...?"

"Yeah. Him."

Calder.

The creepy voice had sounded as though he stood at my shoulder, but no spirits lurked at the riverside, and I didn't dare move my attention from the many-headed monstrosity lashing at the bank. I lifted the saltshaker and ran closer, wondering how in hell I was supposed to finish it off. The creature was half submerged beneath filthy water high enough to spill over the canal's edges, and the hydra's other heads were hidden somewhere in the murky depths.

"I thought the clean-up crew was in charge of removing the dead." Vance's sword lashed out, severing another head, and I sidestepped a shower of decomposing flesh.

"It was too big for anyone to drag it from the canal." I brought my sword down into another writhing tentacle. "I don't have enough salt to take the whole thing out at once."

"Then we'll do it one piece at a time." Vance lifted a hand, and a torrent of salt poured out of the sky, splashing into the murky water.

"Where'd you get that from?"

"The manor's emergency stores," said Vance. "Let's hope nobody needs it."

"No kidding." Last time, I'd killed the hydra by using my magic to incapacitate all its heads at once. Then I'd jumped into the canal—*not* an experience I'd wanted to repeat—and stabbed it in the heart. But stabbing alone wouldn't work now the creature was undead. I needed to change strategies.

Another small mountain of salt crashed on top of the creature, but its teeth kept snapping even as its heads decayed. Fangs snapped at my ankles as my sword bit into scaly flesh. Vance fought a similar battle at my side, using two blades to quicken the process, but it'd take all day to remove all the heads individually.

"Hang on. I've got an idea." I let the blue haze of magic flood my body, forming a shield against my skin.

Vance's blade came down on another head. "What idea?"

"You won't like it." I moved closer to the filthy water lapping over the bank. "Sorry."

Then I jumped into the canal.

Vance shouted my name as I plummeted, my magical shield cushioning my fall and forming a bubble around me that pushed the water away. Darkness closed over my head as I sank downward and rose just as quickly, buoyed upward by the blue haze that encircled me. It was a hell of a weird sensation, being able to see the water rising to my knees without a single droplet touching my body.

I lifted my head and caught Vance's eye. "Can you displace the water while I distract it?"

A tentacle jabbed at my shield and bounced clean off. Vance's blade severed it, and he flashed me an exasperated look from the bank. "Mind letting me in on your plan?"

"Isn't it obvious?" I asked. "You read my old file, but I didn't have a Mage Lord with me the last time I fought one of these fuckers."

"You're standing *in* the canal."

"And I'll be out of it when you move the water."

Vance slashed at another tentacle. "Even you wouldn't be that reckless."

"I'm not going to dignify that with an answer."

I waded further into the canal, magic fanning out around me. The water would have come up to my waist, if not for the shield keeping me dry. If my concentration slipped and I let it drop, I'd get an impromptu swim, but I needed to expose the monster to stand any hope of stopping its assault. Tentacles bounced off my shield and snapping teeth left no impact on my skin. I wouldn't be able to keep up the shield forever—not if I wanted to launch an effective magical attack —but I'd distracted its attention from Vance, which was the plan.

The water shifted sideways and surged towards the blockade at the bridge near the troll's nest. More reptilian heads popped up, no longer concealed by the filthy water. I didn't know if the beast had retained any awareness of its surroundings, but it didn't seem to notice the rapidly expanding shallow trench that had once been deep water. Tentacles thrashed weakly, no longer buoyant.

"Ivy," Vance said through gritted teeth, "I'd appreciate it if you let me know how much longer I need to hold back all this water before I accidentally cause a flood."

"Sorry." I lifted my sword. "Give me five seconds. Ten at most."

Three heads lashed at me at once. I released my shield, no longer in danger of an unplanned soaking, and turned the magic into a shockwave that shattered all three heads at once. Beyond lay a mass of decaying flesh that formed the beast's massive scaly body, formerly hidden beneath the water.

I concentrated all my power into my next attack and aimed straight for its rotting heart.

A blue haze dazzled my eyes as my attack hit. The impact shook the water, the ground, even the bridge, and its remaining heads were flung in all directions as its vast scaly body burst like a firework. The sound of lumpy bits of dead hydra hitting the ground continued in a grisly chorus while I tried not to breathe in.

"Holy shit." I coughed. "I didn't expect it to work *that* well."

"Ivy." The sound of a window cracking suggested Vance had accidentally knocked the torrent of water into one of the lower windows of a tower block. Oops. At least broken windows would be better than being devoured by an undead hydra.

I leapt out of the canal on light feet and landed at Vance's side. "You can let go now."

We both lifted our arms to shield ourselves from the impact as the canal came rushing back at the bridge with enough force to break straight through the dam, swamping the troll's lair and carrying a sea of debris in its wake.

"Whoa." I gave Vance an appreciative look. "We should tell the city council and see if we get a reward for removing the blockage. Pretty sure they've been trying to get rid of all that junk for years."

"It's lucky I didn't flood half the buildings on the bank." He squeezed water out of his cloak. I bit back a laugh at the sight of his usually immaculate hair dripping and his clothes soaked through. "I don't make a habit of moving canals around."

"I'd be worried if you did." As the water levels lowered, I glimpsed bits of dead hydra, alongside... "Oh, *shit.*"

Several pale, half-decomposed bodies lay sprawled over the bank. Humans, not half-faeries. Our presence must have disturbed them, or else they'd been under the water and unable to get out until we'd moved the canal. More than a few people had drowned in there over the years.

I ran to the edge and swung my sword at the undead, sending one toppling back into the water. A second followed suit, flailing, unable to surface.

"I don't think someone used necromancy to bring *them* back." I cut off an undead's hands, and Vance displaced them into the water. "The hydra, though? I didn't see any candles underwater." Obviously. But a beast of that size surely hadn't risen of its own accord. There'd been a summoning circle in the troll's lair for a reason.

Vance stilled. "Don't tell me you want to…?"

"Go into Death?" I finished. "He spoke to me. He wants me to find him, and he was willing to use an undead hydra to drive the point home. I'll be fine."

"No, you won't be." Vance conjured a salt canister to his hand. "I can keep the undead from attacking you while you're gone, but I can't do a thing for the ghosts."

It's just one ghost I'm worried about. Vance was right, but given how close that voice had sounded, its owner was nearby. Watching us.

I would not let Calder play any more mind games with me. "I'll be fine. I'll come back before you know it."

My nerves jangled. The hydra was nothing compared to its summoner. Calder had killed those necromancers, I had no doubt, and his plan was in its early stages. The sooner I found out his endgame, the better.

Despite Vance's presence at my side, I called my magic into a shield so that not a single dead hand would touch me while I was out of my body. Then I closed my eyes and crossed over the veil.

Between one second and the next, I slipped out of my body and into Death. Grey smoke swirled around me on all sides, and I was greeted with a face I'd seen in my nightmares for months.

"Are you really so keen to die, Ivy Lane?" said Calder.

14

Calder's face might haunt me whenever I closed my eyes, but seeing his spectre was both the living embodiment of my worst fear and proof that my subconscious had warped the memories of our last encounter far beyond rationality. I'd forgotten how young he was, twenty at most, with the pointed face and ears of a half-Sidhe. His shoulder-length silver hair was now transparent and wispy; his armour was no more, and no wicked blade was sheathed at his waist. Without the glow of blue faerie magic that had once surrounded him, he appeared as much a faded echo as any ghost. *This is the man who I've been scared shitless of for months?*

"Enjoying Death?" I fixed on a smile with more ease than I'd ever have expected when faced with my enemy's ghost. "I'm disappointed in you, Calder. I knew you lacked subtlety, but an undead hydra? Really?"

His icy blue eyes roved over me. "I want nothing more than to watch you die, Ivy. No cheating death this time."

"You did all this for me?" I faked astonishment. "You murdered Ralph, terrorised the necromancers, caused a riot at the half-faerie prison… anything else I missed? Did you decide to steal from a bunch of orphans and kick some puppies just for the hell of it, too?"

"You haven't changed a bit."

"Neither have you," I retaliated. "You're the same shallow dickhead who got dragged into Death by a bunch of ghosts. Care to tell me how you slipped through the Guardians' clutches? Because you should have been dragged through the gates the second I sealed your magic away."

Calder's mouth twisted. "Did you really think I'd bow to a necromancer and allow them to dictate my fate? I *will* live again, and you'll pay for what you did to me."

"Seems more like you want a chat over coffee." He had no weapon, though admittedly neither did I. My magic remained, though, and I undoubtedly had more power than he did in his current state. "Tell me how you survived. If that's even the right word."

"I am stronger than death, Ivy Lane." His blue eyes glowed like candle flames. "I resisted the gates of Death because it's my fate to become immortal."

His hand reached out and closed around my wrist, as real and solid as though he gripped my physical body.

"You're forgetting one thing," I told him. "I have magic. You don't."

I swung my fist and hit him on the jaw. My hand sailed right through. Apparently, he'd only solidified one hand and not the rest of his body. I stumbled, unbalanced, and he tightened his grip, locking my arm behind my back. Even as a ghost, he was surprisingly strong.

"I deserve to live, Ivy Lane," said Calder. "And you are going to die."

He brought his arm around my throat to crush my windpipe. My feet jerked, passing through empty air. His control surprised me; being able to solidify one part of his body must require a hell of a lot of focus, but he'd had nothing but time over the past few months. Though I felt no real pain, my non-existent body was doing a pretty convincing job of telling me I couldn't breathe.

"Fuck—you," I wheezed, tapping into my magic again. I might have no talisman to back me up, but Death held no shortage of fuel. The lingering misery of the dead ignited in my hands, in addition to the anger burning through my veins in the waking world. This dickhead had killed Ralph for no good reason, not to mention those necromancers and the half-faeries at the jail.

In a burst of light, the grip on my neck disappeared. Gasping, I spun around, but Calder had vanished. Glamour, or a ghostly trick? No matter. Blue light flared from my hands and arms, brightening the grey haze.

"My father's magic," snarled Calder's voice, "was never meant to be yours."

His hand lashed out of thin air. I caught him by the wrist and dug my fingers in, his body flickering back into view. Then I delivered a kick to his kneecap.

Amazingly, the blow connected, though with less force than if I'd kicked him for real. His lack of reaction suggested he felt no pain, but then, why had it had hurt when he'd strangled me? Maybe he was less bothered because he'd been in Death for longer, or perhaps it was a psychological trick that I'd felt anything at all.

No matter. I called magic to my hands and sent a sharp bolt of power crashing into his chest. I'd hoped to blow him to pieces like I had the other ghosts, but he didn't even stagger.

Calder lifted his own palms and sent a torrent of energy at me in return. I dodged the icy air whipping past, my heart giving a lurch in a chest that didn't exist. "How? I bound your magic."

I'd nearly died in the process, too. He shouldn't have access to any power.

"Did you think you took everything from me?" He laughed, sensing my unspoken question. "You might have bound the power I gathered to break open the veil, but that didn't take away my bloodline. I'm descended from a Lord of the Grey Vale, and that won't ever change."

"Neither will you being a massive prick, unfortunately." *Shit.* I'd bound the power he'd gathered to break the veil, but evidently, I hadn't taken whatever magic was bound up in his bloodline, that he'd inherited from his father. And while I'd assumed our power was on a similar wavelength, having come from the same source, that wasn't strictly true. Avalin had claimed the talisman—*my* talisman—after he'd already been stripped of his original magic upon his exile. Calder, I was sure, couldn't have inherited any of that power. Based on what I'd come to understand of faerie bloodlines, his own gift must tie back to whatever magic Avalin had possessed before the other Sidhe had taken it from him and cast him out.

And despite the binding spell I'd used, some of that power still existed, and had followed him into Death.

Not all of it. Avalin had no doubt been a force to be reckoned with even before he'd claimed the sword I now held in my hands, but his son was nothing but a shallow reflection. I could still beat him.

After all, Death was my domain, too.

I extended my senses outward, imagined the raging pain of the spirits trapped here flooding me like it had back in Faerie. Pain and anger burned white-hot, and energy burst from my hand in a shimmering wave of blue light.

Calder dodged, leaping high above the torrent of energy, using a Sidhe's typical agility coupled with the weightlessness of a ghost. *Ack.* I might be able to beat him on raw strength, but I was a total novice when it came to fighting as a spirit. If he'd dealt damage to me, logically I ought to be able to hurt him back... but then, I was alive, and I still had a physical body. He didn't.

Okay. Let's try another tactic.

I lunged at him with a punch that would have knocked him flat if we'd been in the real world. As it was, I careened right through him, not needing to steady myself because there was nothing for either of us to crash into. If necessary, I could use my disembodied state to my advantage, too.

"Going to tell me your plan?" I tried another punch, which he blocked. "I assume it involves tearing the veil open, flipping off the pure Sidhe, and setting your hellhounds on anyone who disagrees with you. Hard to pull off without a physical body, but hey, if it keeps you entertained..."

"I *will* have my life back, Ivy. Your death means little to me."

"I'm just another stepping stone on the way to being the most badass motherfucker in the universe, I get it." My fist connected with his jaw, knocking his head sideways, but even the direct blow barely fazed him.

He recovered swiftly, glaring at me. "Death itself will bow to me, and my kin and I will return to life and take this world for our own."

"Sure you will." I delivered another punch, which he shook off equally fast. "Do the half-faeries know you worked with Velkas to deceive them? They'll never be immortal, and the sooner they accept that, the better."

"Wrong." He dodged my oncoming strike and returned with one of his own. We were equally fast, undoubtedly, but none of my attacks had the impact that I'd caused when I'd stabbed that ghost and shattered its body with my sword. I'd left my weapon behind in the waking world.

"I never lied to anyone, Ivy," he added. "You weren't

willing to hear Velkas out before you killed him. The only way for mortals to gain immortality is to die first."

I raised a shield to deflect his attempt to grab me. "Where'd you pull that one from? Velkas, right? He's the one who fed you those lies in the first place. *He* was immortal before I killed him. You were nothing to him."

"He gave me everything," he hissed. "He taught me to extract knowledge from the necromancers. He directed me to the Lady of the Tree, whose promise enabled me to learn how to conquer death."

"Was that the favour you asked for?" With her dying breath, the Lady of the Tree had laughed at me, asking if I knew which favour she'd offered to Calder. She'd said, *"He wanted revenge on humans, and he'll have it. You've already lost."*

"The Lady offered me immortality," he said. "I will have a new body, and you and your mage will die."

A heavy blow collided with the side of my head. I staggered, falling right into a second opponent. More had appeared from the fog, solid and angry, eyes like blue fire. Half-faeries.

A hit between the shoulder blades sent me flying backwards, struggling to catch my balance without a body or ground to steady me. Three more spirits rose upward to join Calder. Half-faeries, two Winter and one Summer.

"You can't even fight me alone when I don't have my body, huh." I layered derision into my voice. "Pathetic, but about what I'd expect, since you're nothing but a cheap imitation of Avalin. Did you know I met *his* ghost? His wraith was ten times stronger than you are now."

Calder threw magic at me in answer. Blue light suffused the air, mingling with my own, and our attacks both fizzled out in the same instant.

A whipcord of green light shot at me and snaked around my ankle. One of the half-faeries advanced on me, holding the whip's other end, and recognition hit me. "Lucas. Did you know your girlfriend was looking for you?"

He tugged the whip and yanked me off my feet. Since I wasn't on my feet in the first place, I fell sprawling across the air.

"You got us both killed," Lucas spat at me. "I want to play with her a little before you finish her off, Calder."

"Feel free," said Calder. "You'll get to watch her die, either way. I have more than enough time."

"Oh, you won't for much longer." I struggled as the whip pulled me upward by the feet, but my hands passed through bluish smoke as insubstantial as the grey haze around us. This place had no dimensions, and these ghosts had been here longer than I had. Long enough to figure out how to turn being dead into an advantage.

The whip brought me crashing down onto my back and sent a wave of pain up my spine. A punch to my chest knocked the breath from my lungs. The three half-faeries closed in, Lucas still holding the whip as his other hand pummelled at me.

"Fuck *off.*" I rolled sideways, calling my magic into a shield. Blue light flared, and as the whip loosened its hold, I shook myself free and leapt into the air. I didn't need to push off from the ground when I weighed nothing, and I swiftly caught my balance, too.

Once I adjusted to the weightlessness, fighting in Death wasn't too far removed from when I tapped into my faerie-enhanced speed in the waking world. I felt myself relax into the fluid movements I knew well, enhanced by the grace and speed my magic gifted me.

If this realm could trick my mind into thinking I felt pain, there was no reason I shouldn't be able to turn that same trickery on them. As I'd learned from my time with the faeries, reality was malleable. And I'd learned at the Trials that while most half-faeries might be good with magic, their knowledge of hand-to-hand was sorely lacking.

One faerie fell as I hammered a kick into the side of her head. Another reeled from a punch to the jaw. Most of my hits didn't connect, but unlike the half-faeries, I knew what I was doing in combat, and being punched in the face tended to draw the same reaction whether I was solid or not. Lucas flinched away as my fist sailed through his transparent face. Wisps of blue light surrounded me, mingling with the silver-grey light of Death.

Wait... silver?

The grey haze had pulled back, and below, I glimpsed silver-lit trees flanking a path that wound into the distance.

Huh? This can't be the Grey Vale. I couldn't have crossed over without knowing. I wasn't on the Ley Line, for a start. What kind of trickery was Calder up to this time?

I turned back to my attacker, but he'd vanished and so had the other half-faeries. In their place hovered two figures. Not fae but human. A kind-faced woman of average height, smiling at me, while a balding man put his arm around her.

"Mum," I whispered. "Dad..."

It's a trick. The veil had tricked me before, and I didn't need to be in Faerie for its insidious magic to reach into my mind and pluck out my inmost thoughts. These weren't my parents but shadows, distorted by memory and the foul magic that had conjured them.

"Oh, Ivy," my mother whispered. "You could have saved us. If you hadn't run."

I *had* run the day the faeries came, and a familiar series of images burst into life behind my eyes. Fleeing from the school gates, my feet slapping against the pavement. I tasted the fear on my tongue as my too-short legs carried me along until I reached the park, and the figure beckoning me to safety, away from my parents, away from everyone I knew.

Avalin's hand closed around mine. *"Welcome to your new home,"* he whispered. *"I've made it comfortable for you."*

I squeezed my eyes shut to dispel the illusion. "We've been through this already," I said loudly. "You can't use my past to screw with me anymore. I claimed Avalin's power, and I'm free."

"Not everyone would agree, Ivy." Calder's voice was close enough that my eyes jerked open, but my parents remained in front of me, their ghostly forms accompanied by others. Half-faeries. Some I recognised from among those killed in the Trials, or those who'd been arrested following the riots.

"So you recruited a plague of ghosts," I said. "I'm not impressed."

"That's not a nice way to speak to your old friends."

The spirits drew to either side, revealing a smaller group of short, transparent figures. The ghosts of Avalin's victims watched me with reproach and sadness in equal measures.

"Did you forget about them?" Calder's soft whisper trailed down my spine like ice. "They were waiting for you to save them, too."

The spirits from the castle. The ghosts of the people left behind when I'd knocked Avalin's castle down and tore my way out of Faerie using his magic. I'd helped Helena escape, but I hadn't seen any of the others in the illusion of Avalin's castle where I'd faced his wraith.

"They're an illusion." I spoke to convince myself more than anyone else. "Just like the Vale. We're not there."

"Who are you to dictate what is real, Ivy?" Calder laughed. "You know that in the Vale, nobody can truly die. Their suffering is entirely your fault."

Had Calder really gone into the Vale and recruited the spirits of the humans Avalin had killed? It was certainly in line with his usual strategies, but we weren't in the Vale. Of that, I had no doubt. "If you're telling the truth, *you're* the one preventing them from moving on."

The dead moved in on me, Lucas in the lead. I conjured a shield around myself and pushed back against the icy chill. I had one way to prove his illusion was fake… use my magic to draw upon the pain and distress of those left behind in the Vale.

If you're real, please forgive me.

The brightening blue glow brought the echo of a faint scream, but the silvery light of the Vale began to dissipate at once.

Then Calder's hands locked from my throat from behind.

I choked, kicked out. A burning ache spread through my chest. Calder's soft laughter sounded in my ear. Despite my rational mind telling me it was nothing but a trick, an unwelcome question arose. If I was choking here, what was happening to my body in the waking world?

"You're already dead, Ivy Lane," he whispered. "You lose this time."

No. My power came from Death itself, but I was the one who was still alive, not him.

I called my magic, but my shield wavered, too insubstantial to break his hold on my neck. Calder's ice-cold touch blistered against my skin, and my body spasmed so convincingly that my limbs went floppy. I found my hand inching towards my weapon, following an old instinct. If only I'd had my sword.

Blue light flared. My lungs burned, my limbs moving as though I was underwater. My outstretched hands might have belonged to someone else.

Wait. Ivy, have some sense. My hands were free, and while no weapon hung at my waist, wasn't my magic from the same source?

I closed my eyes and imagined my magic coalescing

around my hands as I held them out. Like I was gripping a blade. My mind conjured an image of shimmering light in my hands, and my tingling palms wrapping around a hilt.

Calder's hands released me. My eyes jerked open to a pillar of light in my hands, formed into a distinctly swordlike shape.

Calder gaped at me, shock etched on his face. "What—?"

"Now who's losing?" I brought the blade down in an arc.

The sword never reached its target. A sudden force pulled me backwards, and I crashed back into my body with the force of a car falling from a ten-foot height.

"Dammit." All that came out was a choked noise. My body felt like it'd been rammed through a cement mixer and then hung out to dry at the North Pole. Iciness weighed down my limbs. My vision was so blurry when I opened my eyes that the blood soaking my chest didn't register until the light of a healing spell shone above.

I lifted my head to look at who held the healing spell. Vance, bedraggled and soaked through. "Ivy." He sounded hoarse. "Your shield must have dropped. I'm sorry."

"I nearly had him," I managed to croak.

"You were bleeding out," said Vance, equally hoarsely. "The undead got you."

I touched a hand to my side. "The undead? Seriously?"

Had Calder somehow knocked out my shield while I'd been in Death? Or had I released it myself, too focused on fighting my opponent to remember I'd left my all-too-vulnerable body behind?

"I should have watched you more carefully." Vance brushed a strand of hair from my forehead. "Ivy, you're freezing cold."

"I did just—die." I coughed a rattling breath, and the world dissolved into blue-tinged blackness.

15

Numbness awaited me when I next woke. For an instant, I thought I'd run out of second chances, and death had claimed me for real. Aching coldness filled my bones despite the fireplace across from where I lay, orange flames burning low in the grate. I blinked a couple of times, identifying my surroundings as the room that served as a cross between an informal meeting place and a sitting room for mages who didn't live in the manor. The sofa I lay on was comfortable, I knew, but the pervasive cold prevented me from feeling the fire's warmth.

"Out of the question," Lady Granville's voice drifted in from somewhere nearby. *Great.* Just who I wanted to see right after coming back from a near-permanent trip to Death. "The necromancers cannot be trusted."

"If that's the case," said Drake, "I'm in favour of 'borrowing' the necromancers' extermination gear and exorcising this dickhead ourselves. How about that?"

"If you claim to know *where* this spirit is hiding—"

"I actually have a very good idea," said Vance in his most scarily calm voice. "But I'd prefer to wait until Ivy wakes up, because she has the better chance of exterminating this rogue spirit than any of us."

"Damn right." I tried to stand and fell off the sofa instead. I felt no pain despite the blood I knew must stain my clothes, but I didn't feel much of anything else either. My body ached with coldness so potent that the fire might not have existed. Understandable, given how long I'd spent in Death, but that I hadn't noticed my body had sustained a fatal wound was a major flaw in crossing the veil.

"Ivy?" Vance's soft footfalls sounded on the thick carpet.

"Yeah?" I grimaced, trying to push myself upright. My floppy limbs were presumably another side effect of losing contact with my body, but I sincerely hoped the effect was temporary.

Vance crouched beside me, worry etched in lines on his face. "Are you okay?"

"I can't feel my fingers."

He interlaced his hand with mine. "Does that help?"

"Not really, but it's nice." I leaned up and kissed him on the mouth. His hair had curled at the edges, presumably from showering, and he smelled clean. "Ah, shit. My hand's covered in blood and other crap. Sorry."

"I already used a cleansing spell."

"Just one?" I leaned in as he lifted me back onto the sofa. "I bet it took at least three."

"Four. Your clothes were a wreck."

"Nah, that's their default state." I didn't even want to know what my hair looked like. "How long was I out for?"

"All evening. It's past ten o'clock now."

"Any more…?"

"Ghosts?" he guessed. "A fair few, and the undead are a persistent problem, but Calder hasn't been sighted. As far as I know."

"I hope he's running scared." I flexed my numb fingers.

"Bloody hell. The necromancers never warned me that I'd wake up with frostbite."

"Drink this." Vance handed me a steaming mug.

I sipped the warm liquid and nearly choked. "Ugh. That's not hot chocolate."

"It's an energy restorative. I find it helps when I overextend my own abilities, so I thought it might work on you. Healing spells only regenerate so much energy. I worried when you didn't wake up."

"It tastes more like drinking turpentine," I said, but took another sip. Some of the warmth came back to my fingers.

"I'll ask Quentin to bring you some soup. What happened over there?"

I told him. He listened with deceptive calmness, though when Vance was in this particular realm of quietness, he was thinking of ways to dismember whoever had hurt me. When Quentin bought me a bowl, I devoured the soup, explaining my confrontation with Calder between bites.

"I don't know where he disappeared to," I finished. "I also don't know how he got that powerful, considering we bound his magic and left him with nothing. I'm guessing I was just tired out and that's why my shield dropped, but it felt way too real when he was strangling me."

Vance rested a hand on my knee. "I should have been keeping a closer watch on you. I'm sorry."

"It's not your fault," I said. "I should have gone somewhere safer before I went looking for Calder. I knew he was there, though. Watching us fight the hydra."

"Speaking of which, I sent the deceased necromancers' remains that you found in the troll's nest back to Lord Evander."

"I bet he was thrilled." I finished my soup, now considerably warmer. I'd been out for hours, and Isabel would be worried as hell, but there was no chance I'd be able to go back to the house tonight.

Vance peered at my face. "What is it?"

"Isabel."

"I called her. After I knew you weren't bleeding to death, that is."

"Thanks." I put my bowl aside. "Now I know why the necromancer handbook warns against disconnecting from your body for too long."

"You scared the hell out of me." He brushed a hand over my wrist and cupped my hand in his. "When you were over there, you were like a... like a statue."

"No wonder the necromancers are as stiff as corpses." I felt a lot better after the infusion of warmth, but I made a mental note to take more precautions before my next jaunt over to the other side. "Calder seems to have changed his strategy. Last I heard, he planned to make me watch him kill you before he put me out of my misery, but I guess he couldn't resist the impulse to challenge me to a ghostly duel."

"That's what he did?"

"Him and his allies." I suppressed a shudder, thinking of those forlorn ghosts abandoned in the Vale. I never did confirm if they were real or nothing more than an illusion. "Where's my sword?"

"Over there." He pointed over the sofa.

I leaned over to run my hand over the familiar hilt, wondering how close the illusion I'd conjured up had been to the real thing. "I wish I'd been able to take it with me into Death. Calder wouldn't have stood a chance."

"No." Vance's brow furrowed. "Calder's magic shouldn't be as strong as yours is."

"You'd think not." I released the hilt and settled on the sofa again. "But I never faced Avalin's original power. The one the Sidhe stripped away from him when he was exiled. That's what Calder would have inherited by blood."

"And his allies? Where'd he recruit them from?"

My insides pitched downward. "The Vale. They… died there."

"I thought the dead despised him." His burning gaze told me he hadn't forgotten the circumstances of Calder's death. I'd poisoned him with infected blood, and in the frenzy, his spirit had been dragged from his body by a flurry of pissed-off ghosts who'd fallen for his lies. Vance had finished him off with my blade, since I'd been incapacitated after the Invocation I'd spoken to seal his magic had detached me from my own body.

At the time, I hadn't thought I'd ever want to take a trip out of my body voluntarily. Really, I'd probably needed the reminder that the process was far from a risk-free venture.

"They did," I said. "I'm guessing he slipped into the Grey Vale before he could move on, because the ghosts he recruited are from there. And I—I'm the one who left them behind in Avalin's castle. I'm not saying it's all my fault," I added, as Vance opened his mouth to speak. "Just, you know, cause and effect are a real bitch."

"Mage Lord!" Drake shouted from across the room. "Lord Evander's here."

"Oh, for god's sake." I rose to my feet, but the energy drain dragging at my limbs threatened to pull me down again. "Can't he wait until morning?"

"I'll speak to him," said Vance.

"Not without me." I held myself upright and followed him into the hallway.

The front door stood open, and Lord Evander waited, his smart suit soaked through like he'd been standing in the rain. Which, given the drizzle washing over the lawn behind him, he probably had.

"Finally," he snarled. "I was beginning to think your guards were ignoring me on purpose."

"Lord Evander." I gave him a wan smile. "To what do I owe the pleasure?"

"You can cut the theatrics. Why, after you broke into my headquarters for no good reason, did you leave the delivery of the bodies of *my* people to the mercenary clean-up crew?"

Huh? Oh. He meant the necromancers I'd found in the troll's lair. "I was unconscious at the time, you know."

"That was my choice," Vance said. "Unfortunately, as you refused to respond to any of my mages' attempts to contact you, I had no choice but to call the clean-up crew. I apologise for your loss."

Lord Evander hissed out a breath. "And just how did you know where to find them in the first place?"

"We didn't." Man, I was tired. The front door was closed, but away from the fireplace, the coldness returned to my limbs. How Lord Evander had tolerated a lifetime of living in a place that amounted to a giant refrigerator was beyond me. "An undead troll attacked me at the canal yesterday, so we went to see where it came from, and we found your people in its lair. Plus a summoning circle. And an undead hydra. You might wanna look into that."

"We did," he said. "My examination of the little that remained of my fellow necromancers concluded that they were sacrificed."

"Sacrificed?" My heart plunged. "He killed them to raise that hydra from the dead, didn't he?"

"Who is 'he'?"

"Calder." At his blank expression, I added, "The half-faerie responsible for nearly breaking the veil a few months ago. His ghost refused to move on. Which, you know, is kind of your job."

"I don't know what you've stirred up this time, Ivy Lane, but my people were butchered. I want justice for them."

"You'll get it," said Vance tightly, "if you agree to properly communicate with the mages so that we are able to effectively put our forces together to deal with this threat. My own assistant had to order for salt deliveries throughout the city due to the ongoing undead incursions, which would have been a lot easier to manage if we had known which areas were higher risk."

"What more do you want of me?" snapped Lord Evander. "I already allow the pair of you unfettered access to my headquarters. I allow you to corrupt my apprentices and steal my Guardians away from their valuable jobs. Someone also stole a volume of necromancy and some valuable equipment from our headquarters during your last visit."

"What do I want from you?" I bit back a laugh. "I'm not going to claim it's your responsibility to deal with Calder. He's mine, but if I'm to kill him, I need to know more about how the spirit realm works. Give me access to your knowledge and I'll destroy the bastard before he kills us all. How's that for a deal?"

Lord Evander watched me for a moment. "Our knowledge, I rather think, is not what you seek."

"Oh, I have questions." I pushed on. "Is it possible to reunite a soul with a physical body?"

Lord Evander's mouth closed, then opened again. "No. What you're talking about is impossible. Once the body and spirit have spent too long apart, the soul decays and so does the body. The link is severed, permanently."

"A reanimated body *is* dead, effectively, isn't it? What about putting a soul in a new body?"

"Absolutely not."

"Two of your people got possessed the first time the veil lifted."

His stare turned icy cold. "And you used that as an excuse for committing a terrible crime."

"You of all people should know it's not impossible for a ghost to possess someone in the right circumstances," said Vance. "Especially a necromancer."

"I didn't mean to kill anyone that day," I added. "We need to put this crap behind us if we want to survive whatever the hell Calder's planning to do. It *is* possible to possess someone. Could a ghost do that long-term?"

Lord Evander's jaw worked. "I've never heard of a case where a ghost has survived in a person's body for longer than a minute, especially if the person being possessed is still alive. It's impossible for the connection to be permanent."

"Calder's plans have never exactly been workable," I said. "But he has conviction, and that's dangerous enough on its own. He even managed to avoid the Guardians and stay on this side of the gate."

"You *have* been reading the textbook." His eyes narrowed. "Where is it? Colby was hysterical."

Oops. "I'll give it back when I'm done. What else do you know?"

"Everything I know is in the book you stole," said Lord Evander. "As for Calder, whatever magic he wields, he's in for a disappointment if he truly expects to return to life."

"Don't be so sure," I warned. "He's recruiting other ghosts and preventing them from moving on. Even your Guardians are having trouble dealing with him. Not exactly a typical spirit, is he?"

He gave me an ugly look. "You might think you've swayed my predecessor over to your side, but you're mistaken."

"I'm right about Calder being a threat, though," I pressed. "What's your plan for the worst-case scenario? If Calder does manage to get another body and breaks the veil in the process?"

"Seal ourselves underground like we did in the last invasion."

Well. At least he was being honest.

"Will you?" Vance's every word carried the hint of a threat. "Need I remind you that you have a responsibility towards the people of this city?"

"No." Lord Evander shrank away from him. "You do not, and I highly doubt your smart-mouthed assistant's ridiculous theories are true. As it is, I will endeavour to keep you informed of areas of high undead activity in the future."

"See to it that you do," said the Mage Lord.

The door opened behind Lord Evander, and I shivered in the gust of air. The necromancers' leader gave Vance another wary look before he departed, and when he stepped outside, the door swung closed with enough force to knock him off the doorstep. I grinned at the notable thump on the other side. "Arsehole. Hope he gets soaked on the way home."

"Come upstairs." Vance caught my arm and steered me down the hallway.

My limbs began to sag again, forcing me to lean on him for balance.

"Want me to carry you?"

"I'm fine," I said through chattering teeth. "Your revolting potion worked like a charm."

"Your lips are blue."

"You didn't have a problem with my lips when I was kissing you."

"At least sit by the fire if you're going to be obstinate." He let me keep my dignity and walk upstairs to his room, and I sank gracelessly into the thick, warm carpet beside the fireplace.

"Bloody dead faeries," I mumbled into the soft mat beneath my face.

"You're actually going to sleep on the floor?" He sounded

amused. "The bed's not ten feet away. I can move us there without you having to open your eyes."

"Don't you dare." I reached my hands towards the fire, seeking the heat. "This carpet's thicker than my mattress back home, anyway."

He laughed, a quiet rumble low in his throat, and sat next to me, his long legs stretching beside the fire. I let him pull my head into his lap, fingers trailing through my hair.

"By the way, thanks for telling Lady Granville that I'll be the one to kill Calder."

"Of course." He spoke like it wasn't a big deal, but it was. "Lady Granville might not understand why I insist on involving you, but she'll vouch for me to make the right decision for the people of this city."

"Hope so," I murmured. "Because Lady Harper said you'd choose the mages over me. She said I was your weak link and that I had to step aside for the sake of you keeping your title."

He paused. "You didn't actually believe that, did you?"

"Of course not."

"Good." He resumed stroking my hair. "Lady Harper came here at a difficult time. She worries that Lady Granville will issue a challenge."

"She'd bloody better not."

"She won't. My mentor has a proclivity for paranoia, and a justified one, but she reacted wrongly in your case."

I shifted my legs closer to the fire. "She wasn't wrong to tell me I don't fit in with the council. They all think I'm a royal nuisance."

"The council has been in dire need of some disruption. Personally, recent events excepted, there's been a marked improvement since you started attending meetings."

"Except the murder accusation." When his fingers released my hair, I rolled over onto my elbow to properly look at him. "You know. That small detail."

"The accusation was unfounded."

"Not surprising, though." I sighed. "I know you're the Mage Lord and can overturn any challenge they might offer against me, but the others… they don't want me there. I'm not a mage and never will be."

"You've only been here a few months." He cupped my chin in his hand. "Give it time."

I made a sceptical noise. "The first time I came here I was thrown out on the street."

"What?" Vance's hand slid from my face. "Who threw you out? When?"

"Years ago, when I came back from Faerie." I'd never told him, more out of pride than anything. In truth, I didn't know why I was telling him now, except out of a desire to lay that old grudge to rest once and for all. "I ended up here at the manor and begged the first people I saw to help me. The mages told me they weren't a charity and closed the door in my face. And, you know, every time I look at Lady Granville, I see the same people who laughed at me and left me to sleep on the streets."

Vance drew me into his arms again. "I'm sorry that happened to you, Ivy. I didn't know."

"I was a kid." My voice cracked. "I get that you weren't all involved in that, but fuck, I can't deal with being treated like a criminal."

"That'll never happen again," said Vance. "I already made my position clear, but if necessary, I'll remove the council from the picture myself."

"I'm not asking you to fire the council." I didn't even know what I was asking, except for an end to the impotence of always being at the mercy of someone who held all the power.

"Well, I'd rather re-elect the entire council from scratch than see the woman I love killed by their wilful ignorance."

My breath caught. I might have said, *It was my decision to go after Calder, not the council's,* but all I could think was, *I nearly lost this. I nearly lost him.*

And despite how much of an absolute shit show I'd brought into his life, he'd just declared he'd put his own standing at risk for my sake without a second thought.

Because, inexplicably, he loved me.

And I—

When I'd nearly died saying the Invocation, I'd retreated in terror, pushed him away, because my instincts had known what my conscious thoughts had yet to accept. Even now, some part of me held onto the old fear of exposing my wounds for the world to see, though those same wounds healed every time he looked at me—*really* looked at me, like he saw the person I might have been if Faerie hadn't taken me.

I love you, I wanted to say back, but the words stuck in my throat. Though Vance was close, and the fire was warm, and I didn't fear the past any longer, my mouth refused to speak.

I kissed him instead. Straddling his lap, I leaned into his warmth and let my body tell him what my lips couldn't, not yet. He released a low growl that did more to warm me than the fire did, and I arched my body against his, wanting to feel him inside me and forget everything else. The firelight cast warm patterns on his muscled shoulders and chest as he leaned over me, grey eyes bright with need as great as my own.

Pleasure shuddered through my body as we moved in time with one another. I let my head fall back, let him love me, taking me to the edge and over. His scent wrapped around me, and for a while, there was just us, and the warmth of the fire.

16

Ghostly faces haunted my dreams, and I awoke to the sound of an alarm wailing. With a groan, I rolled over, legs tangled in the sheets. Vance must have moved us to the bed at some point after I'd passed out in front of the fire, but he wasn't here now. My ears registered the location of the wailing—somewhere outside the manor—and then its owner.

The banshee.

I jumped to my feet, ran to the wardrobe and grabbed my spare clothes. *Vance.* Why hadn't he woken me when he'd left the room? Questions cascaded through my mind as I shoved my feet into my boots and ran out of the bedroom. My sword's burning light shone like a torch, reflecting off the white wallpaper as I ran downstairs. I reached the bottom and sprinted to the front door, which lay ajar.

God. No. Please—not Vance.

I hurtled outside and straight past Wanda.

She gasped. "Ivy?"

"What?" I skidded to a halt on the path. "Vance. Where—"

"He's okay. Ivy, but… Lord Evander… he's dead."

The wailing stopped.

So did the world.

I stared at Wanda for a moment, my mind moving sluggishly. "The banshee wasn't screaming for him."

"Banshee?" she echoed. "Is that what that ungodly screaming was? I was going to look, but Vance ordered me to stay behind."

"She screams whenever someone's going to die. Please—stay in here." My legs remembered how to move again, and I continued down the path to the front gate.

A horrible snarling reached my ears, no longer masked by the banshee's screeching. I picked up the pace and sprinted out into the road in time to see Vance leap at the throat of a huge hellhound. His blades flashed out, held in clawed hands, and the hellhound sank beneath him. A second slash cleaved its neighbour's neck, sending its head flying in a spray of blood.

Spying two more beasts across the road, I ran at them with my sword held high. One slash decapitated the first, while Vance ran to help with the second. His blade flashed out and its severed head flew sideways. As he caught up to me, the sword reappeared in Vance's hand, covered in gristle and bone.

"Vance, why didn't you tell me you were being attacked?" I spoke lightly despite the weight of Wanda's revelation hanging over me. "Was it hellhounds who killed—killed Lord Evander?"

"No," he replied. "The necromancers found his body a mile outside the city. No one knows how he got there, or why."

I stared. What had he been doing out there? "And the hellhounds? How'd I manage to sleep through that?"

"You were out cold. I was worried about you."

"I'm fine." More so than Lord Evander, anyway. "Did you hear the banshee?"

"I did." He scanned the street, his jaw tightening. "That's what drew me outside. If I hadn't heard, the hellhounds might have fatally injured one of my security guards."

"Whose death was she warning of this time?" I checked my phone. No messages from Isabel had shown up. She probably didn't know yet. "Not Lord Evander's. If he was a mile outside the city, how'd they find him?"

"A tracking spell," he replied. "His apprentices got concerned when they realised he never came back to the guild last night."

"Shit." I lifted my head when my sword lit up with blazing blue light. "There are more."

The blazing light pointed me to the street's corner—near where Ralph had died—and I ran to meet the hellhound coming the other way. My blade sliced up, magic bursting from both sides, and the hound's head exploded across the pavement.

A flash of fire drew my attention to Drake, who did battle with another monster. As his fire struck, the hellhound's flesh melted from its bones, its protruding teeth still snapping in anger as it fell apart.

"See, I'm not just a pretty face," said Drake, spying me watching him. "Behind you!"

I speared the beast creeping up on me, sending a blast of magic through my blade that took the hellhound's legs out from underneath it. Another blast, and its head exploded into a grisly mess.

"I think that's the last one." Vance pulled his own sword out of what was left of the hellhound Drake had set on fire. "The banshee..."

"Shit, that's who was screaming?" Drake gave a shudder. "I thought someone saw Lady Granville naked."

"Drake." Vance gave him a pointed look. We both swivelled to see Lady Granville herself marching across the road towards us.

Hoping she hadn't heard Drake, I gestured to the hellhounds. "I don't suppose you saw where these charming individuals came from?"

Lady Granville slowed, fury carved on her face. "What the devil is happening here?"

"We *were* under attack," Drake said. "Luckily, some of us were quick on the mark. Did you hear—" He cut off in a hiss of surprise, and I followed his gaze across the road, where grey mist coalesced around an indistinct figure. A ghost.

I tensed, lifted my blade, but the spirit's outline suggested it was human, not fae. And from the expressions on the others' faces, they saw it, too. Even Lady Granville. *Oh, hell.*

Drake turned to me as the mist faded along with the spirit. "Did you see that? Tell me I'm not the only one who saw that."

"The veil," I murmured. "We shouldn't be able to see that from here." Or rather, *I* shouldn't. The others shouldn't be able to see it at all.

A distinct scream—human, not banshee—rang over the rooftops. Drake took a few steps that way, lifting his head. "I don't think we're the only ones seeing apparitions. Fuck me, what's going on now?"

"The veil is unstable," Vance said grimly. "This is one of the side effects."

"And the person who's supposed to handle this kind of thing is dead." The colour drained from Drake's face. "Shit."

Lady Granville gave a disapproving sniff at his language. "Tell me what is going on at once."

"The city is under attack from the dead," Vance said. "Salt has already been dispersed to central locations and barriers are being set up throughout the city on my orders. We're prepared for undead, but if ghosts are appearing en masse..."

"And they can walk through wards." My blood chilled. "We're not safe anywhere. Maybe not even in the manor."

"Is that so?" Lady Granville tutted. "I was given to understand that you had a strategy prepared to handle the person responsible for this."

Damn her for turning Vance's words against both of us. "You worry about protecting the public."

And staying out from under my feet.

"We'll have to put out another emergency broadcast." Drake nodded to Vance. "I'll do it. I have a very soothing voice."

"This isn't a joke," Lady Granville said.

"Oh, I'm fucking terrified," Drake said, deadpan. "But I won't let the ghosts have the last laugh."

Our group returned to the manor, where Vance made calls to the other mages and arranged for them to spread across the city. There weren't anywhere near enough to cover the whole range of possible targets, but it would help if I knew *where* Calder was hiding.

"The other council members are on their way, are they?" Drake was saying to Lady Granville. "Has anyone actually seen Lord Carlisle since last night?"

"What's that?" Vance moved closer, looking between them.

"Lord Carlisle is missing."

"He isn't missing," Lady Granville said. "He hasn't checked in yet. Lady Penrose is on the way."

"Is that true?" Vance faced Lady Granville. "When did you last hear from him?"

"Last night." She met Vance's stare unflinchingly. "I believe it's unwise for any of us to leave the manor."

My phone vibrated in my pocket. Isabel's message said,

"Ivy. There's a faerie outside our house. Outside the wards. She's staring at me."

"Vance." I strode over to him and whispered, "There's a faerie outside my flat. I have to go."

Vance nodded. Without so much as a warning to the other mages—several of whom were trying to talk to him— he transported us to the street outside my house.

Right in the path of the banshee. I swung my blade but missed, unbalanced from our sudden arrival. The banshee recoiled, talons rising in front of her face to protect herself.

"What are you doing?" she hissed.

"Get away from my house." I stepped protectively in front of the gate. "Did you come here to gloat at me about how you murdered the necromancers' leader, is that it?"

"What?" She shrank away from my blade. "No, I came to warn you, human."

"That someone will die? You're too late for that."

"Lying scum," said Vance. "How many more people did you manipulate on Calder's orders?"

As she tried to protest, my sword's tip nicked the skin of her throat. "We both know you're the one who caused the jailbreak and then killed everyone involved. I'm guessing so that they'd have no choice but to join Calder as ghosts."

"No… I didn't." She made a noise of gurgling terror as my blade cut into her neck. "I—I tried to stop them, but I was too late. You don't understand what he's planning. Do you know of the Wild Hunt?"

"Only by hearsay." The Hunt was where the hellhounds had originated, or so I'd heard. "Don't change the subject. You expect me to believe you tried to stop the jailbreak when you manipulated the guards into leaving their posts?"

"I'm not lying." Her eyes bulged, following the stream of crimson where my blade had sliced into the skin of her throat. "I knew Calder when he was alive. I can help you."

"This had better be good." I didn't lower my blade. "If you're telling the truth, why'd you pretend to be guarding the jail?"

"To warn you," she replied. "Death fae are distrusted by most."

"Can't imagine why." I narrowed my eyes. "Your warning was of no use whatsoever. And for the record, I have no reason to believe you aren't the one who lured away the manor's guards—and the necromancers' leader, too. Which of them did you scream for?"

"I told you I never know *who* will die." More blood trickled down her neck. "And I cannot stop their deaths. That is beyond my power."

"Ivy!" Isabel called over the garden wall. Her arms were covered in band-shaped spells, and she held a saltshaker in each hand. "I take it she's not a villain, if her head's still attached?"

"Oh, she is, I'm just deciding how to decapitate her." I ignored the banshee's whimper. "You should probably stay in the house. The veil is acting up all over the city. Unless... do you still have the necromantic equipment you borrowed? We'll need it."

"What's going on with the veil?" Isabel asked. "I've tried messaging Colby, and there's been no response."

"Lord Evander's dead. There are hellhounds on the loose, and Calder's planning an attack." I turned back to the banshee. "*She* promised to tell us more, but so far all she's done is lie."

"I am not lying." The banshee tried to wriggle away from my blade. "You're all in terrible danger."

"We already knew that," Vance said. "Tell us now, banshee. You mentioned the Wild Hunt. The hellhounds came from there, correct?"

"On the rare occasion that war comes to Faerie and blood

is spilled, the Wild Hunt come to collect the dead." Her tone held a hint of reverence that I didn't care for in the slightest. "They say that the leader of the Hunt is a true immortal and cannot be killed, even with iron. He is an entity apart from the Sidhe and can travel through all the realms… even Death itself."

I gaped at her. "If that's true, he hasn't come back to fetch his hellhounds. They've been roaming around here for weeks."

"I would not be so quick to make assumptions." She offered a smile, a quick flash of white teeth. "The leader of the Wild Hunt is also said to possess the ability to return the dead to life…and to immortality."

"Bullshit." Death was final. Even for the Sidhe. Everyone knew that.

"It is true, and Calder intends to call the Hunt for his own purposes." She bared her teeth again, in more of a grimace than a smile. "I am no friend to them either, Ivy. Your realm will suffer greatly when the Wild Hunt rides."

"Bad faerie!" Erwin came zipping out of the house and flew at the banshee.

Startled, she sprang back, impaling her own throat on my blade, and when he landed on her head, she let out a piercing shriek, tearing at her hair.

"Erwin, no." I moved my blade back to avoid accidentally hitting him. "What are you doing?"

"Protecting you!" screamed the piskie.

Oh, dear god.

The banshee let out an inhuman hiss and ran, so fast that she left the bewildered piskie hanging upside-down in midair. I might have chased after her, but if she'd told the truth, we had bigger problems on our hands. The Wild Hunt was certainly a real entity, but that its leader could supposedly return the dead to life… no. It was absurd. Though

Calder had claimed the same, and he seemed to genuinely believe it. Either way, a plague of hellhounds was dangerous enough *without* a leader.

"We need to move." I faced Isabel. "The mages are putting out a warning to the public, but it's going to get really nasty out here. And with the state the necromancers are in, there's no guarantee they'll be in any position to protect anyone."

She sucked in a breath. "He's dead? Lord Evander? Are you sure?"

"Unfortunately yes," I said. "I imagine that's why Colby isn't answering the phone."

"Damn. Wait, what's Vance doing?"

I turned and saw Vance walking back towards the house, holding the struggling banshee in a headlock.

"Mercy!" she shrieked. "I knew him. Calder. I knew him as a child. I know where he lived."

"You're a child, too." She didn't talk like one, but I doubted creepy death fae hung out with regular teenagers. "Tell me where he lived, then."

"It's easier if I show you," she said. "If you venture into the home of the outcasts on your own, you will be taken as a threat."

"Bite me." Outcasts? I assumed she meant in *this* realm, not the Vale, but it was true that there were fae squatting in all kinds of abandoned corners of the city that humans had long forsaken.

Vance swore, releasing the banshee with one hand and grabbing his phone with the other. "They're trying to get hold of me at the manor. I have to go."

"Don't take her with you," I said, though hell if Lady Granville didn't deserve to be serenaded by a banshee. "I'll go with her. If it's a trap, I'll tear off her ears so she can't hear her own song."

"Absolutely not. You can't go alone."

"You need to help the mages," I reminded him. "I can kill her if she turns on me. It's a non-issue."

If the veil was fracturing all over the city, I was in no more danger with the banshee than I was anywhere else. With reluctance, Vance loosened his hold, and the banshee skipped away, massaging her bleeding neck.

"I shall prove my word is true, human." She beckoned a clawed finger. "This way."

17

I followed the banshee's lead, tapping into my magic-enhanced speed to ensure she never left my sight. The walk was long, but taking the bus would have been out of the question even if there hadn't been ghostly apparitions popping up out of nowhere.

Finally, we came to a run-down apartment complex with the same aura of neglect as the mercenaries' place, except with a more obvious faerie presence. Vines snaked down from the roofs and spiked plants sprouted from the windows of abandoned flats, all dull and leafless under the winter sky.

So this was where my mortal enemy had grown up. "Calder lived… here?"

The area was surprisingly ordinary, faerie plants aside. The buildings had once been serviceable flats, but the invasion had hit hard, and the impoverished—and clearly, half-faeries who didn't want to live on the Chief's territory—had moved in. Kids, mostly. When a bunch of teenagers with horns and claws emerged from the overhang outside the largest block of flats, the banshee waved her talons at them, and they scuttled away into the bushes.

"You live here, too?" I guessed. "Not half-blood territory."

"I dislike rules. I heard you do, too, and yet you're the Mage Lord's…"

"Girlfriend and coworker, if you really want to put a label on it," I said, "and I'm not here to talk about him. I'm here to find out how you knew Calder. And how you know about this Wild Hunt. You seem to know an awful lot about Faerie for someone who's never been there."

"So does Calder," she said. "This way."

Gleaming eyes watched us from the shadows as the banshee opened the front door to the apartment building. So many kids, left to fend for themselves. No wonder Calder had turned to Velkas as soon as he'd had the chance. Question was, how had Velkas found him in the first place? Maybe because he'd made no secret of his half-Sidhe heritage and had probably told everyone he met that he was Avalin's son.

It didn't matter, not really. I didn't need to know my enemy. Only how to beat him.

The banshee led me upstairs to the first floor and pushed open a wooden door rotting from its hinges. Inside was a room even dingier than the corridor. Bare floorboards. Furniture barely functional. Only a bed and a bookshelf in the main room. Calder's man cave, I guessed. I didn't know what I'd expected. Curtains made from his enemy's corpses, maybe. There wasn't a weapon in sight, nor any sign of living presence. He *had* been dead for months, though.

"The other kids raided his room," the banshee explained.

"So how do you know I'll find anything?" The place was abandoned, and even if he'd come back here as a ghost, he hadn't been able to manifest in a physical form in a long while. That likely meant a tracking spell would be useless, but it was worth a try.

I called my magic into a shield around myself before I set up a tracking spell on the filthy floorboards.

"There's no need to do that," the banshee said petulantly. "I'm not going to attack you."

"I always cover my back." I crouched down and plunged my hands into the tracking spell.

Green lights ignited. Calder appeared before my eyes so suddenly that I damn near jumped out of the vision altogether. He walked—no, floated—across the bare floorboards to the broken desk. *He's dead.* How long ago had this been? Tracking spells didn't reach very far into the past, but so few people ever set foot in here that the imprint might have lingered for a more extended period of time than usual.

Calder's ghostly form crouched beside the desk and extended his hands over a gap in the floorboards. His face screwed up in concentration that swiftly turned to annoyance as he was unable to touch the floor. *What's he trying to do?*

The vision faded. I rose upright and crossed the room to the spot where he'd been standing. My fingers scraped the floorboards and nudged against a loose edge, and I lifted the board upward. *Gotcha.*

Inside lay a copy of the necromancers' handbook identical to my own, albeit considerably more battered and worn than the one I'd borrowed from the guild.

"I wonder if Lord Evander ever noticed *he* stole this?" I muttered to myself as I picked it up. He'd turned the corners of several pages down, including the one depicting a map of the UK criss-crossed with lines. The text above read, *the spirit paths.*

"What does all this mean?" I lifted my gaze to the banshee. "A necromancer handbook isn't going to mention the Wild Hunt of Faerie." Though it did confirm he'd been dabbling with necromancy before he'd passed beyond the veil himself.

"He intends to summon the Hunt," said the banshee. "That much I know."

"Summoning creatures from Faerie isn't the same as raising the dead." Not that either was good news with the veil in this state. Calder would wake up more than ghosts if he continued on his bizarre quest to immortalise himself.

I flipped to another marked page and found a brief layout of how to conduct a summoning. I'd already read the same section in my own copy of the book. The gist was that a summoning had two main requirements: a circle of candles to contain the spirit being summoned, and a surge of concentrated energy aimed to pierce the veil in a controlled manner.

The rest, according to the book, depended on what was being summoned. The rules were clear: only summoning the ghost of a person was contained under the necromancers' sacred oath. No other summonings were permitted, though the textbook refrained from going into any detail on what those might be. I guessed it had been too much to expect a handbook the necromancers gave to novices to contain details of illegal rituals.

Is summoning the Wild Hunt really the same as summoning a spirit? I was pretty sure Calder had never used a summoning circle when he'd called the hellhounds, though admittedly summoning circles were a safety measure and nothing more. I'd proven that a skilled necromancer didn't *need* a circle to travel into Death, if you were willing to take the risk. Calder, I was certain, didn't give a shit about safety.

As for the second requirement? A mass of concentrated energy might come from anywhere. Necromantic candles themselves contained enough energy to call back almost any spirit, and that was where the textbook drew to a definitive halt. I knew, though, that summoning hellhounds required more than a few candles. And that was assuming it worked the same way as the sort described in the handbook. I doubted the necromancers and the faeries had ever compared notes.

I lifted my gaze to the banshee. "How much did Calder tell you? *Can* the Wild Hunt be summoned like a ghost? They aren't spirits, are they?."

"They are, in a way." A smile curled her lip. "They are echoes of the dead, yet so much more."

"What the hell does that mean?" I dropped my hand to my sword's hilt, not trusting the glint in her eye.

"I'm trying to help you." The smile slipped from her face. "I have no desire to see the Hunt ravage my home either."

"You knew what Calder was doing, but you never challenged him?" My hands curled into fists. "I assume you also knew when he was drugging people at the Trials?"

"Anyone who refused to join him met an unpleasant end." Her mouth turned down at the corners. "My death magic scared him enough that he didn't dare try to recruit me."

"Then how'd you figure out what he was doing?"

"He talked to himself." She gestured to the book. "I didn't see that, but I can guess it is where he learned how to tap into the spirit paths."

"There's nothing about the Hunt in here." There *was* a lot about screwing with the boundaries between life and death, which was also very much of interest to Calder. He'd planned to become immortal long before he'd met his demise. "What spirit paths? The Ley Line?"

Spirit paths. I flipped back to the page he'd marked. That was the official name for places like the Ley Line, where our own realm overlapped with the next world. The Ley Line had gained notoriety due to being the site of the faerie invasion, but it was far from the only path into Death. The entire country was covered in a web of interconnecting lines, and key points formed where two lines intersected.

Places of power. They didn't have to be on the Ley Line at all.

Is that why we haven't been able to find him? He's hiding on another spirit line? Did the other lines lead into the Grey Vale, too? All of them were tied to Death in the same way, and given the number of lines spiderwebbing across the page, it was no wonder the ghosts were appearing all over the city, not just at the Ley Line.

I fished my phone out of my pocket, keeping one eye on the banshee, and typed out a message to Isabel. *Do you have a map that shows all the spirit lines? I think Calder's been using one that isn't the Ley Line to hide out on. And it's where he plans to summon the Wild Hunt, according to the banshee.*

The last part might not be true, but if the necromancers had neglected to watch the other spirit lines outside of the main one, it explained how the undead problem had spread across the city so fast. Who needed a summoning circle when the spirit lines themselves were formed of pure concentrated energy, uncontrolled and untamed? The textbook didn't spell it out, but it wasn't hard to add two and two. Or to guess that Calder's plan involved harnessing those same spirit lines.

A response came from Isabel: *Didn't they find Lord Evander's body outside the city?*

I swore softly. The necromancers thought he'd been sacrificed, and if he had, I'd bet my sword it'd been on a spirit line. And the death of the most powerful necromancer in the city would certainly trigger a surge of energy on a level capable of summoning worse than a hydra.

I messaged Isabel back: *can you get Colby to give you the location?*

Failing that, I'd ask him myself, but Lord Evander had died hours ago. We might already be too late.

Isabel's next message: *They mentioned it was on a spirit line. I'll ask if they know which one.*

The banshee let out a scream when a ghost stepped out of the wall. I jumped to my feet, grabbing my sword with one hand and attempting to cover my ears with the other.

"Ivy." The ghost's face blurred into someone I knew.

"Ralph." My mouth dropped. "Erm. Sorry you're dead. What're you doing here?" I assumed the veil had brought him back like the other spirits, but how had he known when to find me?

"I came to warn you, Ivy." His voice was quiet, subdued, and free of its usual derision. "One of the Mage Lords is stealing from the storeroom."

"Ralph…" A thousand questions exploded in my mind, but thanks to the banshee's squalling, all I managed to say was, "I'm sorry, what?"

"A mage is opening the storeroom where you put the talisman."

"*Who?*" Impossible. The wards kept out hostile threats, and the only people able to access the stores were the five Mage Lords.

"A man," said Ralph. "Older. I don't know his name."

"Lord Carlisle." Hadn't he been unaccounted for? Oh, fuck.

"He was stealing—" Ralph recoiled from the banshee as if seeing her for the first time. "Why are you meeting with a harbinger, Ivy?"

The banshee ceased her screaming and gave me a wide grin. "A mage stealing from the storeroom? I told you I wasn't the traitor, Ivy."

"Don't push me." My hand clenched around my sword. I was closer to the mages' storeroom than I was to the manor, but not telling Vance first was out of the question. "The mage you saw has been missing since this morning. Maybe since last night."

The banshee might easily have bewitched him earlier. She

wasn't off the suspect list, but I didn't have time to stick around and play mind games with a death fae. I'd got all the information I'd come here for. The rest could wait until the mages were safe.

I tucked the book under my arm and ran out of Calder's flat, using every ounce of faerie-enhanced speed to propel myself downstairs and out the front door. The half-faerie children stared as I ran out of the cul-de-sac, the blood thrumming in my veins.

I'll kill your mage first.

When had the enemy got to Lord Carlisle? It had to be recent. The manor was warded against threats, but we'd learned from the two bewitched guards that someone could walk in while under the influence of faerie glamour and it wouldn't trip the alarms unless they made a direct threat.

Lord Carlisle hadn't. The enemy wanted him to get into the storeroom instead. *Why*, I didn't know. Maybe he wanted a means of reversing the Invocation I'd used to seal his magic, if such a thing was possible. If not, the life-drinker was an equally likely target. It had once belonged to Velkas, so Calder probably saw the blade as rightfully his.

I got out my phone and fired off a message to Vance, hoping I remembered the way to the storeroom. Mist drifted in patches, but I didn't stop for long enough to see if any ghosts materialised.

A message came from Isabel pinged my phone and nearly caused me to trip over mid-sprint.

At a key point a few miles outside of town, three lines intersect. That's where they found Lord Evander.

Fuck. If *three* lines intersected in the same spot, I could only imagine the concentration of raw power that would result from sacrificing a high-ranked necromancer.

I pocketed my phone and renewed my sprint, picking up speed when I recognised the route I'd taken to find Vance in the cemetery. My sword's glow frequently warned me of nearby fae, but I ignored them all, like I did the ghosts. Nothing mattered but getting to that storeroom.

I skidded to a halt at the road's end, hardly winded. Faerie magic sure came in handy sometimes, though I had the worried suspicion that my power was enhanced due to the state of the veil. With Death spilling into this realm, it was natural that the faerie realm pressed closer, too. The two were entwined far more profoundly than anyone knew. I might have run through a dozen spirit lines on the way here without having the slightest idea.

I followed the country lane where the depository sat. The unassuming brick building appeared little changed since my last visit, but my sword's warning glow told me hostile fae lurked nearby.

I ran to the door and kicked it open. The corridor on the other side stank of the dead, but the man who stood inside was undoubtedly alive. Lord Carlisle was in the process of leaving the room that contained the mages' most valuable artefacts, and he held the parchment that contained the Invocations in one hand.

"Get away from there," I told him. "You've been bewitched, or… something." I trailed off when he turned around, his expression not the blank slate of someone under a spell but a mask of uncharacteristic anger. His eyes had turned the bluish silver of a Winter Sidhe—which was impossible.

"You're Ivy, right?" The voice that came from his mouth sounded like someone much younger. "I just needed some assistance."

Holy shit, he's being possessed. By a half-faerie. What better way to break into a depository that only the Mage Lords had access to?

"You can't speak those," I said, one eye on the shimmering parchment.

"You can."

A pressure hit the back of my head. I gasped, my vision fracturing, as pain split my skull. Images burst inside my mind, violent and bloody, and enough for me to realise the bastard was trying to *possess* me.

I hit out, but punching Lord Carlisle had zero effect on the ghost. Agonising pressure burned inside my head, like flames licking the inside of my eyes. I clenched my jaw and willed my blade to absorb the pain, to drive it straight back at its owner.

Magic blasted from my hand, mercifully hitting the spirit and not Lord Carlisle. The spirit had let go of his host in the hopes of switching to a more valuable one, but I would *not* let my body become a vessel for one of Calder's twisted-minded lackeys. Fuck that.

I had a talisman from a Sidhe Lord. This dickhead wasn't even alive.

The blast of magic knocked him back, and the spirit lurched forward, his mouth twisting in anger.

"Go to hell," I told him.

"I'm already there, Ivy."

Pressure burst behind my eyes again, but my sword came up in a blur of light. The spirit's blue eyes widened as his ghostly form broke apart into fragments. The parchment fluttered free, and I reached to snag it between my fingertips. As the text passed my vision, words leaped to life on my tongue, and I clamped my mouth shut against the sudden compulsion. Did the Invocations *want* me to speak them? I hadn't held the parchment in my hand since I'd bound Calder's magic, but I had no intention of voicing an unknown spell that might summon the Wild Hunt for all I knew.

I need to put this thing back where it belongs. I faced the door to the Invocation chamber and felt the resistance of the wards built into its surface. "I'm not here to steal anything."

I tentatively pushed on the door handle and released it as my hand burned like I'd placed it on a hot stove. Ow. *Dammit.* That the wards had let in the possessed Lord Carlisle but refused access to me was a glaring hole in security that I'd definitely have to mention to Vance.

Wait a moment. I crouched beside Lord Carlisle, who'd slumped against the wall. His eyes were closed, but he had a pulse. And for the purposes of the security room, he counted as a Mage Lord whether he was conscious or not.

I pulled his arm forward and pressed Lord Carlisle's palm against the door to the Invocation chamber.

The wards flashed, once, and the door swung inward. I met another layer of resistance when I tried to put the Invocations into the room, so I shoved the parchment into Lord Carlisle's hand instead and draped his arm over the entrance until he let go. Leaving the Invocations on the floor wasn't ideal, but it would have to do until another Mage Lord showed up. Hopefully this one wouldn't be possessed.

Vance. Where are you? He couldn't know what was going on—Ralph had come to me, likely because he'd known I'd be more likely to be able to see and interact with him—but if one Mage Lord had been under the enemy's influence, might the same apply to the others? Lady Granville didn't need to be possessed to be an obstructionist. I was pretty sure no spirit would tolerate being in her head for longer than a minute, but still.

A thud sounded outside. I grabbed my blade and ran to the door.

"Vance." Relief flooded me to see him on the doorstep, coat fluttering in the breeze stirred up by his arrival. "Thank god."

"Ivy." His eyes widened at the sight of Lord Carlisle's unconscious body. "Is he...?"

"He's alive," I said. "He was possessed. By a half-faerie ghost."

Horror dawned on his face. "I never thought... but it makes sense. He's part necromancer, and with the state of the veil..."

"He is?" Damn. How long had the spirit been hitching a ride in his body? Surely not before today, or else he'd have broken in much sooner. "Ralph came to warn me he was stealing from here. He nearly took the Invocations."

Vance swore. "And the banshee?"

"I left her at Calder's apartment." I held up the necromancers' handbook. "He was using this before he died, and I figured out what he's up to. The banshee claims he wants to summon the Wild Hunt, and I think that's why he sacrificed Lord Evander. The place where they found him was at an intersection of three spirit lines."

"Three?" His eyes widened. "Not the Ley Line?"

"No, but there are spirit lines all over the country, and three intersecting in the same place is bound to be the site of some serious power."

Vance's expression darkened. "The Wild Hunt... that means the hellhounds? He's intending to summon more?"

"Worse." I pushed on. "The banshee also claimed their leader is a godlike being who is essentially a true immortal. And that he can make others immortal, too. No idea if it's true, but isn't that what Calder's been claiming he wants to achieve all along?"

"Yes." His voice was tight. "True or not, we have a problem. Lady Granville is still insisting that the mages stay at the manor rather than dispersing throughout the city, and I have no doubt she'll redouble her efforts when I tell her of Lord Carlisle's possession."

"Pity she's not the one who got possessed." Hadn't she been against looking for him in the first place? "What, she wants you to hide?"

"She claims we need to leave the cleanup to the necromancers."

"Whose leader just died." As a sacrifice. "Are you sure she isn't...?"

"No, she isn't possessed." Vance leaned down and hoisted Lord Carlisle's unconscious body over his shoulder. "You destroyed the spirit, I assume?"

"Yes, but Lady Granville doesn't need to be possessed to be working against you." With or without Calder. The result would be the same: if she had her way, all the mages would look the other way while the city dissolved into chaos. "We'd better go."

Vance transported the three of us to the manor's doorstep. The mages had assembled on the lawn, and Lady Granville swooped in on us immediately. When she saw Lord Carlisle, her mouth formed an expression that was probably supposed to show relief but instead looked more like she was chewing on a lemon. "You found him."

"Yes." The chill in Vance's tone would have given a Winter ghost a run for their money. "He was possessed by a ghost who was attempting to manipulate him into stealing from the depository, but luckily, Ivy was able to get rid of the spirit."

"He was *possessed*?" she asked.

"Yes, and when he wakes up, he needs to be questioned to determine how much information he gave to the enemy." Ahead of us, the manor's door opened. Vance gestured ahead. "As the spirit in question was likely involved in Ralph's murder, it seems appropriate for you to conduct the questioning yourself, doesn't it?"

I bit back a laugh at her huff of disbelief. "You wanted to

stay at the manor, right?" I said. "You question him, and we'll deal with the dead. Everyone's happy."

"Or we're all equally miserable." Drake sauntered over. "Ivy, your friend's outside."

"Isabel?" I figured the pair of them could handle Lady Granville between them. "I'll be right back."

I hurried to the front gate. Isabel waited on the other side, accompanied by Colby of all people. The apprentice's skinny frame was bowed under the weight of a heavy-looking rucksack.

"He was the only necromancer I could get hold of," she explained. "The others are scattered, but Lord Evander tried to ground him for losing his textbook. That was before he…"

"Died." I looked apologetically at Colby. His face was flushed and his eyes reddened, like he'd been crying. "Sorry. It's not good news for the rest of us either. Isabel, you didn't run into anything nasty on the way here? I did tell you not to leave the house."

"I figured the mages could make use of some of the necromancers' equipment." She hefted a rucksack over one shoulder. "You're okay? Did I miss any new world-ending apocalypses while you were gone?"

"Only a Mage Lord getting possessed and breaking into his own storeroom," I replied. "I took care of it, don't worry."

Vance swept in behind me. "Isabel. And you're Lord Evander's apprentice?"

"Y-yes." Colby looked as if he might pass out from being in the Mage Lord's presence. "I can wait outside."

"He and Isabel brought equipment from the necro-mancers in case anyone needs assistance," I explained. "Did you get Lady Granville off your back?"

"For the time being," he said. "Yes, we can certainly make use of that equipment. Did you bring sensors?"

"And exterminators," Isabel added. "And—oh, Ivy, is that the necromancers' handbook?"

She'd noticed the book I held tucked under my arm.

"This one used to be Calder's." I swivelled to Colby. "Sorry, I should have asked before I borrowed yours. I can give it back now I have my own."

Not that I relished the idea of keeping anything Calder had put his slimy hands on, but at my words, Colby nearly burst into tears of gratitude on the spot.

"Thanks," he choked. "I need that textbook to remember my incantations."

"The equipment?" Vance said.

Colby awkwardly dropped the rucksack at his feet. "There are candles in there as well as sensors. Everything I could get."

"Excellent." Drake sprang up behind us. "Is this the necromancers' ghost extermination gear?"

"This is a sensor." Isabel held one out to him. "It detects spirits, but we'll mostly need to use the emergency backup weapon built in. Just hit the button and any spirit in its path will dissolve into ectoplasm."

"Point, shoot, and the ghost explodes. Got it."

I snorted. "I hope there's enough for everyone, but we need to deal with the source of this."

"The spirit line." Isabel gave me an anxious look. "What you said in your message… do you really think Lord Evander was sacrificed intentionally? What's this Wild Hunt?"

"Bad news," I said, nodding to Vance. "I don't know if that's his goal, but sacrificing a powerful necromancer at an intersection of three lines is bound to have knock-on effects, and I'm assuming Calder's still hanging around out there."

Hearing, Colby swayed so violently that he had to grab the hedge for balance. "What? My master…?"

I ignored him. "I can't imagine whoever sacrificed him picked the location at random."

"I'll assemble a team," Vance said. "We'll head there immediately. Drake, you'll stay in charge of the mages here while we're gone."

"Oh, I'm not staying out of this one." He folded his arms, one hand holding the spirit sensor. "If Calder's still a ghost, I'll happily explode him myself."

"Someone needs to make sure Lady Granville doesn't cause any problems while we're gone," Vance said in a low voice. "I've distracted her, but I have little doubt she'll use Lord Carlisle's confusion to her advantage with me gone."

Drake scowled but didn't argue. Vance picked out a few mages and directed them to the black cars parked outside the manor. Eyes narrowed, he muttered, "It's outside of the range of my abilities. We'll have to drive."

"Dammit." I might have suggested using my magic-boosted speed in the same way as my wild dash across the city, but since I didn't know where I was going, I was more likely to end up running in circles around the English countryside instead. "Fine."

Isabel hugged me before I got into the car. "Drive safely."

"At least it's not Drake at the wheel."

I got into the front seat beside Vance and swiftly took back that statement when Vance broke every traffic law into a hundred pieces within seconds of hitting the engine. I hung onto the door for dear life as he one-handedly drove while displacing anything unlucky enough to get in our way, ranging from road blockades, wandering undead, and, once we reached the countryside, a runaway sheep.

"Don't you even think about lecturing Drake for breaking traffic regulations ever again." I jerked in my seat as he took a sharp turn down a country lane. "Do you even know where we're going?"

Fields lay on either side, unkempt and overgrown. Rolling hills extended into the distance, dotted with patches of woodland. Rain spattered the window as we drove. To make the end of the world even more unpleasant, good old British weather had decided to chime in. Between the rain and the intermittent flickers of grey mist that materialised in the road, I wouldn't have known if Calder himself was standing in front of us.

Vance slowed the car. "There's someone out there."

"Oh boy." Through the haze of rain, I glimpsed several cloaked figures crossing a field. "I think they're necromancers."

"They are." He pulled over at the roadside, near the wet, bedraggled necromancers. I didn't see Lord Evander, but I'd assumed they'd retrieved his body a while ago.

"Hey." I rolled down the window. "Can you tell me if we're near any spirit paths?"

The necromancer at the front startled at the sight of us. "Who are you?"

"I don't have time to explain." I opened the car door. "Someone sacrificed your leader at a point where three paths intersect. It's part of a plan to summon... look, you should probably get out of here. There are a lot of people back there in the city who'd appreciate your help."

"And we need to know where you found his body," added Vance.

A deafening howl rose upward from somewhere over the hills. I winced. "No need."

I slammed the door and Vance kicked the car into gear again, and we left the rain-drenched necromancers in the dust.

"Hellhounds," he said. "They're already here."

"Yeah." My heart drummed in my chest. "I guess the banshee was right."

The howl became a chorus, and the deafening sound of a thousand hellhounds' footsteps tore through the air.

18

Vance drove faster, towards the noise. Within the haze of rain and mist appeared a mass of furry bodies, heading right towards us.

"Hell." I turned to Vance. "If we're not careful, we're going to drive straight into them."

Tyres screeched and mud spattered the side window, mingling with the rain. I threw the door open and drew my sword, leaping out onto the roadside. Damp grass cushioned the impact and I rolled upright, swinging my blade at an oncoming hellhound. Blood gushed, thick and hot, and my blade's glow illuminated countless more beasts barrelling across the field.

Ah, shit. Vance and I had left the other mages far behind, and the two of us alone hadn't a hope of taking on an army.

Vance appeared at my side in a whirl of rainwater. "I called the mages to send another backup team. The others should be right behind us."

"There aren't enough of us." That much was abundantly clear. "I need to find…"

"Calder." He'd be hiding near where he'd sacrificed Lord

Evander, and all I'd need to do was follow the trail of hell-hounds. Preferably without getting killed on the way. "Vance, you wait for the other mages. I'll run ahead…"

"No."

"Don't argue with me on this one."

He would, and it came as no surprise that when I broke into a run, he was right behind me. The hellhounds were all moving in the same direction—westward—but some stragglers broke away. Any that crossed our paths met their ends at the point of my sword or were cut down by Vance, who was getting harder and harder to see in the lashing rain and thickening fog.

A sudden blue flash halted my steps. Calder hovered in front of me, his ghostly form more vibrant than the last time I'd seen him. "You won't stop them, Ivy. It's already too late."

"You didn't think I'd sit back while you brought an army into the city, did you?" I had to raise my voice over the thunder of giant paws and howls. "It's you I want to stop. You're long past your expiry date."

I swung my sword in a blaze of light. As long as he had a physical presence in this realm, I *could* kill him, like I had the others. I just needed to put enough power into it—and here, at the intersection of three spirit lines, there was no shortage of that.

He dodged, teeth bared, and cold hands grabbed at me from behind. *More ghosts.* I swung around, decapitating the spirit who'd grabbed me. Its head floated oddly above its body before my magic shattered the spirit to fragments. I pivoted, intending to do the same to Calder, but he'd vanished.

His ghostly voice rang out from thin air. "Unless you wish to be trampled before I can kill you, Ivy, I'd suggest you step aside."

Ah, shit. The hellhounds had changed direction, veering southward towards me.

I sprinted out of their path, putting on a burst of speed. Hot breath burned the back of my neck. My blade sliced upwards and out, slicing throats and severing heads. I used a fallen hellhound as a springboard to leap out of the fray, landing on bare grass. Nearby, I saw Vance expertly diverting the air currents to drive the hellhounds out of his path as he ran towards me. Flashes of fire told me Drake was there, too. That was fast. Unless he'd been behind us all along, which wouldn't have surprised me.

Where's that fucker Calder hiding? Skirting the hellhounds, I squinted into the fog, my gaze picking out a dense black mass on the horizon. Was that the key point? The hellhounds certainly seemed to be coming from that direction, and as my vision adjusted a little, I glimpsed a telltale shimmer in the air.

I was on a spirit line.

One blink and a familiar sight flickered into view. A path without end, flanked by silvery trees and bathed in an unnatural light.

The Grey Vale. The three realms overlapped, merging into one another as the veil thinned and Death spilled over into the mortal realm. As if I needed any more confirmation that the Ley Line wasn't the only path into Faerie.

The thunder of hellhounds filled both realms, and my flickering vision told me they were running *out* of the Vale. I blinked to clear my vision, but it was all I could do to keep myself anchored in the human world as I ran alongside the hellhounds, following an instinct I couldn't name.

When the ground ran out, I went sailing straight over the edge.

My feet skidded. I caught my balance, arms pinwheeling, and gave a double take. A stone building sat across from me.

Other than that, everything—the hellhounds, the rain—had vanished as though Vance's ability had transported me somewhere else entirely.

What is this place? It wasn't the Vale—the grass was too green, the building simple and manmade in its appearance— but I no longer felt the spray of cold drizzle on my face and the fog had lightened notably. The pounding of hellhound feet was still audible, though muffled, as if I stood on one side of a soundproof wall.

I trod closer to the building, my skin prickling. It was the size of a garden shed at most, yet its unobtrusive appearance was overshadowed by the sheer *presence* that hit me when I faced its closed door. My skin itched all over, and unfamiliar wards pressed against me, power whispering over my skin. Not the sort of wards I was used to, but more akin to the feeling that hit me whenever I walked into the room that contained the Invocations or when I'd faced the sleeping body of the shifter god. The sense of being around something ancient and primal, beyond my understanding.

Rippling light shone on the walls, and a gasp lodged in my throat. The walls weren't plain stone as I'd first thought, but had been laced with iron bands, the metal and stone merging into one another in a manner that could only have been achieved with magic. *But what kind of magic? Not fae.*

This place had been constructed by humans, I was sure, but the humming in my ears and the taste of magic on my tongue told me that an Invocation had been used in its creation.

Like the one I'd used to seal away the sleeping god.

The iron-laced walls gleamed, images flitting through my head as my human mind struggled to make sense of the glyphs forged within the iron. One had been repeated, over and over. Its meaning slid into my mind.

Forget.

I jerked back from the door at a sudden rush of pure hatred. A foul taste came to my lips, sour and metallic, and the blue glow around my blade reached outward, drawn to the building. The sharp touch left me with little doubt that my magic *hated* whatever was inside that place.

The door opened. I recoiled; I hadn't touched it, but my magic had, as though it had gained a life of its own. Blue tendrils extended, and I pulled them inward, drawing on every ounce of willpower I possessed. The magic seethed, and beyond lay a sight so startling that I forgot all about the incongruity of my own power slipping from my control.

This was no shed. It was a tomb.

Inside, a coffin stood upright against the back wall. Its transparent lid showed a *person*, or something that looked like one. Glyphs were carved into the walls on the inside, mirroring the ones on the outside laced within the iron and stone. That same word, over and over. *Forget.*

Whoever had built this place hadn't just sealed the tomb. They'd used an Invocation to ensure nobody remembered it existed. Including, perhaps, the person sleeping inside.

"Twenty years, he's lain here," whispered Calder's voice in my ear. "Twenty years, since he was sealed away in the invasion. Thank you for opening the door, Ivy."

I tried to speak, but my magic gave another violent lunge. I reeled in the threads, the blue light illuminating the face of the man sleeping inside the coffin. Or rather, the Sidhe sleeping within. He couldn't be anything else, and while I might have wondered why he'd been imprisoned and not killed when the building itself was made of iron, the man himself was in no condition to answer.

At my side, Calder watched the tomb with nothing short of reverence. "He's been sleeping for so long… it's time to open the door."

"No," I croaked. "Don't. You're a fool. No Sidhe would fight on *your* side, whoever he is."

I released my seething magic and aimed at Calder rather than the man in the tomb. Glyphs ignited along my blade, but a sudden tremor underfoot unbalanced me and sent me staggering sideways. Had that vibration come from the tomb? If that Sidhe was anything like the shifter god, it might take a magical trigger to awaken him, and my talisman seemed all too happy to oblige.

Stop it, magic. Stop that.

"Who *is* that?" I held my blade upright, willing its anger to fixate on Calder instead. He was the person I'd come to kill, to banish beyond the gates of the afterlife in a place that he would never return from again. "For that matter, where *are* we?"

"Somewhere that not a soul has set foot in since the invasion." He gave me a chilling smile. "He is Lord Fionn, master of death. He has lived a thousand years, and he holds the secrets to bringing me back to life."

"He's..." The Wild Hunt's leader. The person the banshee had alluded to. *Lord Fionn.* "Will he be pleased you stole his hellhounds while he was sleeping?"

"I plan to take far more than that." His smile gained a vicious edge. "I shall claim his body and use it to command the Wild Hunt."

"You want to... *steal his body*?" And I'd thought Calder's plans couldn't get any more unhinged. "What if he wakes up?"

"He won't, not yet, but when the time is right..." His eyes lit up. "He will grant me a place of honour in his Hunt."

Well, shit.

As he moved towards the tomb's entrance, I barred his path. "What do you say we finish our battle first? I was just about to kick the crap out of you when we left off."

In answer, he flung a whipcord of magic at me. I dodged, raising my blade and driving it into his ribs. No blood spilled, but my magic gave an alarming lurch sideways, a physical pull drawing us both towards the tomb. *Stop that!*

Calder laughed, noticing. "Having some trouble with my father's talisman, are you?"

"For some reason, it wants to kill that guy." I jerked my chin at the tomb. "I might let it try after I finish you off."

Magic whipped from his hands and brought an icy chill to my limbs. I should be able to win now that I wasn't fighting him as a spirit, but the sleeping time bomb was a major distraction, and blasting him with magic had no effect.

"Why." I blasted him. "Won't. You. Just. Die?"

A final burst rattled the tomb's door and my heart sank, certain I'd disturbed its occupant. Seizing the advantage, Calder's whipcord of magic spun around my legs and tightened, cutting off the circulation.

"Stay there." He lifted his head. "Good. He's ready."

"Hey!" I squirmed, trying to free myself. "Who's ready?"

Another ghost appeared in my peripheral vision, gliding towards Calder. Though his feet didn't touch the ground, his body appeared almost solid.

And in his hands, he held out the life-drinker sword.

19

"How?" I knew how. Lord Carlisle must have removed the sword before he'd picked up the Invocations, and this guy had taken from him before I'd shown up at the depository. He shouldn't be able to hold it in his ghostly hands, but with the state of the veil, the usual rules were obliterated.

Calder took the sword from the spirit's outstretched hand. If the talisman objected to being handled by someone who wasn't the wielder, the pair of them being ghosts would protect them against any damage, and the roiling anger of my other talisman masked all other sensation. The other ghost melted away, while Calder held up the life-drinker to examine its shimmering edges.

"You know I'm the one who claimed that sword, don't you?" I called to him. "It's lucky you're dead, or picking up someone else's talisman might not have gone well for you."

"Now I have everything I need," he said. "It's time for you to die, Ivy."

A fist connected with my jaw, sending me sprawling on the hillside. Its ghostly owner flickered into view—*Lucas*—

and someone else kicked me in the ribs. Ow. My mind told me they weren't real, but my senses told me otherwise, and my body shook with the impact of a dozen punches and kicks hitting at once.

"The Grey Vale never forgets," said Calder. "You will pay for your past mistakes, Ivy."

"What?" *Oh. Oh, no.*

Were these spirits the same ones I'd seen in that illusion I'd witnessed in our last fight? The spectres of Avalin's prisoners who'd died when the castle had collapsed?

No. It's not them. Some were familiar, though, including Lucas. And Alain, hovering behind him, staring at me with accusing eyes.

"You got us all killed!" she shrieked.

"I really didn't." Had Calder dragged them into the Vale to help him? Was there no end to his depravity?

It didn't escape my attention that this setup mimicked exactly how Calder himself had died, pulled into the afterlife by the enraged spirits of the people he'd killed. Doubtless he'd staged everything in an attempt at poetic justice, but I refused to believe these spirits had come with him willingly. They'd joined forces with Calder because they'd felt they had no choice. He'd shut them out of the afterlife and prevented them from moving on.

I conjured a shield, pushing the ghosts back. Their fists pounded, trying to reach me. Another tremor ran through the earth, reminding me of the more significant threat. My magic thrummed, and I wondered what Calder planned to do if the tomb's occupant woke up before he completed his plan. If I was lucky, the so-called master of death might do everyone a favour and send Calder scurrying into the distant afterlife, but the universe was rarely that cooperative.

Calder stood in front of the open tomb, extending the life-drinker sword to reveal the glyphs carved along its length. Words spilled from his mouth, familiar and foreign all at once. The glyphs on my own sword squirmed and writhed, and my tongue numbed as my ears struggled to comprehend the Invocation he spoke. A grinding noise rang through my bones, the sound of the coffin opening.

Calder vanished. I ran towards the tomb and halted when my magic lashed out of its own accord. The air sizzled with static. Gritting my teeth, I reeled the magic back in. A series of creaks and thuds came from the tomb.

The Sidhe Lord strode out.

Out of the coffin, he was much larger than I'd realised. At least six and a half feet tall, cloaked in armour that made him look even bigger. His face was almost rugged, not at all like too-pretty Calder or Velkas, and it was jarring when Calder's voice spoke through his mouth.

"That was easier than I expected." He lifted the life-drinker sword. "Now all that remains is for me to keep my promise, Ivy Lane. Remember? *I'll kill your mage first.*"

"Fuck you." I lunged after him, but he was gone, vanishing from the patch of hillside with a Sidhe's swiftness and leaving me alone with the ghosts.

He actually did it. He'd possessed the leader of the Wild Hunt, and to add insult to injury, he'd taken the life-drinker sword.

Ghostly bodies swarmed me as I tried to follow. Magic formed a shield between us, no longer drawn towards the tomb now its occupant was gone. Its glow brightened, drawing in the anger of the ghosts whose fists battered at the shield.

"There's no point in trying to hurt me," I told them. "Calder will sacrifice you all for his ambition without a thought. You must know I'm right. He literally already did that when he got you killed."

"You're lying," shouted Alain, and a dozen other voices echoed her words.

My shield brightened, their emotions flickering through. Resentment, remorse, anger, despair. All those emotions lapped against me, but I made no effort to forge them into a weapon.

"I don't want to fight you," I told them. "I promise to set you free, and I'm not lying. Calder is. He won't give you what you want."

"Wrong," Lucas said. "He'll make us immortal."

"Looks more like he left you behind." I turned to Alain, looked for one face within the crowd who might believe me. "He's out for himself alone. Even if it's true that he can become immortal, does he look like he'll be inclined to share the secret with the rest of you? He killed you because you were more useful to him dead than alive. Now your fates are in his hands. Unless you let me help you move on."

"There's no moving on," said a younger half-faerie ghost. He couldn't have been older than fourteen. "There's no way through."

"Through what?"

"The gates."

The gates of death? What had Calder done?

"Enough!" Lucas leapt at me, his ghostly form colliding with my shield. His hands clawed, magic flaring out, his eyes positively demonic. "Just die."

I raised a brow at him. "You know, if Calder blocked the gates of death, that means *I* won't move on if you kill me. I'll stay here and make your afterlives a misery."

Lucas's forehead wrinkled as though puzzling that one out.

Alain shrieked. "What's *that?*"

I looked. Past the ghosts, on the periphery of where

Calder had disappeared, a blur of darkness gathered. *That doesn't look good.*

I took a step. Glanced at the ghosts. "Feel free to come with me or stay. It's all the same to me. Just know I'm committed to taking Calder down, and it'd be great if you come to your senses before he destroys everyone."

I walked, then ran. Within moments, drizzle soaked my face, and dark clouds blotted the sky. Roiling darkness surged overhead, and a clamour filled the air, the braying of horses mingling with the roars of hellhounds.

And from within the surging darkness came giant horses bearing armoured riders.

Ah, I thought. *So that's the Wild Hunt.*

20

Calder had got his wish. His army awaited, and whether they thought he was the true Leader of the Wild Hunt or realised he was an impostor didn't matter when innocent people were the ones in the path of his army.

If not for the vibrant glow of my sword, I wouldn't have been able to see where I was going. Clouds cast dark shadows on the hillside as though it was the middle of the night and not morning, though spirits were visible as pinpricks scattered around the grass, and the cluster of ghostly figures behind me. No longer attacking me. Their attention, too, was riveted on the sky, and on the pillar of darkness that rose upward from the hillside.

Definitely not a good sign. What was the source? The crack in the world had opened on the spot Lord Evander had been sacrificed, I assumed, but there was no summoning circle to contain the surge of energy. It rippled up and down the spirit lines, uncontrolled, and with it came an army that defied description.

Calder watched too, or the Sidhe he possessed did. He

stood on the hillside, head tilted back to watch the sky. Upon spotting me, he smiled. "Isn't it beautiful?"

Once again, hearing Calder's voice from the mouth of such a huge man was jarring. The warrior was a fearsome specimen, packed with muscle beneath the heavy armour yet surprisingly light on his feet. Plates encased his arms and legs and covered his wide shoulders and chest. He carried a sword strapped to his waist, though the life-drinker didn't look out of place in his huge hands.

Calder's voice, by contrast, sounded like it belonged to the kid he really was. "Like my new body?"

"Nah, recently-resurrected-from-the-dead isn't generally my type."

I had to admit the guy was unusually rugged by Sidhe standards. His square jaw might have been carved out of rock, while his eyes were the most arresting shade of glassy blue I'd ever seen. His vacant expression somewhat dulled the intimidating image. The real guy was asleep, and I fervently hoped he'd never wake up.

So did my talisman. A tugging sensation almost like the pull of a vow seized my hands, and tendrils of magic snaked towards his armour. Calder didn't even seem to have noticed.

"You've lost, Ivy," he said. "The Hunt answers to me now."

"Did you forget you're still dead?" I queried. "You aren't bound to that body yet. And I reckon I can pull you out."

I lifted my blade and let go of any subconscious impulse holding back my magic. My talisman's anger leapt out, and so did I, aiming for a gap in his armour.

He slammed a kick into my ribs. *Holy shit.* He moved as fast as a Sidhe at full strength, and the weight of the kick sent me flying a good five feet into the air. I landed on my back, the wind knocked out of me. Ow. Possibly a broken rib or two as well.

Magic encased my body and the stabbing pain in my ribs

disappeared. That my healing abilities had kicked in so quickly said volumes for how close I must be to the Vale, but getting rid of Calder had to take precedence over undoing the damage he'd done.

I leapt to my feet and deflected a swing from the life-drinker. While I felt no draining effects from its magic, he shouldn't be able to wield another person's talisman at all. Was the lack of consequences due to him being a ghost, or more to do with the formidable Sidhe he'd possessed? This guy had been on the same level as Avalin, I was sure, if not higher.

Master of death. What that meant among a bunch of immortals remained to be seen, but he'd better appreciate me evicting Calder from his body. Even if I did a little damage in the process.

I swung at him. My blade glanced off his armour and blocked the life-drinker from reaching my throat. "That's *mine*," I snarled between my teeth. "I won that blade. You didn't."

I'd beaten the Lady of the Tree, and unlike this guy, she'd been the talisman's actual wielder. He was nothing but a poser squatting in someone else's body. Okay, the body in question was that of a Sidhe Lord with 'I am a badass' tattooed on his forehead, but the principle still stood.

Time to try another tactic. I threw up a magical shield and plunged into Death. The first thing I saw was Calder—the real Calder, not the Sidhe whose body he'd hijacked—hovering amid the grey. *Thought so.* He hadn't taken full control of his new body. If I gave him a strong enough push, I might be able to knock him loose.

Around me hovered the ghosts who'd accompanied him. Alain and the others. They hadn't got close enough to attack me—repelled by my shield—but I took one last chance to plead for help.

"Does he look like he's going to ask the Huntsman to bring you back to life?" I asked of them. "Would *you* offer a favour to someone who possessed your body against your will?"

Nobody replied, but their emotions lapped at me, and their anger and confusion added to the current of pure hate that drove my talisman towards its target. Even in Death, that hatred remained, and its collective force slammed into Calder.

I shifted back into my body as Calder—or rather, the Sidhe—stumbled. My vision doubled, showing me his ghostly hands reaching out as though fighting to maintain control over the body he was possessing.

Encouraged, I resumed my attack. He still blocked every swipe, but the movements were slower, less fluid, and the blankness in his eyes even more pronounced than before. I conjured a shield and shifted into Death, intending to knock him loose this time.

Calder was nowhere in sight.

I stared around the greyness, uncomprehending. Where was he? Did his disappearance mean—fuck, he hadn't managed to complete the possession, had he?

As I shifted back into my body, the Sidhe Lord batted at the air. "Who are you? Begone!"

His voice didn't sound like Calder any longer. Not at all. It was too deep, too layered, and with a faintly melodic tint that put me in the mind of an opera singer.

Oh, fuck.

The body's original owner had woken up.

He spoke, in that same deep, unfamiliar voice, uttering words in a language I didn't know. I braced myself in case they hit with the impact of an Invocation, but no obvious effects came.

His gaze locked onto me. My throat went dry. Calder...

fuck, he'd left *me* to deal with this guy. How to explain how he'd ended up out of his tomb and in a field? Should I mention that Calder had been trying to possess him? A thousand cascading questions jostled for attention, chief among which was why my magic seemingly wanted him dead.

Even through my shock, anger rippled through the blue glow around my body, disconnected from my own emotions. Attacking a dangerous Sidhe would end badly even if he hadn't been holding one of my own talismans, but I couldn't bring myself to lower my weapon, either. The guy had been imprisoned for a reason. Whoever had put him in that tomb had gone as far as to erase all memory of its existence, or close to it. Calder had found out, after all.

Dammit, say something, Ivy. I couldn't keep staring at him, but it was all I could do to keep my magic from projecting hostility at him. Blue tendrils crept outward, and he studied them through those strange glassy eyes.

"Avalin."

"No." I licked my lips. "I'm not him. Obviously. I'm Ivy Lane."

"Ivy Lane." His accent was... strange. Polished, every word clearly enunciated, and yet without the same inflections as the upper-class mages I'd spent so much time with in the last few months. "You're human."

"Really? I had no idea." *Why me?* I hoped he and Avalin hadn't been friends, or else this might get even more awkward than it already was. It didn't help that his voice sounded like one I'd heard before, though I couldn't put my finger on why. Regardless, what in the hell was I supposed to do now? My past experience with Sidhe Lords had taught me they were unpredictable at the best of times, but I'd never dealt with one who'd just been awakened from a decades-long slumber.

"And you are the one who summoned me?" He lifted his

gaze to the blackened clouds and the army within. His army. The Wild Hunt. Worse, thanks to Calder, he held the life-drinker talisman in his hand and didn't even seem to have noticed. "You have Lord Avalin's magic?"

"Yes." He already knew, and it hit me where I thought I'd heard his voice before. Avalin had spoken in the same manner; his voice, melodic and enticing, had lured in thirteen-year-old me like bait dangling from a fishing rod. That same attraction had soured into terror within minutes of arriving in his castle, but one of the prisoners had confided in me that she thought Avalin's voice changed with everyone he spoke to. Everyone heard a voice that attracted, enticed, and reassured them in the same instant, and language didn't seem to be a barrier either. According to other whispers I'd heard during my imprisonment, all Sidhe had a similar aura that ensured they both looked and sounded like whatever the person they wanted to entrap believed to be the most appealing.

This guy? He had that in spades, and I might have fallen for the act if not for my magic trying to leap clear of my blade and strangle him.

"I killed Avalin." I lifted my chin. "I claimed his talisman, and then I claimed that one, too. That blade is mine. I'd appreciate it if you gave it back."

"This?" His gaze dropped to the life-drinker, mild surprise flickering through those pool-like eyes. "Is *he* here?"

Did he mean Velkas? "Nobody's here but you and I, and a bunch of angry spirits. One of them wants to possess your body. I don't think you were supposed to wake up in the process."

He was imprisoned for a reason. That was obvious, and since this guy led the Wild Hunt, I doubted he'd have any intention of calling the hellhounds off. And thanks to Calder's disappearing act, someone else had to deal with the fallout.

The last time I'd been faced with an immortal entity with world-destroying power, I'd used an Invocation to send the beast into slumber. The words had come to me by instinct, through the glyphs on my sword, as though the magic itself carried their memory.

I opened my mouth. The first syllable had scarcely pushed past my tongue when the Sidhe lord raised a hand and I gasped, choking on my own breath. *A tongue-tying spell.* I'd never had one used on me before, but I'd seen the effects enough times to know the words were locked behind my throat, my lips unable to move.

Fuck, now I'm in trouble.

21

I gasped and choked, reaching for my throat as though to rip away the spell that had stolen my voice.

Then the scene changed, from a darkened hillside to a stone balcony overlooking thick, dense forest. The silvery sheen to the trees told me where we were, and vertigo hit when I looked down the sheer wall. *This isn't Avalin's castle. It can't be.*

"Would you look at that." The Sidhe's soft, melodic voice raised the hairs on the back of my neck. "It's the same as the day I left."

Was this an illusion, or were we truly in the Vale? The tongue-tying spell shoved all my questions back down my throat. I glared at him instead, putting every ounce of fury I possessed into my expression. If looks could kill, he'd have burst into flames.

As it was, he laughed. "I'd have liked to have seen you outwit Avalin, human. You have trickery written all over you."

Damn you. This was hardly the place for a duel, but I wanted that talisman back, and who knew, maybe I'd get lucky and send him plummeting off the balcony to his death.

I called upon my magic. Anger returned, potent and sharp, and the choking sensation disappeared from my throat as I extended my blade to point at his throat. "Give me the sword. It's mine."

He appeared unsurprised that I'd shaken off his spell. "What would a human want with Eraenar's blade, I wonder?"

Hearing the god's name from his mouth jarred me into forgetting what I planned to say. *He knows...* damn, he hadn't *met* the god, had he?

Focus, Ivy. Worry about that later. "I won that sword," I said. "Its allegiance is to me alone."

"Is it?" He turned the blade over, admiring the glyphs on its edge, and lightly tossed the hilt from one hand to the other. "That explains it."

He threw the sword back to me. My reflexes kicked in and I caught the hilt in my left hand, bewilderment kicking in an instant later.

"That's it?" I'd expected more of a fight. Expected a clash to the death, even.

"You won the sword yourself. I have no need of it now... but I'm very curious as to *how* you won it."

His voice glided across my skin and brought a wave of goosebumps to my arms. Some of my shock receded, giving way to good old-fashioned fear. He was too calm. Too controlled. Based on my experience with the Sidhe, that meant he was about to start breaking things.

"I killed its owner, twice over. Who *are* you?"

"Lord Fionn," said the man. "Leader of the Wild Hunt. I see you called my hellhounds."

"Not me," I said firmly. "An egotistical half-faerie ghost called Calder is the one who called your army and disturbed your tomb. He's Avalin's son."

"Is he?" He looked down at me—not hard, because he was an absolute giant—and smiled. "You don't look like him."

"That's because I'm not his relation. I'm a hundred percent human."

"His lover?"

"Avalin's?" I gave a shudder. "No. He captured a bunch of humans when you and your friends decided to lay waste to our world. I eventually outsmarted him and stole his magic."

He threw back his head and laughed. "What I wouldn't have given to see his face when a human bested him. Humans never cease to amaze me."

His huge hand reached out. Instinct took over, coupled with the festering anger beneath the surface, and my blade snapped upward. Straight through his palm, bursting through the other side in a frisson of blue light.

A momentary startled expression flashed through his eyes, then he laughed. Loudly. Fionn stood with his mangled hand outstretched, laughing like I'd told a hilarious joke.

My skin crawled. I wanted to back away, but I didn't. "Are you done?"

"Humans have changed a great deal during my slumber," he mused. "I remember how pathetic they were... how they begged for help even as I stripped the skin from their bones."

Ice slid through my core. If I hadn't already suspected he'd been involved in the invasion, I knew for sure. He and his allies had ravaged our world, and as punishment, he'd been locked in that tomb.

Because nobody could kill him?

Who had put him there? His tomb had held the same odd combination of Invocations laced into iron walls. Two elements that should be incompatible with one another. Humans couldn't speak Invocations. Sidhe couldn't touch iron.

Fionn's hand knotted back together, splintered bones

reforming and muscle fusing before my eyes. In a snap, his hand was whole again, and he extended a crooked finger to beckon me closer.

"I seem to be missing part of my memory, human. Perhaps you and I can get comfortable and you can fill me in on what I missed."

Was he *flirting* with me? After I'd stabbed him in the hand? Revulsion aside, I didn't have time for this. The Wild Hunt might be rampaging towards the city as we spoke, and Calder was still out there somewhere.

"Sorry," I said. "I have a ghost to catch. I'll have to decline."

"Were you assuming I made a request?" He gave another laugh. "No… though I confess I'm intrigued as to how you planned to get down from here."

Magic. The same magic that buzzed beneath my skin and hummed in my blade's hilt, longing to strike him down. His gaze followed the blue sheen, a wicked grin forming on his lips. "Ah… of course. I'm curious, human. You won over Avalin's magic, but can a human like you truly understand how to wield power of such magnitude? Avalin held the talisman before you even came into existence."

"Oh, I understand enough." I gave him a level stare. "You, though… you don't understand humans at all. We survive. It's kind of our thing."

Part of me knew he had a point. I knew so little of Faerie compared to someone who'd lived there for millennia, and even speaking Invocations felt more like the magic was acting through me, using my voice, than a force that I held mastery over.

But I was used to being outgunned, used to facing odds stacked heavily against me. Simple numbers told me that I had two swords and he had one, and he'd been trapped in an iron prison for at least twenty years. Those facts might not undo centuries of training, but they had to count for something.

He moved fast enough he might as well have read my thoughts, drawing his weapon in the time it took me to raise both swords to block him. Green light from the life-drinker mingled with Helena's raging blue, and yet he didn't so much as stumble. A bluish-white sheen flared along the blade he held in both hands, his grip loose, blocking both my swords as effortlessly as if they were made of plastic.

I pushed back, magic thrumming through my body until I trembled from head to toe, but I barely gained an inch.

Pain shot through my ribs. I glanced down in disbelief at the curved dagger sticking out of my chest. Threads of wire-thin magic wrapped around its hilt, and when Fionn gave a casual flick of his wrist, I glimpsed more threads fanning outward from his blade. The knife twisted, too, and I screamed. Blood drenched my middle. I couldn't pull out the knife with my shoulders and arms burning with the strain of keeping both swords upright.

Blue light encased the wound, encircling the dagger twisting under my ribs. My magic was trying to heal me, but it was impossible with the knife embedded in the wound.

Fionn studied me like a cat contemplating a stray beetle. "So you do have accelerated healing. I did wonder."

The dagger escaped in a rush of pain, swiftly extinguished by my healing magic. Fionn reached out with his free hand and caught the weapon in mid-air, flashing me a smile. I coughed, tasting blood. How had he thrown a dagger at me without my noticing? He was far stronger than Velkas, and certainly much more powerful than the Lady of the Tree. She hadn't been her talisman's equal, while he'd dwarfed two of mine.

Was he even stronger than Avalin? I'd thought—hoped—that

Avalin was the worst Faerie had had to offer. That no Sidhe I faced would ever be his equal.

"I think that's enough games, Ivy," said Fionn. "It's past time I retook what is rightfully mine. Don't you agree?"

He shouted a command in the same language he'd spoken when he'd first returned to alertness. The sound of hooves rang out, and a thrill of dread raced through my nerves. He'd called the Hunt.

Horses descended, far bigger than any I'd seen, their hooves skimming the air as they galloped towards the castle. Most bore riders dressed in black armour that covered every inch of skin. Their faces were masked, their features hidden, and frankly, they creeped me the fuck out.

Fionn waved. A single horse without a rider came down to the balcony and paused near the edge. Waiting for its rider. Fionn reached for me, a wide grin stretching his face.

"Don't you dare—"

He seized my arm and leapt onto the horse's back. A scream jammed my throat, lost on the wind as the Wild Hunt swept us away in its midst.

22

Riding with the Wild Hunt was like being caught in a mosh pit. If your average mosh pit typically consisted of armoured horsemen riding frightening black steeds and accompanied by dogs as big as the horses, of course. It was bloody hard to keep my balance on horseback and hold two swords at the same time. My thighs squeezed the horse's vast neck and I tried not to look down at the wickedly sharp hooves that would trample me if I lost my balance.

Fionn had settled behind me, wearing a wide grin as if we were riding a harmless fairground ride. I made several attempts to angle my swords to stab him—first one, then the other—but he countered with a firm hand on my back.

"I wouldn't," he said, his fingers brushing my neck. My gut twisted with nausea. "You don't want to fall."

"Fuck you." I leaned forward as we hurtled onward, below roiling clouds and dense fog. I couldn't have said whether we were in the human realm or Faerie, in Death or in the Vale. The Wild Hunt encompassed every realm and carried us along silver-leafed paths, grey fog, and grassy hillside. I zeroed in on the latter, scanning for the mages, but the Hunt moved too fast for me to see anyone.

"Extraordinary view, isn't it?" said Fionn. "Oh, were those your allies we just passed? I suppose that answers my question about whether the mages survived."

Survived... the invasion? Had *he* been the one to kill the original Mage Lords twenty years ago?

"Oh, they did." *Vance.* He was out there in the fog somewhere, fighting for his life alongside the other mages while I was trapped in a sea of hellhounds. My temper snapped at his soft laugh and I drove my foot back into his knee. The heel of my boot bounced off his armour.

"The hell do you even want?" I snarled over my shoulder. "You don't have a clue what's happened in the past twenty years. You didn't even summon the Hunt yourself."

Yet now we were riding full tilt towards the city I called home in the company of an army of monsters, and he showed no signs of turning away from Calder's plan.

"Now I finish what I started, of course," he said. "In the end, your fellow humans could only postpone your fates."

"Oh, I don't know," I said. "You might live longer than us, but we rebuilt a whole civilisation in the time it took you to have a nap."

"And yet you die so easily." Fionn's voice gained a contemplative note. "I always thought it was a waste, how Avalin kept that talisman locked in his castle while he busied himself tormenting helpless humans. Did you know he once ruled a quarter of Winter's territory? How the mighty rise, and how they fall into dust. A thousand earthen empires pass in the blink of an eye, and all that's left is... us."

"How very philosophical. Don't touch anyone in this realm again." I couldn't tell if we were anywhere near the city yet, but it was only a matter of time before the Hunt reached an area of human habitation.

The riders of the apocalypse were here, and I was the one who'd brought them to our realm.

No. I leaned over the horse's side, reckless daring seizing me. This would hurt like hell and would probably end in my death, but I had no other route of escape left.

Fionn's hands reached for me and closed over empty air as I rolled off the horse's side, conjuring a shield as I did so. Hooves skimmed overhead without touching me, and I held both blades as I rolled again, trying to regain my feet amid a frenzy of stomping.

A hand caught me by the scruff of my neck. One of the riders had caught me mid-gallop, and as I dangled, gawping, he rode straight *out* of the Wild Hunt. Rain drenched my face as we left the mass of hellhounds behind, and Calder's voice spoke from the masked rider. "Caught you, Ivy."

"Calder?" What had he done, possessed another body? I swung my legs, trying to free myself. From my precarious position, I saw the back of the Wild Hunt, or as much as was visible from the human side. A crack split the air down the hillside where the three spirit lines intersected, out of which furred monstrosities continued to emerge.

"Thank you," said Fionn's voice from behind. "We were having such a fascinating conversation. It'd be a shame to ruin it."

Calder—or the rider—went completely still. *Guilty.*

"You know, Calder," I whispered, "I feel like your application to join the Wild Hunt is going to be automatically rejected. You know, on the grounds that you stole its leader's body."

In answer, Calder leaned over the horse's head and hissed a command into its ear. The horse changed directions, breaking into a faster gallop as it did so.

"You seriously think you can outrun the master of the

Wild Hunt?" I yelped, dangling in midair. "Whatever happened to asking him for a favour?"

He was panicking, evidently. I swung from his outstretched hand, feet skimming the horse's smooth hide. Angling my blade downward, I drove the tip against the horse's flank.

The beast tilted, and Calder let go of me. I fell head over heels, the wet grass slowing the impact, and rolled to my feet. Calder leapt free of his steed in a clatter of heavy armour, straightening upright.

"Well done." I gave him an eye-roll. "What did you expect when you possessed someone who was still alive? Do you even know who he is?"

"Master of the Wild Hunt," he said. "And master of death."

"He'll be a master of *your* death if he decides you deserve punishment for possessing him." Not that I intended to let anyone else take over. This shithead was mine to kill.

In answer, Calder threw a bolt of Winter magic at me. I raised the twin swords, and his attack bounced harmlessly away. After Fionn, fighting him wouldn't be as much of a challenge, but the brute he'd possessed was bound to have a few surprises in store. More to the point, I didn't *care*. I'd beaten him enough times, and though he might refuse to die, he was no longer the prevalent threat. I wished I could lock him up in a tomb and throw away the key, or…

A word flashed into my mind. *Forget.*

I deflected another burst of icy energy, but I noticed that he hadn't drawn his sword yet. The warrior moved fast even with the heavy armour encasing his new body, but from his movements were hesitant enough that I knew his coordination wasn't totally on the mark.

Neither was mine. I moved fluidly, but my arms ached with the weight of the twin blades, and I was distracted by worry for my friends. How long did we have until that army reached the city? Minutes?

I risked a look at the sky, and Calder strode forward and punched me in the jaw. Stars burst behind my eyes. Before I could recover, Calder delivered a punch to my solar plexus that drove the breath from my lungs and left me gasping like a fish on land.

Above scudded dark clouds, emanating from the fractured spirit lines. The crack I'd seen before, the source, must be where Lord Evander had been sacrificed. His death had called the Hunt, but did that mean Calder commanded the hellhounds—or Fionn?

Calder leaned over me, his borrowed fingers grasping my throat. I sucked in air, tasted the word on my tongue, and screamed the Invocation in his face.

Forget.

Calder reeled. So did I. The Invocation burned in my blood, its metal taste on my tongue, and all remaining air fled my lungs until Death's grey hands carried me away.

Calder greeted me on the other side. He hovered outside the body he'd been possessing, a blank expression on his face. *Did it work?*

"Calder?" I said uncertainly.

He didn't respond to his name. Not a trace of awareness shone in his bright-blue eyes, the only part of his ghostly body that looked alive. "Where am I?"

"Someone will explain," I told him. "Do you remember *who* you are?"

"I… no, I don't." His stammer banished all doubts from my mind, as did the tentative smile he offered me. "You look familiar. Do I know you?"

"No." I let the greyness fade away as I left Death and returned to my body. "Not anymore."

23

Fionn's laughter greeted my return. I gasped, sprawled on my back where Calder had left me, one sword clutched in each hand and the roiling sky above. Fionn was beside me, sitting astride his horse, but I could no longer hear the thunderous roar that had accompanied the Wild Hunt's charge.

Did they leave when Calder lost his memories?

I sat upright. Stood on shaky legs, the Invocation's aftermath lingering on my tongue. More horses were littered through the field, but the bulk of the army had dispersed.

Fionn didn't look angry, more amused. "That was interesting. A nice bit of improvisation from you, Ivy."

"Oh, I got the idea from your jailors." My chest ached a little, but I'd suffered no lasting damage from the fight. "What did I miss?"

What are you going to do now? That was the real question. He commanded the Hunt—or the horsemen at least—and there were at least a dozen freakishly strong warriors waiting for orders.

"Very little." He gave me a broad smile. "You successfully

drove off my hellhounds when you wiped their commander's memories, and I believe that little disturbance on the spirit lines is repairing itself as we speak. All that is left is to decide our futures, and I would like to offer you the chance to join me in the Hunt. As a wielder of the talismans of two Sidhe lords, you're more than qualified."

"Absolutely not."

"So quick to deny yourself a chance at glory." His smile widened even further. "I do hope nobody was standing at the intersection of the spirit lines when the hellhounds fled."

"What?" My voice caught on the word. *What is he implying?* "What do you mean?"

"That enterprising friend of yours was certainly thorough in his preparations to summon the Hunt," said Fionn. "He must have had close to a hundred hounds there, and at an intersection of three spirit lines, I can imagine the effect that would have had on the souls of any unfortunate mortals attempting to move on."

That's how he blocked the gates of Death? The hellhounds?

"As I said, I hope nobody living was nearby when they left," he went on. "As I imagine the sudden dispersal of energy will have dragged those unlucky souls out of their bodies and into Death. I thought I should warn you, Ivy, as I'm fairly sure I spotted a cloaked individual attempting to get into the liminal space in which you found my tomb."

"You're lying." *Vance.* If anyone might have been trying to reach me, Vance would, but I refused to believe a word that came out of Fionn's mouth. "Why didn't you try to stop Calder from stealing your army?"

"I rather hoped to spend a little more time catching up on the past few years before riding with the Hunt," he said. "And rebuilding my ranks, of course. I respect your choice, Ivy, but I can assure you that it will work out in your favour to ally with me."

I gave him my best attempt at an angry mercenary stare, under the circumstances. "I'd rather be on anyone's side but yours."

Refusing an invitation from the master of death would doubtless come back to bite me as surely as a hellhound's teeth, but he hadn't seriously expected me to accept, had he? And what was his plan now? To leave, to rebuild his army and conquer Earth another day?

"If you change your mind, my invitation is still open."

My magic seethed, wanting nothing more than to rip his face off, and words formed on my tongue. I opened my mouth to speak the Invocation, and my throat locked up. I gasped, trying to force out the words past the spell that held me captive.

Fionn nudged his horse with a leg and winked at me. "Until next time, Ivy."

He rode away at a fast gallop, leaving me alone. Or not. Spirits drifted over the hillside, none interacting with me, nor seeming to notice they had living company. All were moving northward, in the same direction, as though pulled by a magnetic force.

Towards the intersection of the three spirit lines.

Fionn might be a liar, but I'd never risk Vance's life. If he'd somehow ended up in Death as a result of the hellhounds fleeing, I had to bring him back.

I floated out of my body, joining the flood of spirits heading north. Some were human, some half-faeries, but none of the latter showed any of the anger or distress they had when we'd fought. The pull of Death was relentless, drawing everyone towards…

It's real. A vast pair of gates, extending to either side as far as the eye could see. Though transparent, the gates held a certain solidity that nothing else in Death possessed. The spirits converged towards a gap where both gates met, wreathed in mist, and when they passed through, they vanished from sight. I glimpsed Alain and Lucas, hand in hand, among the dead. In the end, they, too, were moving on.

Two exceptions hovered on the gate's right-hand side, watching the passing spirits. Lord Evander and Frank both locked eyes with me as I drifted over to meet them.

"Sorry you're dead," I said to Lord Evander.

"You aren't," he said. "You—"

"Are still alive," said Frank. "I'd advise you to return to your body. The force blocking the gates has gone, and when it was removed, it caused a significant shift in the veil. I can't promise another won't occur when this number of dead people cross over at once."

"A shift in the veil?" My heart gave an unpleasant jolt. "What if someone was—standing nearby? What would happen to them?"

"At the key point?" he asked. "I should hope nobody was there. They might have…"

"Been dragged out of their body." I scanned the mass of spirits, desperately trying to pinpoint a single figure. *Please don't let him be here. Please…*

There he was. Floating towards the gates along with the rest of the dead.

"Vance!" I shouted. "Vance!"

He lifted his head. No recognition showed on his face. *Shit. Please tell me my Invocation didn't hit him, too.* It couldn't have, surely. He hadn't been anywhere near Calder.

"Vance!" I threw out my arms in front of him, barring his path.

"Sarah?" He looked right past me, his eyes unseeing. "I have to find her."

"She isn't here." His distant expression tore at my heart. Maybe his family were on the other side of the gate, same as mine, but the veil's trickery was a lie. "Vance, you're alive. Please come back with me."

He shook his head. "I have to go."

"No." I took Vance's hand in mine. Our fingers passed through one another, but I persisted, gripping tightly enough that I almost believed I felt his fingers curl around mine, too.

He looked down at our interlinked hands. "Do I know you?"

"You know me. You love me. I love you too, Vance, and I'm going to stand here and hold onto you until you remember. Sarah's dead, and—I'm sorry. But you're alive, and so am I." My tears spilled over. "Please. Please come with me, Vance. Trust me."

Please, please let me bring him back.

I closed my eyes and held him tight until the greyness faded away.

———

I blinked awake. I lay on the hillside, my hands clenched around the two swords. I was bloody freezing, but not so much that I couldn't stand.

Calder was gone. The spirits who he'd forced to serve him would be free, the gates of Death once again wide open… but I'd still let Fionn get away.

"You fucked up, Ivy," I murmured.

The silence was palpable as my feet trod through the dead grass mixed with mud and fresh blood. Hellhound, mostly. The blue tinge of faerie blood shone unnaturally bright under the dim sunlight streaming between the clouds.

Sunlight. The Wild Hunt had gone. Fionn had spared us, and while Calder stealing his hellhounds had doubtless played a part in his choice, he'd also been sleeping for twenty years and had his memories screwed with. In his eyes, there was no sense in destroying the world before he learned how much had changed in the interim. Unlike Calder, he seemed to have a modicum of patience. For the time being.

Light burned through the gloom, revealing cloaked figures gathered on the hillside. The mages. None had got close to the site of the summoning, except for one. Vance lay on his back, alone, and the sight brought me to my knees in the dirt. My face damp with rain and tears, I leaned over and squeezed his hand. It was cold as death, but my fingers detected the flutter of a pulse.

"Vance." I gasped. "Vance?"

His eyes opened.

"Do you… do you remember me?"

"I remember," he said slowly. "I think you told me you loved me, but I might have imagined that part."

Oh. "Yeah. No, you didn't imagine it."

"Good." He took my hands. His were as cold as ice, but then, so were mine. "Thank you. For bringing me back."

"Anytime." I leaned over and kissed him on the mouth. "I also mean it when I say I'm freezing my arse off here."

Vance sat up, groaning a little. I slid an arm around his back and he half leaned on me as he got to his feet.

We limped over to join the other mages. There were more present than I'd initially thought. The apprentices like Wanda would have stayed behind, but I recognised Rod, Bailey, and a dozen others who'd come to support Vance despite Lady Granville doing her best to persuade them otherwise.

"Do you have any idea how hard it is for a fire mage to fight in the pouring rain?" Drake shook water from his hair. "I'm glad you got rid of those hellhounds, Ivy. Or I assume it was you. Is it over?"

"Yeah." I nodded but didn't quite manage a smile. "It's over. We can go home."

24

Vance drove us back, slower this time. After a healing spell took care of my various bruises, I explained everything from the passenger seat. He didn't stop to ask questions, only listened, while Isabel sent me updates from the city. Apparently, she and a handful of necromancers had joined the mages in exterminating any ghosts they came across, but they'd had a narrow escape. The Huntsman's army had mostly dispersed before the bulk of the hellhounds had reached the city, and while the emergency alert would be up for a while, Fionn's horsemen had never ventured beyond the borders.

Strangely, his supposed generosity was in no way reassuring at all.

"Are you all right?" Vance watched me in the wing mirror, a worried frown on his face.

I forced a nod. "What's going to happen to Lord Carlisle?"

"He'll be removed from the council until it can be determined if he acted of his own free will or not."

"I doubt he had any say in the matter," I said. "I killed the ghost that possessed him. He might not even remember what he did while he was being controlled."

"Nevertheless," he said, "the fact remains that an outside influence was able to slip past our wards. The council has good reason for concern, but it leaves me with the choice between condemning an innocent man and giving the impression that we are willing to overlook the attempted break-in and theft."

"As the person who actually got stolen from, I'm not pinning the blame on the guy who the faeries manipulated. It happens to the best of us." The life-drinker rested against my knee, while Helena was sheathed at my side. Not the most comfortable arrangement, but I refused to let either out of my sight.

His expression remained dark. "Perhaps, but I can guarantee that's the argument Lady Granville will use, and we can't afford any more upheaval in our ranks. The necromancers are already without a leader in a time when they sorely need one."

"Yeah. It's a mess." I clenched my fists on my lap. "Now there's a Sidhe out there with enough power to level the city. If I'd stopped Calder sooner..."

"Don't blame yourself." Vance took one hand off the wheel and rested his palm on my knee. "This is Calder's fault."

"And Avalin," I said. "His magic started everything. And you know, there's some history there, I'm sure. My magic wants to rip Fionn's face off every time I go near him. But I'm no match for him. He blocked two talismans like it was nothing. If he hadn't called off his army..."

His hand found mine and squeezed. "He did. There's no point in dwelling on the alternatives."

"Yeah." I smothered a sigh. "Shit, I thought I'd be glad to

be rid of Calder, but he's left me to clean up his mess. Again. That tomb…"

"You said his prison was made of iron," said Vance. "Who imprisoned him?"

"No clue. Iron rules out another Sidhe, but I can't see a human having the power to put a Sidhe under an Invocation either. I thought the same when we found that god's prison, too." Mysteries built upon mysteries, and the only possible source of answers I knew of was the capricious immortal who was now wandering the realms, unchecked.

"Maybe the humans and Sidhe cooperated," he suggested.

"Sure would help if they did the same now."

"Yes," said Vance. "I have to wonder if that forgetfulness spell on the tomb affected more than Fionn."

"How'd you mean?"

"The invasion," he said. "I assumed, for a long time, that all witnesses were killed. The situation might be far more complicated."

"No kidding." I looked out the window at the fields rushing past. "Does the Chief know, do you think? That one of his people was buried out there?"

"I doubt it, but he might have heard this Lord Fionn's title," said Vance. "He knew of the Wild Hunt."

"All the faeries do." It had been the banshee who'd first mentioned Fionn's name, and now I thought back, I hadn't seen her among the Wild Hunt nor Calder's forces. I could only assume she'd told the truth when she'd claimed not to be on Calder's side, which presumably meant she was out for her own self-interest alone. Not entirely out of character for a death fae. "You know, if Fionn was imprisoned the same year Avalin took me, maybe the Hunt's been gone the whole time, waiting for Fionn to wake up."

"Not the hellhounds."

"No, those faeries on horseback." I shivered. "I don't

know if they were Sidhe, but they creeped me the hell out. And they're still around somewhere, with Fionn."

"We'll handle them another day," he said. "Fionn might not have called off the attack for magnanimous reasons, but he's given us time to prepare."

For what, though?

"A more immediate matter," said Vance, "is that a certain council member was all too swift to take advantage of my absence."

"Lady Granville." I swore. "What's she done?"

"I don't know yet, but I intend to deal with her upon our return." His tone held an undercurrent of decisive anger. He didn't plan to dissolve his own council so soon after the battle, did he?

We pulled up outside the manor. The road was half flooded with rainwater, mingling with salt and the remnants of old spells. A group of bedraggled mages converged on the car and began asking Vance questions.

"The threat is taken care of." Vance opened the door and got out. "The Wild Hunt has gone."

Yeah, but what happened here? On the other side of the manor's gate, Lady Granville had rallied a group of fellow mages around her. Lady Penrose was prominent among them, and the two stood huddled with a handful of others I'd seen in council meetings.

"Ah, Lord Colton." Lady Granville addressed Vance as if he'd been running an errand at the corner shop, not saving the world. "We have sentenced the traitor to death."

"Lord Carlisle?" Vance's tone sharpened. "You can't make those decisions without the backing of the full council."

"At the time, half of the remaining council members were absent." She offered a smile with as little sincerity as a goblin trying to sell you a cure for acne. "Therefore, I decided to take certain steps in the event that you failed to return."

My hands curled into fists. "What did you do?"

"I have been chosen as interim council leader," she said, "with Lady Penrose as my second-in-command."

"The hell you are." Drake marched over, dripping wet. "Where were you when we were fighting to protect the city?"

"Doing our jobs," Lady Granville said. "The traitor will be sentenced to death, and I will choose his replacement myself."

"You can't kill someone for getting possessed," I said, appalled.

"His heritage would have made his fate inevitable. A detail, I note, that you did not share with the rest of us, Lord Colton."

"You..." I gaped at her, lost for words. "You think he deserved to die for being part necromancer? You don't choose whether you inherit the spirit sight. Besides, with the veil in that state, any of you could have been possessed instead."

"This is out of the question," said Vance. "I might have been absent, but you have no authority over the rest of the council, especially given the dire emergency that threatened our city."

"Yeah, you don't get to choose." She had some cheek giving orders. Not only was there not a single speck of dirt on her, but given that she hadn't been drenched to the skin like the other mages, she'd either used a rain-repelling spell or else stayed indoors throughout the whole battle. Anger chased away the weariness dragging at my limbs. I was through with her bullshit—and by the expression on his face, so was Vance.

"None of this is your business, Ivy Lane," said Lady Granville. "Lord Colton, you know our reputation is at stake here. There's chaos in the streets. The necromancers are without a leader, and their people are responsible for this catastrophe."

"Actually," I corrected, "the person responsible is the Sidhe lord I killed twenty years ago. His son's ghost is gone, and so is the army he summoned. Thanks to Vance and me, no mages were killed either."

"And if they had been?"

"If I had hesitated, more would have died," said Vance. "In diverging from my orders, you might have cost us the city."

"Your orders?" she repeated. "I was acting as Head Mage."

"Were you?" The air trembled, and a breeze kicked up, rustling the hedges. "Do you challenge me for leadership, Lady Granville?"

Oh, boy. I vaguely remembered Vance telling me the East Midlands division of mages had chosen their current leader by staging a duel between the contenders. *Please tell me that isn't his plan.*

"Yes." She lifted her chin. "I do."

"If you win, I'll step aside," Vance said. "Lose, and you will no longer be welcome to serve on my council. I think it's best we settle this as quickly as possible before we lose face, as that seems to be your major concern."

Whoa.

Lady Granville raised a brow again. "If that's the only language you speak…"

I bit the inside of my cheek. This was Vance's fight, though damn if it wasn't tempting to yank her off her high horse.

"The time for diplomacy has long gone," said Vance. "Quite apart from the fact that we've lost a council member and an ally, and the necromancers have fractured, your decisions might easily have cost the lives of my fellow mages. I won't stand for it."

He threw his coat aside, eliciting a gasp from the surrounding mages. Wait. He planned to challenge her *now*?

"Vance—" I broke off. *Dammit. He has to do this. There's no other way to be rid of her.*

The mages—injured or otherwise—began to move to either side of the lawn, leaving a sizeable gap in the middle big enough for them to face one another. This was really happening. A duel for the title of Mage Lord. It might have surprised me that someone like Lady Granville would agree to settle the matter with a bout of magical combat, but I had to admit this was more my language than a council debate. I hoped Vance knew what he was doing. He'd just fought a gruelling battle against the hellhounds and taken a trip into Death with no rest in between.

Without his coat, the difference between him and Lady Granville was even more pronounced. Usually, Vance embodied control and order. Now, covered in blood with his shirt torn and his shoes muddy, hair curling into his eyes from the rain, he looked like he'd walked out of a riot. But then, so did the rest of us. We'd gone to war, and we'd been lucky enough to come back in one piece. Lady Granville might not have a hair out of place, but if the decision had been up to her, the entire city might have been flattened beneath the Wild Hunt.

As the two faced one another, Drake laid down a spell that conjured a shimmering barrier around the edges of the makeshift arena. Presumably they wanted to ensure no stray attacks hit the other mages, but I wasn't entirely convinced the barrier would keep Vance's ability contained. Lady Granville was an earth mage, so the worst she could do was tear up the lawn. Doubtless the mages would return the garden to normal within five minutes, but Vance might well tear off the roof if he lost control.

Why, Vance. Why now?

"In three," Drake called. "Two. One…"

The match began. Lady Granville and Vance watched one another, neither betraying whether they'd attack first. I didn't know the rules of mage combat, but I assumed Vance wasn't allowed to use his abilities to conjure up any other weapons. Knowing Vance, he wanted a fair fight, a decisive one that cast aside all doubts of his worthiness as leader.

The ground shifted, then a wave of wet earth rose upward. He immediately conjured a shield, displacing the air to knock the soil aside before it struck him. The soil rose upward again, barring him from reaching her, but he didn't move nearly as fast as usual and there was a marked absence of scales or claws. He might be tired after the battle, but I was more inclined to think he'd suppressed his shifter instincts to fight as a true equal. As a mage, not a shifter.

"Fools," growled a voice from behind me.

My shoulders tensed when a figure marched over, leaning heavily on a cane. "Lady Harper."

Both her hands rested on the top of her cane as she cast a dismissive glance over the arena. "They're fools, the pair of them."

"I'm told this is how you typically handle disputes over leadership." I was far from in the mood to argue with her. "Where were you during the fighting?"

"Who do you think stopped the rogue spirits from inflicting any substantial damage on the city?"

This was news to me. "What did you do, break into their minds to fuck with them like you did with me? I didn't know you could do that to a ghost."

At her piercing stare, I tensed and readied myself for an attack, but she merely grunted. "No need."

Okay…

"What do *you* think about Lord Carlisle?" I queried. "A

faerie spirit possessed him. I don't think that warrants being sentenced to death."

"Did anyone ever tell you what happened to the previous head of the Mage Lords?" asked Lady Harper.

I frowned at the change of subject. "No. It's never come up."

"He was Lord Carlisle's brother," said Lady Harper.

My breath caught. *"Oh.* I know Vance killed him…"

"There was an incident with a rogue necromancer last year who summoned a number of ghosts." Lady Harper sniffed disapprovingly. "Lord Carlisle's brother was possessed, and the force possessing him was also able to gain control of his mage powers. He was halfway through a killing spree before Vance cornered and killed him, as a mercy."

"Ouch." I winced. "Is that why he's fighting to help Lord Carlisle keep his position—and his life, too?"

"Yes, it is."

"*That* makes sense, but this?" I gestured to the arena. "A public duel seems like a hell of a weird way to decide the future of the council."

"It's tradition." She drummed her fingers on top of her cane. "Unlike anything *you've* been involved with. You fought a Sidhe lord, didn't you?"

"You don't need to ask me that."

"You wield two talismans," she went on. "You speak Invocations. You are no ordinary human."

"Really? I had no idea." I watched her through narrowed eyes. "Does that make me more worthy to stand at Vance's side? Or are there some other criteria I don't fit?"

"Power alone is worthless," she said. "Even the Sidhe know that."

"You speak like you know them personally."

She made a disparaging noise. "After all the years I've

lived, Ivy, nothing surprises me, including people. And yes, I count the Sidhe as people."

I didn't know where to begin with that, so I turned back to the fight. Vance gestured, and the swirling curtain of earth Lady Granville had conjured lashed outwards, knocking its owner off her feet. Before she could retain control, Vance had her pinned down beneath the torrent of earth. Sweat stood out on his forehead, but her struggles weakened by the second, and eventually she slumped onto her back.

"Do you surrender?" he asked.

She looked up at him and spoke in a clear voice. "Yes."

He released her. The loose soil slid away, piling onto the ruined lawn, and she climbed to her feet. Without a word, she began dusting off her suit. I had to hand it to her for showing class in her defeat.

Vance's eyes roved over the crowd. "You saw with your own eyes: the bout is decided. I will remain head of the council, and Lord Carlisle will face a fair trial. The new council will be elected on the fifteenth of the month. You may all leave now."

Nobody raised an objection. It was pretty impressive that he'd managed to answer all their questions in five seconds flat. Most of them, anyway. Even I had no clue where the Wild Hunt had gone, or if they would return. And Fionn...

If I'd managed to stop him awakening—I shut the thought off, knowing I couldn't change the past. I'd come to terms with that a long time ago.

When Lady Granville and her allies had departed, I picked my way across the ruined lawn to Vance's side. "You won."

"Of course." He gave me a questioning look. "Were you talking to Lady Harper?"

I glanced behind me, but there was no sign of the old mage. I did, however, see Isabel peering through the front gate, trying to get my attention. "I think your wards have locked Isabel out."

I ran to the gates where Isabel waited, with Colby the necromancer hovering behind her.

When the gate opened, Isabel leaned in and hugged me. "Sorry, I probably smell of the dead."

"So do I."

"Actually, you smell more like you've been rolling around in a field."

"That's not far off the mark." I caught Colby's eye over her shoulder. "Everything okay out there?"

"I wanted to ask the mages if we can clear the roads," he mumbled. "People are complaining to the guild because they can't drive without hitting a blockade."

Vance came up behind me. "Yes, you can remove the road blockades. I'd advise everybody to take the usual precautions until the undead properly disperse, but the danger has passed."

"You're the Mage Lord." Colby gawped at him. "I thought… you were someone else."

Ha. Admittedly, I could count on one hand the number of times I'd seen Vance look more of a mess than I did, so his confusion was understandable.

"I am," said Vance. "I'd strongly advise you nominate a new leader as soon as possible. The new mage council will be on hand to assist in the process, if you so desire."

The apprentice gulped, nodded, and then bolted down the road.

"I'd vote for Colby over Lord Evander," I said in an undertone. "Maybe they need someone who'll be easy to convince to stay out of our way."

"I've no doubt Lord Evander will prove just as much a hindrance as a ghost as he did as a living person," said Vance.

I pulled a face. "Yeah, you're probably right."

"You know, that Colby has more nerve than I expected," said Isabel. "Considering he came outside to help while most of the other necromancers hid."

"They did just lose their leader," I said. "How bad was the damage?"

"On a scale of zombie night to faerie invasion? Maybe a five." She studied me. "I know that look, Ivy. You're blaming yourself for something."

"I'm not," I said, ineffectually. "Okay. I killed Calder, but I let another maniac with world-destroying ambitions escape. Does that count?"

"As a victory? Yes." Isabel poked me in the arm. "Stop that. Most of us are just glad not to have zombies pawing at the windows. And for the record, if I was a maniac with world-destroying ambitions and I heard your name, I'd run screaming in the opposite direction."

"She's right," Vance said. "We've also evicted another significant problem from our lives."

"What, Lady Granville?" That was true, and a long-overdue change. "Please let me watch you kick her out."

"I imagine she's already leaving through the back door," he said. "The manor will be ours again shortly."

Ours. A hint of doubt remained even now. "I'm not a mage. Not even an honorary one."

"That doesn't matter," Vance said. "As long as I'm Mage Lord, you'll have a place here, and I don't plan on giving up the position anytime soon."

"And if Fionn comes back…?"

"We'll take him down."

"All right. I'll believe you." I lifted my head to the sky, savouring the brief trickle of sunlight streaming through clouds that had roiled with darkness not so long ago.

It was hard not to feel hopeful with the sun on my face

and the knowledge that whatever might come tomorrow, Vance and I would face it together.

ABOUT THE AUTHOR

Emma is the New York Times and USA Today Bestselling author of the Changeling Chronicles urban fantasy series.

Emma spent her childhood creating imaginary worlds to compensate for a disappointingly average reality, so it was probably inevitable that she ended up writing fantasy novels. When she's not immersed in her own fictional universes, Emma can be found with her head in a book or wandering around the world in search of adventure.

Find out more about Emma's books at www. emmaladams.com.